Writing, Written

Several of the stories of this collection first appeared in the following periodicals, to which the author and publisher extend their thanks: *Agni Review, Boulevard, Eckleburg Review, Harper's Magazine* and *New England Review*.

Writing,
Written

Stephen Dixon

FANTAGRAPHICS BOOKS

Contents

To Elizabeth Lightfoot
and Andrew E. Burnett
for their friendship

1

In This One

IN THIS ONE he'll only have one daughter and no other child. In this one he'll be divorced and his ex-wife will live in California. In this one he'll live in a one-bedroom apartment in Manhattan and not in a house in Baltimore. In this one no one will live on Riverside Drive or West 75th Street. In this one he'll be a novelist who's written only five short stories in his entire writing life. In this one he'll have finished a novel a month or so ago after working on it for more than three years. In this one he won't use the expression "or so." In this one he'll have a dog instead of a cat. In this one he'll want almost desperately to start a new novel but can't come up with any idea for one. It's never happened before, not for more than fifty years of writing, and in this one he's getting anxious he'll never come up with something to write again. In this one no one will go to a concert, recital or opera and no music will be played on a radio or CD. In this one his daughter tries to fix him up with a woman about ten years younger than he whom she becomes friendly with at work, but nothing comes of it. They have lunch a couple of times and in this one he finds her attractive but not interesting and she tells his daughter she doesn't find him interesting or attractive. In this one other people besides his daughter try to fix him up with women, but it never works out, mainly because neither is interested in most of the things the other is. In this one he doesn't make a play for women much younger than he. In this one no one goes down in a ship in the North Atlantic or is killed by a fallen tree or a huge chunk of concrete that comes off a building. He doesn't dream in this one, or if he dreams he doesn't describe them. In this one there are no conversations in cars. In this one he hasn't been a reporter or news editor or waiter or bartender or cabby or artist model or gardener or luncheonette counterman or department store salesman or middle or junior high school teacher before he becomes an assistant professor. In this one he hasn't made love for more than three years. In this one the last woman he made love to wasn't his wife. In this one his wife doesn't get very ill and no one he knows is dying or dies. In this one there are no funerals or memorials and no one gets taken to Emergency in an EMS truck. Did he already say that? In this one he never says or thinks, "Did he already say that?" and right after it, "Even if he did." In this one he's not going to fall apart or cry or shout hysterically or drop to his knees and bang his fists on the pavement. In this one he's not going to have any trouble with his memory and letter by letter have to go up the alphabet to get someone's first or last name or a book title, and there'll be no talk or thoughts of writers and books. In this one he won't feel he'll never have a chance to make love to a woman again. In this one the last woman he makes love with is someone he was engaged to almost fifty years ago. In this one, after not being in touch with her for almost forty years and not even realizing she lives in the city and has for about twenty years, he bumps into her in front of a Rembrandt self-portrait in the Dutch wing of the Metropolitan Museum. In this one they have dinner the following night and after dinner she invites him to her apartment for a drink. In this one no one calls a drink like that a nightcap. In this one she says while he's finishing his second brandy and she's nursing her first, "So, my ex-dearie, care to have a go at it for old time's sake?" In this one, though he knows what she means but wants a little more time to think about it, he says, "Excuse me but a go at what?" and in this one he's not going to use the expression "says" or "said something like." In this one, what he says or said is just that. In this one he won't wonder, for instance, if he's using the word "expression" right or if it sometimes shouldn't be called "phrase." In this one she says, "Excuse me yourself, but what do I have to do, spell it out for you? I'm being open and honest and forward and I deserve a mature and honest response." In this one no one used the expression or phrase "the least," as in "the least I deserve," or anything like that. "Sex. Act of love. Love act. Two bodies coupling," she says. "You want to add to that, do. We're certainly of age, but not beyond it, thank goodness, and because we both work out so much, appear to be in pretty good shape for our seventy-plus years. You're not in danger of having a heart attack, are you?" and in this one, because he's used the word too many times too, there'll be no mention of a stroke. "Spare me and yourself if there is that danger. Not only don't I want you to be sick, but having an attack like that would be devastating to us both. If you simply don't want to go to bed with me, that's perfectly all right too. We could still see each other as friends, but I doubt we would. And help me. You, having been a writer for so long and of God knows how many sentences and books, must know if I used 'for old time's sake' correctly or if it should have been 'for old time sake.'" "Whatever it is," he says in this one, "and I have to admit that at the present moment I don't know which is right, yes. I'd like to. Go to bed with you. Would love to, in fact," and in this one he'll use the expression or phrase "in fact" and the word "anyway" only once. "Anyway, one thing you should know is that I'm not sure I'll be able to perform in bed all that well. I'm not saying I won't, but there is that chance. It's been a while. And last time—I should say last three to four thousand times—was with my wife, whom I loved deeply and probably still do, and deeply miss too. That could affect my performance, I hate calling it, but you know what I mean. It's possible I won't even be able to get started. I've warned you, so please don't criticize or blame me if it turns out to be a bust. If you're still willing to go ahead with it, after that spiel, I'm game." In this one she gets out of the chair she's been sitting on across from him. In this one he's also in a chair. In this one there's no mention of a sofa or couch and he doesn't sit on one next to a woman. In this one there's a Hollywood bed with pillows on it against the wall but she tells him it's full of cat hair and is uncomfortable and he shouldn't sit on it unless he wants to be brushing off his pants for the next two days or get them dry-cleaned. In this one there's no kissing before they go into the bedroom. In this one the only time they kissed that night before they were in the bedroom was when they met in front of the restaurant, and that was on the cheek. In this one she says after she stands up, "The bedroom's through there," and points to a short hallway. In this one she says, "Wait a minute. I'm not being a good host and I don't want to rush you. Would you like another drink before we go to the bedroom?" He says, in this one, "I'd actually like to—the brandy was delicious—but it's getting late and it might tire me and affect my performance, again, for want or wont of a better word, so I won't. What I would like is to clean up a little—wash my face and hands and brush my teeth. Do you have a spare toothbrush? And may I use the towel in the bathroom? If not, for my teeth, I'll clean them with this," and holds up his right index finger. "I have two," and she says in this one, "both in the holder, and you can use either one. Toothpaste should be in the cup there, and there are face towels on the towel rack you can use. Why don't you go first?" In this one, he goes into the bathroom and shuts the door. After he comes out, she goes into the bathroom and he goes into the bedroom and sits on the side of the bed nearest the door, waiting for her to come into the bedroom. It's been a while, as he said in this one, since he's been with a woman for the first time, or what seems like it—more than thirty years—and he's not sure what he should do. Should he take off his shoes before she comes in here? He thinks in this one. Also his socks? Should he put his socks, if he takes them off, in his shoes? If he does, he thinks in this one, where should he put his shoes, under the bed on the side he's sitting on? Or should he leave them on the floor but not under the bed till he finds out which side of the bed she wants to be on? In this one he leaves his shoes on. In this one, each of them spends a few minutes in the bathroom. In this one, while he's in the bedroom, she shuts all the lights off in the rest of the apartment and brings their glasses into the kitchen and puts them in the sink. In this one she comes into the bedroom after she leaves the bathroom and says, "I left a nightlight on in the bathroom in case you have to go there later on." In this one she says, "The cat hasn't made an appearance yet, but give him time. Don't be alarmed if he tries to get in bed with us when we're sleeping." "If he does," he says in this one, "can I push him off the bed?" "I'd prefer," she says in this one, "you pick him up gently and set him down on the floor." In this one she starts undressing first. Each takes off his own clothes, in this one, and then gets in bed, she by the side furthest from the door. In this one they kiss for the first time while lying in bed. In this one the sex isn't as good as he last remembered it with his wife and he was hoping for with her. He does okay, though, in this one, mostly because she was so helpful. In this one, it's a relief when he finally completes it and more of a relief in a different way when a few seconds later she starts it too and he can still help her. In this one, after they make love they lie on their sides facing away from each other and he doesn't hold her from behind and isn't held from behind as he falls asleep. In this one he gets up three times at night to pee. After he comes back to bed the third time, she says, "Is anything wrong?" and he says, "No. I don't know what it is. It's just pee, though, no discoloration, and probably from all I drank tonight. Good thing you had a nightlight to leave on." In this one, in the morning while she's still sleeping, he lies in bed and thinks he doesn't ever want to make love with her or even see her again. In this one he doesn't have a prostate problem. In this one he isn't taking medication for high blood pressure. In this one no one has MS or Parkinson's disease. In this one he doesn't have precancerous scalp lesions that have to be burned off by a dermatologist every six months. In this one he isn't bent over a little from an arthritic lower back and is the same height he was when he was twenty and hasn't shrunk three to four inches the last five years. In this one he has blue eyes instead of nondescript brown and has no acne scars and he's lost only a little hair at the temples and none in back and is just slightly gray. In this one he works out every other day in a health club in New

York and swims a mile in its pool twice a week, instead of in so many of the other ones working out in the Towson Y in Maryland every day and not once getting into its pool. In this one he's a soon-to-retire professor in New York rather than a retired one from a university in Baltimore. In this one he reads two to three books a week of various lengths rather than a single average-size book that usually takes him a month to read. In this one he speaks decent Yiddish he learned from his grandparents on his father's side when he was a boy and is fluent in German and French. In this one all his grandparents were alive when he was born instead of all of them being dead for several years. In this one he has no sisters and his only brother is three years younger than him and in excellent health. In this one his father was a doctor instead of a dentist or pharmacist or textile salesman in the Garment District and his mother was a stage actress for many years and not, in her early twenties, a dancer in Broadway musical reviews and former beauty queen. In this one he doesn't meet a woman at a cocktail or dinner party, or did he already say that? If he did, then that'll be the only time he forgets something in this one, if he didn't already say that too. In this one he tells his daughter on the phone how lonely he sometimes gets since her mother left him, but not to worry about it and he's sorry he brought it up. In this one, without first telling him what she was going to do, she registers him with an online dating service and writes his resume and sends it and a recent photo of him to the service. In this one he doesn't respond to any of the women the service tries to match him up with and the ones his daughter thinks might be right for him and asks her to unregister him...deregister him...just get him out of the system, which he'd do himself if he knew how. In this one he tells his daughter that probably the only way he'll get to meet a woman he'll be interested in is by accident—in a movie theater lobby, for instance, when both are waiting on line to be let inside, or at a bookstore in the fiction or literary criticism or poetry section, and more likely the first two. In this one he sees from the street, after he stands up from retying the shoelace on one shoe, an attractive woman sitting alone at a small table in a coffee shop near where he lives. She's reading a book and on her table are an untouched chocolate croissant and a mug of some coffee drink with a thick mound of white foam on top. Means she must have only recently sat down, he thinks in this one. He also, while looking through the window, thinks his wife liked to do the same things when they lived together in New York: sit alone in a coffee shop—usually the Hungarian Pastry Shop on Amsterdam Avenue—and read a book and have a chocolate croissant or almond horn and a cappuccino with lots of foam and sometimes whipped cream on it. In this one—still looking through the window but prepared to quickly turn around if she looks his way-he thinks he'll never meet a woman again to go out with unless he makes an effort to. He goes inside, gets a double espresso—a single, he thinks in this one, would be consumed in two sips—and sits with it at a small empty table next to the woman's, reads a page of the book he has with him and then starts a conversation with her about the book she's reading, which he's heard is very good and always wanted to read but for some inexplicable reason has put off. In this one they talk about the author of the book she's reading, contemporary Austrian fiction, late nineteenth-century Austro-Hungarian fiction, which she wrote her doctoral dissertation on and he's completely unfamiliar with, and teaching—she's also an associate professor but a visiting one for two years at a university downtown. In this one they talk for about half an hour. Then she looks at her watch, says, "Oh, my gosh," stands up, collects her things, says it's been nice talking to him but now she has a dental appointment to go to, "something I should have thought about before I got a chocolate croissant, of all things," and leaves. In this one, still sitting at the table, he thinks he should have asked if she'd like to meet him one day for coffee or lunch and got her first and last names. After all, he thinks in this one, they've similar interests, she seemed to enjoy talking to him, they live just a few blocks from each other, and he also found out in their conversation that she's divorced—a year longer than him—has one child, a son around his daughter's age, and a grandchild. He did, though, he thinks in this one, still sitting at the table, break the ice with a woman he was attracted to and, far as he could tell, seemed right for him. In this one, a month later, he stops in front of the same coffee shop window and looks inside, which he's done, he'd say, about a dozen times since he last saw her, hoping she'd be here, and sees her sitting at the table he sat at and the one she sat at is empty. She's reading a book, and a half-eaten chocolate croissant and mug of some coffee drink are on the table—probably the same drink she had the last time he saw her, but this one has no foam. Don't pass up this chance, he tells himself in this one, because who knows if he'll ever see her here again. He goes inside, goes over to her and says, "Hello, what a pleasant surprise. May I join you after I place my order?" and she says, "If you don't mind, and please don't think I'm being rude or unfriendly. But I have to finish this book in the next fifteen minutes because I'm teaching it in an hour, and I still have my extensive notes on it to read." "By all means," he says in this one, and thinks should he leave? Should he stay? Should he get a coffee and maybe a pastry of some sort to make it seem as if he really did come in for them and sit at the counter or a table far away from her and read his book and never look at her, and leaves.

2

This Guy

THIS IS GOING TO BE a short one. I haven't put any of it on paper yet but in my mind it seems like it'll be short—five typewritten pages or close to it—as there isn't much to say and I don't think there'll be much to elaborate on.

So, to start: I've seen this guy lots of times before at my local Whole Foods. I'd say, half the times I've shopped there the last two years, which is every other Thursday, sometime between noon and one, when the cleaning woman's at my house. I can't get much work done while she's there. The vacuum cleaner noise makes it especially hard to, even when she's vacuuming furthest away from the room I'm in—my bedroom, and the door's shut tight. So I always leave the house for about three of the four hours she's there. If I have some work to copy, I go to the copy store first. Then, or I start off with it if I've nothing to copy, the Y, and then some errands I save for this day—bank, drugstore, liquor store, places like that—and finally Whole Foods, the only time I go there, unless my daughter's visiting me and she wants to buy special foods and drugstore stuff I don't have and which she says the kinds she wants she can only get there. I've elaborated a little. Maybe that's inevitable with me. Maybe I should set the scene up while I still remember it and later, in the final draft, if I finish the first draft and like it enough to want to work on it, weed out what isn't needed and put everything in chronological order. But probably I should just go on. I said I only see this guy in Whole Foods. Well, in Whole Foods I've only seen him in the small eating area by the exit of the store. I have a feeling he hangs out there more than just between noon and one. In fact, I think I've seen him there a couple of times I was in the store at other hours. I always stop in this area after I've shopped and paid up, and sit at one of the tables for two there. Or at the one long table if all the two-tables are taken, and read a book I always bring with me there and eat a little from the container of prepared foods I bought—and just a little because I want to have enough to eat for dinner that night—and also have a coffee I get from one of the thermoses near the eating area. You're supposed to pay for the coffee at the checkout counter when you go through it—there's a price list stapled to the wall behind the thermoses for small, medium and large—or at the express lane by the thermoses after you've gotten your coffee—but I never do. Oh, a couple of times I told the person at the checkout counter when I was going through it that I was also getting a coffee and gave the size and it should be added to my bill. Probably, those times, for some reason I felt I'd get caught not paying for the coffee after I sat down with it at a table. Store policy might be not to ask the customer if he paid or intended to pay for the coffee. Maybe they rely on the honor system. But my feeling is that with all the business I've given this store over the years, I deserve a free coffee—and I only get a small cup of it and rarely fill it up. I know those are pretty weak reasons for not paying, but as my mother liked to say, there's a bit of larceny in us all, though I can't think of a time there was in her. So I see this guy in the eating area—I've never seen him in any other part of the store—and, as usual, he's sitting alone on a stool at the short counter against a wall and reading a folded-up newspaper and drinking something out of a paper cup. It could be coffee—they don't provide tea bags or hot water in this Whole Foods—but something tells me it's water from the water fountain in the eating area and the cup's from one of the three upside-down stacks of them by the thermoses. Small, medium or large? I don't remember noticing what size cup he was drinking from, not even today. And now that I think of it, I do remember him from other days getting off the stool and getting water in a cup from the fountain. A funny thing to remember, but I do. Also—a few times, I'd say—leaving the eating area for what was probably a trip to one of the two restrooms much further back in the store. I assume it wasn't to buy something in the store, since he always came back empty-handed. In fact, I never saw him with anything but a cup and folded-up newspaper. What paper it was, I don't know—probably the Sun, but it wasn't thick enough to be the Times. Again, now that I think of it, he could have left the eating area some of those times to help himself to the food samples they always have out in this store. After all, it's usually between noon and one when I see him, so that might be his lunch. But what I'm getting at with this, and I know I've gone way off the track in telling it, is that today, though this guy never looked healthy—his face, from the first time I saw him, was always too gaunt and a little sickly looking and his body, especially his arms and legs, much too thin—he looked like someone close to death. What made me think that? First of all, I have to say I've never been good at describing people. Places and things too. If a sunset is pretty, for instance, I say it's pretty. I leave the reader to picture his own pretty sunset. I think I have that right. Same if a woman's beautiful. I just say she is but don't say why the narrator or storyteller or whatever he is thinks that. Also, for the last fifty years I'd say, I haven't liked reading descriptions of people and so on, possibly because I've never been able to do them well myself and now don't even try, but I don't think that's why. So what is it? I just feel, although I really haven't thought about it much, descriptions stop the momentum of a piece and hold the reading up. Hold it up in the sense that they delay it—maybe not delay it but slow it down, cut it off, whatever it does but something like what I'm doing right now with this, not in describing but in other ways, like rambling and rattling on how I'm not good at descriptions. Oh, damn, I've created such a mess here, I don't know how I'll ever get out of it. Maybe I should chuck the whole thing into the trash and start something new later today or tomorrow. But there's something here, not much but enough to make me think I should go on with it. I've plenty of times come out okay if I worked long and hard on something that wasn't at first working and seemed almost hopeless. I can already visualize all the stuff I'll have to cut out of it. Probably half; maybe more. And about this guy's close-to-death look, I have to say I'm familiar with it. My wife, my younger sister, my father and also my mother, though less so with her than the others. Also a painter friend of mine, Jim Alderman, who I ended up giving morphine shots to. But what was I talking about? It was so long ago, I forget. I think it's that if I had to describe this guy's look today—and if this isn't it, that's all right too, so long as I continue with it—I'd probably resort to an easy comparison…reference…or whatever the right word for it is—I can't think of it this moment but it'll come to me and then I'll work it in: a concentration camp inmate on the day he's liberated. I'm talking about Auschwitz, Belsen, death camps like that. Most adults are familiar with photographs of these prisoners. Lying in their bunks, two to three in a space that can barely fit one, too weak to get up or sip water from a tin cup or even swallow. Most—oh, who knows? But I'm guessing that most of them that thin and weak, after their guards fled and the camps were opened up, didn't survive. Same with the ones, again in photographs taken by their liberators, clutching the non-barbed part of a barbed wire fence, possibly because they can't stand on their own and need the fence for support, staring at the photographer or just into space. That's whom this guy at Whole Foods mostly resembled. And I still can't think of that word. It's not "resemblance." Sunken eyes, hollow cheeks, conspicuous bones, and so on. Also, completely bald, when before he had a full head of hair, from what I assume are radium treatments or chemotherapy or both for cancer or some illness just as bad. And purple marks on his arms where the IVs must have been in or when he had blood drawn, which might mean he was only recently discharged from a hospital.

Or maybe he's so sick that he doesn't heal as fast as someone not as sick, and he got out of the hospital weeks ago and the purple marks take a long time for someone in his condition to go away. His clothes also show how thin he's become. Dress shirt and trousers several sizes too large for him when they probably once fit him. Of course they once fit him. These are his clothes, and it was always an old dress shirt with no tie he used to wear. Belt holding up his pants, though at times I'd think one of his hands had to hold them up too or they'd slip off him, buckled at the front but wound halfway around the back and tucked into a belt loop there. I forgot to say, and this is important because of what it leads to, in the past, if we happened to look at each other at the same time, I'd always, at least the first time if we happened to look at each other more than once at the same time, nod or smile at him and then look away as I would to anybody I didn't know whom I'd been caught looking at, however accidental it was on my part, while he never nodded or smiled back at me but he also always quickly looked away. Anyway, one of us looked away from the other first. Today, though, one of the times I looked at him, and I looked at him more than I ever did before because of how changed his appearance was—it's for sure something like that was making me look at him so much, for what else could it be?—he was staring at me and didn't turn around when I nodded or smiled at him or maybe I did both. Just kept staring at me from where he was sitting at the counter against the wall, no expression—nothing; his face was blank. Fact is, I can't remember his face ever being anything but blank or a little angry or disapproving, at what I couldn't tell. I also don't remember him ever saying a word to anyone in the eating area and I certainly don't remember him being with anyone here. He may have, but I don't remember. Finding his staring a little uncomfortable, or I just did this instinctively, I quickly looked away from him, but as far as he was concerned, maybe not quick enough. I read from my book opened on the table—a history, or biography of a book, someone reviewing it on public radio said, of Ulysses, which I was finding very interesting. All these different literary characters and what Joyce had to go through to get the book published. And I'm a sucker for that period and Paris and Joyce and Pound and

Sylvia Beach and really anything about that book. Drank some coffee while I read and with a plastic fork I got from the utensil tray there, dug into my container of prepared food for a chunk of balsamic chicken and a few small cubes of sweet and sour tofu I got from the steam table. The chicken and wheatberry salad and the fake chicken strips, which I'll never get again—they were practically tasteless and felt a bit like chewing rubber—I got from the cold foods bar next to the steam table. I know the rubber comparison is a familiar one, but so what? I also know I'm using the word "familiar" a lot, but again, so what? Both of those can be fixed up in the second go-round of this piece, if there will be one and I want them to be. Couple of short paragraphs later of the book I'm reading, and I really couldn't absorb much of it because of what's happening with this guy, I look up at him, this time to see if he's still staring at me—I didn't think he would be—and he is, that is, if he didn't turn away from me before and read his newspaper or do something like that after I looked away from him the last time and then resume staring at me before I looked at him again, and says "You. What are you looking at?" "Me?" I say. This is the first time we've said a word to each other since I first saw him here around two years ago. "Excuse me?" I say. I thought of looking around me for the person he might be directing this question—or accusation, you could call it—but nobody takes you seriously when you do that. And I think I've gone from present tense to past tense and then to present again, and maybe did this a couple of times in this piece. Well, makes no difference, since I can fix that up too. So he says, "Yes, you. Don't try to fool me," and I say, "I'm sorry. I didn't mean to give that impression or to make you feel uncomfortable." "Who says I feel uncomfortable?" and I say, "Then I'm glad you're not. But look. You want to talk, or discuss this, I can come over to you or you can come here." I don't know why I said this. Maybe it's because I felt sorry for him. Of course that's it or almost must be. So sick, or looking like it and probably coming off a really bad illness and possibly still in one that's life-threatening and going through it all alone. And I knew he was lonely and might want to talk. He was, as I said, always by himself here. So am I most of the times I'm here. But he seems like someone—his shabby clothes; his expressions or lack of one. Not any of those but something about him I can't quite put my finger on or not even come close—who rarely speaks to anyone no matter where he is: home, here; work, perhaps, though I doubt he has a job and I suspect no family. Certainly no children. I can just tell—his looks, demeanor, and the rest of it—and I'd be very surprised if I were wrong. Anyway, and I'll obviously have to work on that last passage too, if I keep it, he says to what I said about him coming to me or my going to where he is, though I don't like those high stools and also wouldn't want him to think I'm staying long, so I'd probably stand: "I like it fine where I am. And why would I want to talk or discuss anything with you? But I will come over for a brief visit because I have nothing better now to do and I've some questions for you to answer." He gets off his stool—it seems, from what I can remember from before, with a little more difficulty than in getting on. I don't know what to expect now. He looks like someone who can get really upset. Even explode. Though he's a little guy—five-six or so and of course slight and not in good health, so it wasn't that I was afraid. I just didn't want a scene. His use of the words "brief visit," though, makes me think nothing will happen. He comes over to my table, puts his folded-up newspaper on it—I see it's the Sun, but it's so beat-up that it could be yesterday's or the day before or taken out of a trash can—and also his cup of what I now see is half filled with water. He stays standing, doesn't sit at the one chair across from where I'm sitting on the long bench against the wall, or settee, or whatever it should be called. I suppose both are okay, though "settee" is a bit fancy for me and most people wouldn't know what it is. Oh, most of that has to go. Just have him come over with his newspaper and cup. I don't even have to say where he puts them, although I think some people might wonder what he did with them if he didn't put them down, so it's better I say he did. "Now," he says, "why were you looking at me so hard? And by 'hard' I mean where you couldn't take your eyes away. Do I know you? Do you know me?" "No, but I've seen you here a few times." "Big deal," he says. "I've seen you here too. What of it? It's a public place. But does it give you the right to stare?" There's one other person in the eating area, a woman, also on the settee or bench, and an almost constant parade of people passing the area with their shopping carts and bags to leave the store through the automatic door here. And I've mentioned, I think, the eating area's very small: three two-tables, two of which the woman and I are at; a larger table that could fit up to six people at it; all told about seven chairs; the short counter with its three stools, and the settee or bench. I haven't made up my mind yet as to which I'll use. Also, a breakfront, I suppose you could call it, with a microwave and napkin dispenser and utensil tray and various condiments on it, and a trash can inside the breakfront that you can dump your non-recyclable trash in through a hole in the top, and the water fountain. High up on a shelf attached to the wall, a flat-screen TV set that I've only seen on during Ravens' games and the World Series once. This woman, whose table is next to mine, is around forty, heavyset, gobbling up spoonfuls of food from her container. I don't know if I mentioned this guy's age. He looks to be around sixty, but could be ten, possibly even twenty years younger than that, but his current or recent illness and he's gotten so thin and his clothes hanging so loosely on him and what I'd call an old-man's shirt and of course his hairless head make him look much older. I forget what age I thought he was, if I thought of it—I probably didn't—the last times I saw him. I only brought up his age now because I gave what I thought was the woman's age, though her age has nothing to do with anything I'm doing here either, or much less so than the guy's. No. His age is relevant; hers isn't. She could be in her early twenties, and what would be the difference? And that list of just about all the furniture in this eating area, or most? Scenery. Not needed, or not in such detail. "Three stools. Table for six. Ravens' games," etcetera. The woman looks up from her container of food, a little worried, it seems, as if she thinks a dispute's about to take place and maybe get out of control. This guy says to her "Don't worry, lady"—so he must have picked up on how she felt—"I'm not going to cause any trouble. Don't call the cops yet. I'm not a tough guy, and they know me here, so go back to your lunch or brunch, if that's what you're having." She smiles at him—doesn't look like she entirely believes him, if I'm reading her right—and goes back to her eating. Again, his face through all this, including our brief exchange, is almost bland, flat, no sign of any emotion one way or the other, and he didn't smile back at her or change his expression in any way when she smiled at him. Maybe that's part of his illness. Nerves in his face paralyzed, preventing much movement there? I don't think so. From what I can recall, his face was like that the previous times I saw him, when he always looked frail but nowhere near as sick. If he did, I would have noted it. After he had that exchange with the woman—not "exchange," since only he talked—he turned to me and said... But there I go again, switching to past tense. I'll stick with present. He says to me, "You still haven't answered my question why you looked so long and hard at me. No answer?" "Well, to be honest," I say, and paused—pause because I think what was in my mind to say would make things worse or more complicated or open up something I didn't want opened between us, so best not to say it, and he says, "Yeah, be honest. What else should you be? We're having an honest and serious talk." "Okay," I say. "I was a little concerned about you. Do you mind my saying that? And I'd be that way about anybody in the same situation." "I'm listening," he says. "Go on." "Even, I have to admit, a bit shocked by your changed appearance." I look over at the woman. She's putting the cover back on her container and gets up and dumps the plastic spoon and I now see a fork into the trash can. "You finished?" the guy says to me. She sits back at her table, doesn't look up at us, opens her cellphone and presses a button on it and holds the phone to her ear. "I'll go on if you want me to," I say to him, "though it's all done, I want you to know, in...what's the expression?" And he shrugs and says, "You have my permission." "Okay. I don't like saying this, but you said it's okay, is that you seem to have lost considerable weight since the last time I saw you here. That wasn't long ago. A month or two—I'm not good at being precise about past dates—and your face has gotten somewhat gaunt. So what I was thinking when I first saw you before, and I'm still thinking, of course, and I know I'm getting my foot stuck in this and it's none of my business, is if you were all right," and he says, "And what would you do if I wasn't? You don't have to answer. But you're holding back and what you're really saying is I look like death warmed over, as they say, and my body and face obviously show it." "That's not what

I was saying," and he says, "Don't go lying to me. Or try to pull the wool over my eyes, to be more polite in what I say. But I know what you're thinking. In spite of what you said—all the nice things—you have no concern for me. Your concern is for yourself. That I'm ruining your lunch by my looking like someone on his last legs. And you want to know something, while we're at it? You don't look so good yourself. Like I said, I've seen you here before—noticed you, as they say—and you used to look healthy but now you don't as much and you also lost lots of weight and there's no color in your face. All that I remember from before, though you're not the only one I observed here, you'll be happy to know." "My doctor, at my last checkup, told me to lose ten pounds, and he was being conservative, he said, at what he wanted me to lose, and I did. Maybe more. So maybe that accounts for it. But I feel a lot better from it." "Don't listen to doctors," he says. "That's what I found out from all my dealings with them," and I say, "Then who would you listen to if you got sick, which I haven't or nothing worse that I had, or want to stay healthy? I think I had a point there but I forgot what I intended to say." "Listen to yourself. Doctors are killing me, or would if they could. Get better on your own. These days you can Google your way to complete recovery and good health. You know, you're not such a bad guy as I initially thought. So we're friends?" All this without any change from his stony expression, and he sticks his hand out to shake and I say, "Sure, of course. Not friends so much, although I know what you mean. I meant no harm by my remarks. I was, to repeat, only concerned about you, and you seem all right too." His hand is back at his side—we didn't shake; I don't know why we didn't. It could be I was a little reluctant to touch him—and now I put my hand out and we shake hands. It's like shaking skinny bones. No flesh there; almost no palm, it feels like. "Now that we've settled things," he says, "let me get back to my newspaper and observations post," and I say, "Nice talking to you." "Ted," he says. "For Theodore. But I like Ted." "Nice to talk to you, Ted," and he says, "You're pulling the wool over me again, but I'll take it as a compliment. Sparing my feelings, but I could use a compliment or two, so thanks. See you again, I'm sure," and he takes his newspaper and cup of water from my table, sits back on his stool, or one of the three there and had to grab the counter to help him get back on, unfolds the newspaper to another page, folds it, reads, or seems to be reading, and while he's reading, sips from his cup. "That's nice," the woman says to me, so low I almost don't hear her, so I suppose said that way so Ted wouldn't hear. "I'm glad there wasn't a row." "And what's your name?" Ted says from the counter. "You mean me?" and he says, "Yes, you. Not the lady. You have a name, or is it because you don't want to?" "No, I'll give it," and I give it and he says, "Good. Now I know what to call you next time we meet, if I don't forget it by then. If I do, no harm done. I'll just ask it again," and he goes back to his newspaper. I don't want to stay here anymore—in other words, I just feel like going—and I close my prepared food container, wrap the rubber band around it that the cashier had originally put on, stand, drop the plastic fork into the recycling can for plastic there and paper napkin and my coffee cup with some coffee still in it into the trash can, grab my book and bag of groceries with the container now in it and smile at the woman and start to go. "I hope I didn't chase you out of here," Ted says, and I say, "Not at all. I just got to be going. See ya," and I go. I get in my car and am about to start it up when I realize I forgot my cap. Left it on the bench I was sitting on. It's a good cap and was expensive. Bought it at the Wooden Boat store in Brooklin, Maine, near where my wife and I and then I alone rented a cottage for one to two months the last thirty summers except for the two when she was very sick and couldn't travel. When I was waiting in line in the local fire station to vote last November a man who just used one of the voting machines came over to me and pointed to the logo on the front of the cap and said, "Wooden boat." "That's right. How'd you know?" and he said, "You think you're the only one who vacations in Maine, or did you buy it from their catalog?" "No. Bought it there." "Same with me," he said, "but I save mine for the sea. My wife and I spend two weeks every summer there for the last five years working on a boat we've been building under their guidance. We should be finishing it this summer and then we're taking it out. Pray that it doesn't sink." That happened more than once, someone recognizing the cap I was wearing when I wasn't in Maine. So it's a cap I like very much. I think the only reason I realized I'd forgotten it in Whole Foods is because if it were on my head when I was about to get into the car I would have had to take it off first or it'd be knocked off or pushed over my face by the top of the door frame. What I'm saying, and I know I wasn't too clear with that, is I knew right after I sat down in the driver's seat that I'd left my cap behind. Either I haven't figured out something about getting into the car from that side or the driver's entrance wasn't designed well for slipping into the seat and it's always going to be a tight squeeze. The same thing doesn't happen on the front passenger-seat side because, of course, there's no steering wheel there. I always take the cap off before I get in the car and toss it, if nobody's there, to the front passenger seat. If someone's sitting there, I take the cap off before I get in the car and stick it in the narrow space to the right of the driver's seat or in the sleeve on the driver's door. I actually have two of these caps. A purple one, which was my wife's and which I inherited, you can say, because my daughter didn't want it. She didn't want any of her mother's clothes, and they were around the same size and had similar tastes, except a silk head scarf. The other cap, which I bought the same time my wife bought hers, is navy blue. I forget which cap I was wearing today. But if I had to choose the one I'd feel worse losing, it'd be the purple, even though the blue cap's in much better shape. I think one reason for that is because I have so many photos of her in the cap. She had very fair skin and winter or summer—any season, if the sun was out—she always wore something on her head, and she knew she looked good in that cap. So I have to go back to the store and get the cap. I don't want to but have to, and I'd do it even if I knew it was the blue cap. Another thing: the purple cap is the only article of clothing of hers I kept, for obvious sentimental reasons but also in case I lost the blue one. No, her fleece-lined moccasin slippers too, not for sentimental reasons but because I sometimes wear them at night when the weather's cold. My large feet can fit in them because I bought them for her as a Christmas gift several times larger than her shoe size so her swollen feet could fit in them. Someone—my therapist, or maybe my daughter—asked me if I think of her when I'm wearing her cap or slippers and I said no more than I think of her when I drink from one of the mugs she liked to drink out of or have lunch at a restaurant we used to go to or sleep on what was her side of the bed, and so on. So I go back to the eating area through the exit door when someone pushes a shopping cart out of it. Otherwise I'd have to go in the front entrance, which is closer to where I parked my car in the store's lot, but then have to walk through the entire store to get to the eating area. "Well look at you," Ted says. "Back so soon? It can't be because you missed my company," and I say, "My cap" and grab it off the bench and hold it up to show him. He says, "I saw it there when you left and would have gone out after you but knew you'd come back for it. A man becomes attached to his hat." "Thanks, nevertheless, for even thinking it," and he says, "I don't know why, but lately I've become such a slug. Maybe it's best what I did, and that was to do nothing. Because how would I have found you outside with all those cars?" "Good point," I say. The woman's gone. A young couple are sitting at the table she sat at, woman on the bench, guy on the chair opposite her, both eating sushi out of one container, using chopsticks. I put the cap on—"Best way not to lose the cap again: keep it on my head"—and hold my hand up but stop just before I'm about to wave at him, and go. He doesn't smile. I think he couldn't care less, but so what? He has good reason to be surly and crabby and unhappy and unfriendly and even ill-tempered and sarcastic and certainly glum. I don't. What I've got is nothing compared to what he's going through and I think has to look forward to, or should I say "what he has to face"? He also, as I said, probably doesn't have a child. Again, just seems so. So that's it. Maybe something more at the end: I get back in my car. I drive home. I'm sure he doesn't even have a car. Just walks to Whole Foods from where he lives close by, and walks back. Coming to the store might be his main activity, and it's possible he's in the eating area, reading his newspaper, drinking his water, for hours almost every day. I just thought of that, but that's what I now think he does, and always on a stool at the counter. I see—knew this long before but just kept going—I didn't keep this first draft as short as I thought I would. Nowhere near. I'm sure I can cut it in half. Cut the length. Maybe pare it down to a quarter of what it is now. Do this when I go over it tomorrow morning with a pen before I start working on the final draft. But something tells me it's not going to become anything and I should dump it. Or put it away in my "unfinished stories" folder and then, half a year from now or thereabouts—that's been the pattern, I think I can use the word that way, for lots of other stories I wrote first drafts of but didn't feel were worth going any further with the next day—probably store it and eventually dump. So that's what I did. Read the first draft the next morning, didn't see the sense in wasting my time on something I felt had little to no potential to be a short story or at least not now, and titled and dated it—"Theodore"; "8/5/14"—and put it in the "Unfinished Stories" folder I keep on my work table. There are about a dozen first drafts of stories in it and odds are I'll never turn one of them into a finished story, or maybe just one. One out of a dozen is about my success ratio with the first drafts I have in this folder. So: I can't think why I thought my encounter with this guy could be a short story. And I haven't seen him again since. I've been in the store many times since then—ten, twenty—and every time but once—the exception was when the Ravens were in the Super Bowl or the run-up to it and the eating area was jammed and there was no place to sit—I even think the tables and chairs and stools were removed so there'd be more room for people to watch the game on the TV there—I sit on the bench at a table and have coffee and maybe something to eat from my prepared-foods container or just the heel of a bread I bought and had sliced at the bakery counter but with nothing on it, and read and look at the people walking past. He could be in a nursing home. Or got too weak to make the trip from his apartment or house to the store. Or maybe, God forbid, as we used to say, he died. That's how bad he looked the last time. If he was such a familiar figure in the store, and I believe it, I could always go over to the service booth—it's close to the eating area, just a few feet to the left of the stand with the coffee thermoses and creamers and such on it—and ask someone there if he or she knows what happened to him. If they didn't know whom I was talking about, I'd describe him. "His name's Ted. I don't know his last name. Around fifty or sixty years old; it's hard to tell. Very thin; even emaciated. Height around five-four;

maybe five-six. Looked very sick the last time I saw him here. Last time, also, purple blood-test or IV marks on both arms. It was August. He was wearing a short-sleeve dress shirt, which is how I was able to see the splotches and marks. The one feature of his that really stood out the last time I saw him here was his being completely bald from what was probably chemo or radiation treatments or both. He always sat at the counter in the store's eating area, or whatever you call it—on a stool, reading a newspaper folded lengthwise into quarter strips and drinking water from one of your paper coffee cups. I don't think he ever bought anything in the store, or not while I was here. He just seemed to hang out in the eating area, saying very little to anyone, and always by himself. Another thing: never a smile or greeting or anything like that to anyone, and his face usually kind of stony-looking, almost expressionless, as if frozen, which might be a part of his illness or just the kind of person he was. Reason I'm asking," I could add, "is not because I'm nosy or I was a friend of his in any way, though I did get to talk to him once, but because I got concerned about his health, so just want to know." I don't know why, but I never asked anyone in the booth about him or the woman who seems to be the store's main clean-up person for the eating area, who I think if anyone would know, she would. Could be I just didn't want to find out.

3

The Cap

COULD I TURN this into a story? I finished a new one yesterday and got it photocopied, always like to have something to work on—fact is, I get agitated if I don't and longer that goes on, more agitated I get so here goes. Doesn't work, I'll find something else—later today or tomorrow or the day after, but usually no longer than that. So if something always comes, and something always has, why do I allow myself to get agitated? I don't know. Maybe it's an incentive to get something done, but I'm just guessing.

I'm calling it "The Cap" because it's about a cap and my fear that I lost it and my efforts in trying to find it and, not to be elusive, but all that's involved in the search and what it says about my life, and probably other things. That could be clearer, but don't stop. Starts with me leaving Graul's, the local supermarket just a mile or so from where I live. Whenever I go there I take off my cap and put it in my shopping basket or cart. Almost always a shopping basket, as I live alone—my daughter visits me about once a month for a couple of days and I only occasionally have a friend or two over for drinks and crackers and cheese and a chat—so I don't buy much at any one time and I also like going to the market just about every other day. Breaks up my routine and gives me something to do that day other than write and read for hours and go to the Y and take a short jog in the morning and a short walk later that afternoon. If I know as I enter the store that I'm going to buy a watermelon, or kitty litter—heavy things like that, though I can't think of anything else—laundry detergent, the big can size—I get a cart.

After I leave the store but before I get to my car I realize I'm not wearing my cap. I always wear it outside and, to be safe, even on overcast days where there doesn't seem to be any sun. I was instructed to by my dermatologist about five years ago because I have precancerous lesions on my scalp that she treats with what looks like a blowtorch every six months and which she said can turn into skin cancer if I don't keep the sun off them. "Even if you're only outside for fifteen seconds and the sun's out with you or peeking through clouds," she said, "wear a hat or cap. Last thing you'll want to confront is bumping into me somewhere while it's sunny outside and you're not wearing anything to protect your scalp."

First thing I do when I get back to my car, even before I put my shopping bag down, is look through the window at the front passenger seat. I thought I might have left my cap there. Then I open the door on that side and look at the floor in front of that seat because the cap might have fallen there when I got into the car at home and threw the cap on the seat. I don't like driving with the cap on. There's a better chance—it's happened a few times—of running over the curb on my right when I wear the cap. It's because of the peak, my daughter said when she was in the car with me and I was turning a corner and ran over a curb. I really don't know what the reason is—that might be it—but since then I've stopped wearing the cap while I drive and haven't run over a curb since.

I go back to the store and look at the stack of shopping baskets by the door. There are about ten of them. When I get to the market

I always take off my cap and put it in the basket I'm using. I don't like wearing a cap inside a store. Inside any place. It's as if I'm trying to look much younger or hiding my baldness. There's also something not quite right or just impolite in a man wearing a cap or hat or any head covering but a yarmulke, really, inside a store or movie theater or house or subway car or places like that. Maybe it all stems from something I was repeatedly told to do as a kid—"Take off your hat," I can hear my father saying, "you're not outside"—but for some reason it still seems true.

I pick up the first few baskets and then look through the openings of the rest of the stacked baskets to see if my cap's in one of them. I remember that when my groceries were being rung up at the checkout counter, I put my now-empty basket into the top basket and went back to the counter to swipe my credit card. But I don't remember taking off my cap in the store and putting it in my basket. Still, I had to check.

I go over to the cashier who took care of me before and say, "Excuse me, but did I leave my cap on your counter?" "No," she says. "What kind of cap, in case I see it?" "Blue. And like a baseball cap, with a peak." She's ringing up a customer while she's talking to me. "Check with the office. Maybe someone found it and turned it in." "It's only been around ten minutes since I lost it, but you're probably right."

The office is next to the last checkout counter, about two feet off the ground, with only a short fence-like enclosure around it. I suppose so nobody falls out of the cramped space and also so whoever's in it can observe the front of the store. I'll have to go back and picture that better and maybe also bring in the three to four steps up to the office and the gate at the top of them with a latch on it, but after I finish. There's one person in the office, a woman—I think she's one of the owners of this small chain of stores—and I ask her if anyone's turned in a blue baseball cap in the last ten minutes or so. "And not a navy or baby or light blue but somewhere in between. The blue of stone-washed denim jeans, I think best describes it, and the cap could even be denim—I forget." She says, "Nothing like that's here, I'm sorry. But if someone does turn it in, this is where it'll end up. Check with one of us later."

I go through the entire store—it's not that large for a supermarket, maybe a quarter the size of one of the Giant or Mars stores in the area—looking at the baskets of customers shopping with one. Most are being held; a few are on the floor while the customers are getting something from the bakery or deli or prepared foods or meat or fish departments. I don't stare hard at the baskets; just glance. It still must seem a bit peculiar, this guy without a shopping basket or cart, going through the store looking at their baskets. I just had to make sure, though, that someone didn't take the basket with my cap in it off the stack of baskets when he or she came into the store, but without noticing the cap inside, I'm saying. And, of course, before I went through the stack of baskets myself. I know the chance of that happening is slight—of someone not noticing the cap in the basket. And also, if they did see the cap there, I'm sure they would have taken the next basket and returned the one with the cap in it to the stack or taken the cap out of the basket and, if they didn't intend to bring it to the office or one of the cashiers, left it somewhere near the baskets. But again, if I'm going to be thorough, I had to check.

I leave the store, walk quickly to my car because of the sun. I drive home, now thinking maybe I didn't take the cap with me when I went out the last time, and left it where I almost always leave it when I come into the house: on the dryer by the kitchen door.

I can see through the kitchen door window that the cap's not there, even before I unlock the door. Driving home, in my head I even pictured myself putting it there the last time I came into the house: late yesterday afternoon when I got back from my walk. One other place, and that's it for the house: the coat rack in the living room, which is where I hang the cap when I don't leave it on the dryer. Usually, when someone's coming over for drinks and I want the kitchen and really any room we'll be in to look neat. So everything gets put away: book and cap on the dryer, dishes and silver in the dish rack by the sink, a coffee mug in the sink I might not have washed, which I do and then dry and put it in the kitchen cabinet.

But what's so special about this cap that makes me want to find it so much? I don't know. Or I do. I like the looks and feel of it on my head and of course it protects my scalp from the sun. Other caps could do that, but this one I know I like. Even the Wooden Boat insignia in front of the cap above the peak. Maybe because it's a modern untraditional design for a cap—doesn't exactly look like the hull of a wooden boat, which I'm sure it's supposed to be unless I'm missing something. And it could also be—why I like the cap so much—because very few people would be able to identify the cap and where it comes from as many would almost immediately the insignia, let's say, of the New York Yankees or Baltimore Orioles on a baseball cap. So: the latent snob, or something, in me. If I have lost the cap—lost it for good, I mean—to get another one I'll have to phone the Wooden Boat store in Brooklin, Maine, where I bought it three summers ago I think, and have it sent to me. But there'd be a good chance they'd send a cap with the wrong color blue because I wouldn't know how to describe the color well. "Somewhere between navy and baby or light blue" doesn't quite get it. And then I'd have to go through the trouble of sending it back if I didn't want to just keep it and wear a cap whose color I don't like and which I probably don't look good in or not as good in as the one I lost. So: vanity, too. But if calling the store's what I have to do to replace the cap, and I'll do my best to get the same blue as the one I lost, that's what I'll do and ask them to send it not express—that'd cost too much—but Priority. Anyway: right away.

First, though, I should look around for it some more. Coat rack doesn't have to be the only other place in the house the cap could be. I can be absent-minded. Wearing—it's happened a few times over the years—a cap in the house without knowing I still had it on. Or putting the cap someplace other than on dryer or coat rack when I come into the house. So I go through all the rooms, paying special attention to the dressers and bed, and then the porch and last the patio outside. I need "outside"? Patio's patio. Maybe "outside to the patio." Cap's not anywhere I look, of course, but I still shouldn't give up. Maybe I'm forgetting something. And I've always been good at finding lost or misplaced objects. I don't know where it comes from, but I've been that way almost my entire adult life. It could be related to my writing, which I've been doing my entire adult life: focusing in on one thing and sticking with it despite all the setbacks and doing it every day for three to four hours straight, at least the last five years. Before that, with my wife, I didn't have as much time to write, but I still did it every day. I think there's something to some of that. The reasons for my doggedness, you can say. Maybe. Though more I thought of it, less it seemed right. My wife used to compliment me on what she called my "finding knack." Say to me sometimes when she lost or misplaced something in the house, "Could you help me find it?" And once: "Your eyes are twice as good as mine and seem to see things most people can't or don't," and I'd first check the places she covered and then the places she didn't, and often found it. If our daughter lost something in the house or outside and was upset about it, my wife would say, "Ask Daddy. When it comes to finding anything that's lost—keys, wallet, eyeglasses; all the things that frustrate us the most at losing, especially when we're in a rush to get out—he's the guy to go to." And again, I'd go on the hunt and three times out of four, I'd say—as with my wife's lost items—I found them. Even the collar the cat manages to get off its neck every so often. I'd be petting him and see the collar was gone, or just realize I wasn't hearing its bell. I'd first look around the house—it was never there. Then check the patio and slowly walk the grounds around the house—a big incentive to finding it was that the collar, with its bell and engraved name tag and with my phone number on it, costs around seven dollars each—and sometimes I'd be out there for half an hour or so and I'd find it about once every two times I looked. One time, though, my next-door neighbor—an avid birdwatcher who every so often reminds me to make sure my cat's wearing a collar with a bell on it—did I know that the bird population in Baltimore County dropped by fifty percent the last ten years, mainly because of cats on the loose?—found the collar under one of his bird feeders, and put it in my mailbox with a note: "I'm sure Lewis misses this."

Sometimes I think it all started—my finding knack—with an incident in San Francisco in 1968. Should I go into it? Why not? Got this far and I think it's interesting. I'd moved into a one-room apartment way up the hill on Clay Street that day. I had few belongings: a mattress, lamp, typewriter table, fold-up chair, some dishes and silver and a tea kettle and bread knife and linens I borrowed from the woman's house I'd moved out of after our final breakup the previous day, but no pillow, and some books and of course my typewriter and one pot and one pan. A good can opener, too. I was very pleased with the place. The cheap rent, heat and electricity thrown in—all I needed was a hot plate—and from its one narrow window that ran almost the entire length of the room, I could see the ocean, or maybe it was the bay, and the top of one of the city's two big bridges—I forget which one. I always got them mixed up. One went to Oakland, but I don't think that was the one I saw. I drove to Golden Gate Park, a few minutes away by car, for a run. I didn't stick to the paths but ran through bushes and around trees and up and down grassy hills, and felt great after it. When I got home an hour later I discovered I'd lost my wallet. It must have jumped out of my back pants pocket, which didn't have a button on its flap, while I was running. Or maybe it was in the apartment somewhere or on my car seat, and I checked both places. Well, that's it, I thought; you'll never find it. Besides, it was already dark. But you've nothing to lose and everything to gain by going back to the park to look for it. The wallet had my driver's license and last forty bucks till my next unemployment insurance check in two weeks. I drove to the place I parked in before I took my run and with a flashlight—so I also had a flashlight, or borrowed it from my landlord who lived on the first floor of my building, an eccentric old guy, though at the time he was around ten years younger than I am now, whom I won't write about here but some other day might—I retraced what I thought were my steps. If I don't find the wallet, and there's almost no chance of it, someone tomorrow will and no doubt pocket the money and toss away the wallet. And what do you know? Surprise of all surprises. It was one of the most ecstatic moments of my life. It would almost be impossible to describe how I felt but believe me, I felt great. I'd walked maybe five minutes with the flashlight beamed at the ground in front of me, getting deeper into what I knew at this hour and in the dark could be a dangerous part of the park, and there it was—maybe I had a bit of moonlight to help, but no streetlights; that I remember noting when I told my sister the story the next day—my brown leather wallet, bound by a rubber band to keep all its contents in and because the wallet was falling apart. It just shows, I told myself as I drove home, and I've done the same thing with other things I've lost since—good fountain pens, mostly, also jumping or sliding out of my side and back pants pockets—reminding myself that if I'd given up looking for my wallet as I thought of doing before I drove back to the park that day, I never would have found it and other lost things since. So, and because I really have nothing better to do right now, that's what I'm going to do: retrace my steps, so to speak, since I left the house about an hour ago on a series of errands. Then, if I don't find the wallet—I mean, the cap—unless I can think of some other place it could be, I'll give up.

First place I drive to is the first place I drove to when I left my house on this series of errands: the post office about a mile away to mail two of my books and a literary magazine that has a story of mine in it. Someone out of the blue had asked me to sign the books and then sent me them and the magazine in special protective wrapping. In my letter back to him I told him not to bother including the return postage for the books. Because he paid for the books, and I don't care if he bought them new or used, I'll take care of the cost of sending them to him. He didn't say he was also sending a magazine and I didn't know where to sign in it—nobody has ever asked me to sign one before, or I don't remember anybody asking—so I did it as close to the way I always do it in my books, unless asked otherwise: under the story's title on the title page.

There's just one person working the counter in the post office, no customers, and I ask her if she saw or anybody's turned in, in the last hour or so, a blue baseball cap I lost. "I don't see myself taking it off and putting it down somewhere and forgetting it, but I might have." "Nope," she says. "If it does show up—and you see it's such a small place, I would have seen it by now—I'll set it aside in our Lost and Found box and you can ask for it next time you're here. I know you. You mail a lot." "It's true; I do. By the way, do you remember if I was wearing a baseball cap when I got my package mailed? No, why would you—you see so many people in a day. Thanks."

I next drive to the farmstand I went to after the post office, about two miles away, near the expressway. Bought one cucumber, two corns, beets with the greens attached, cantaloupe and a pint box of grape tomatoes. Went there originally to buy a sugar boy watermelon or whatever it's called—sugar baby?—which I love but thought it too expensive. Eight dollars, for such a small melon, when it was six a week ago, which is how long it takes me to finish one and shows how much I like them. Instead, I got a cantaloupe, at three dollars, and huge, about the size of a sugar baby or sugar boy watermelon, though I don't like it as much and it's not as easy to cut up, and the other stuff—three peaches, too—because everything looked so fresh. I ask one of the two women working the stand—and I wonder if "farmstand" should be two words. I looked it up once in the American Heritage College dictionary on my work table and it wasn't in it. I could have then looked it up in the much larger Webster's Third New International dictionary in my wife's old study, but didn't. I can do it later. So I ask the younger of the two women—the older one's with a customer—if she happened to see a blue baseball cap left lying around in the last hour. She looks at the older woman, who shakes her head, and she says, "No. Sorry. You could look around for it, though." "Nah. I can see very quickly it's not here. I was just checking, going to all the places I might have lost it at. And you wouldn't remember this—nah, it's silly to even ask, though it could cut down on my searching for this cap—" and she says, "What?" and I say, "If I was wearing a cap when I bought some things from you before." "I don't remember," and she looks at the older woman, who shakes her head at her while putting some corn into a bag for a customer. "No. Neither of us." "Didn't think so." "It must have been a very special cap for you to go so far out of your way for," and I say, "I'd say it was my favorite. You know how you get attached to a certain article of clothing. And it was expensive. Fifteen bucks, and that was a number of years ago. Today, it'd be twenty, twenty-five. And I didn't come too far out of my way. But thanks."

Place I went to after that was the dry cleaners, a few stores away from the supermarket. I bought in a wool blanket to be cleaned. The cat had thrown up on it about a half year ago and I'd folded it up, thrown-up part on the inside, and left it on the floor of the guest closet and intended to have the blanket cleaned but forgot about it all these months or didn't want to deal with it for some reason. No, I know why. I don't like that cleaners. About ten years ago they lost the curtains to our bedroom picture window and refused to make good on the loss for more than a quarter of what my wife said we paid for them. She told me not to do business with them anymore, but I continued to without telling her. They were convenient; a short drive from the house and always a parking spot. About a year before they lost the curtains they ruined a silk blouse of hers and wouldn't even give back the cost of the cleaning. They claimed the stain was in the shirt before it was cleaned and they got out half of it. I didn't press them on the matter as my wife wanted me to and told her they reimbursed us for the cleaning fee. After the incident, she told me we should think twice before using them again.

I ask the woman behind the counter, the same person I always seem to deal with the two to three times a year I bring in something to be cleaned or altered, if I left a cap here about an hour ago. She opens a drawer under the counter and takes out what looks like a child's purse. "Maybe this? Someone left it behind today. I don't know who." "No. A cap. A blue baseball cap." "No hat. Nothing like that today. I know you. You came in and gave me a cashmere blanket to clean." "You mean wool," I say. "I hope you're not going to charge me for cleaning a cashmere blanket, if there is such a thing. I didn't check the ticket—it's in the car—or what you're charging me, but I'd think cashmere would be more expensive to clean than wool, maybe as much as it would to clean silk. Am I wrong on that?" "No worry," she says. "No worry. Everything will be fine." She sits down behind the counter and turns up the same piece on the Baltimore classical music radio station I was listening to when I drove here from the farmstand and resumes sewing a button on a man's shirt cuff. Now that I think of it there's usually classical music playing on the radio here, but I don't think there was when I dropped off the blanket. Outside, I think maybe she thought I said cashmere when she asked me that first time the reason for bringing in the blanket and I told her my cat had thrown up on it. Cashmere. Cat. They sound somewhat alike, or could, and English isn't her native language or what she speaks to the other person working here.

I go to the drugstore next to the cleaners, where I bought a container of Naprozen—my sister said it'd help relieve the pain in my lower back—and a box of self-adhesive number 11 letter envelopes. I ask the pharmacist—Jack, I think his name is—who's in the prescription-filling booth, I'll call it, in back of the counter, and like the supermarket office is a foot or two above the ground—if he's seen or anyone's turned in a blue baseball cap in the last hour. "So, you've misplaced it again," he says, and I say, "What do you mean? Have I done it before?" "Only kidding, my friend." He puts aside what he's filling or mixing up there—"dispensary," that's what I think it is—and goes through a side door and comes down to the counter. "Baseball cap?" Shakes his head. "And I'm the sole body working here the last two hours. But I realized after you left that there's a filled prescription waiting here for you. The last of the three you called in for, but which I couldn't refill till I got the fax go-ahead from your physician. Darn, they sometimes take a few days to get back to me." He takes a small paper bag off the shelf behind him. "In fact, two: Losartan and Tamsulosin. You must be close to running out of them. Now that wouldn't be good, especially the Losartan." "Thank you," I say, and I pay for them.

Then, as long as I'm near the supermarket, I should try it again for the cap. It's been about an hour.

I park in the store's lot, go inside, start to check the stack of baskets, thinking maybe the cap's in one that's only recently been added to the pile, then think no, not possible. Next I ask the cashier who checked out my groceries before if she's seen any sign of my cap since we last spoke. "Nothing," she says, "and I've kept my eye out for it." "That's very kind of you. I know how busy it can get. Thank you." Cashier at the next check-out stand says to me, "You lost a hat? I thought I heard a lady before say she found a hat." "Mine's a cap, but it could also be considered a hat. Do you know what she did with it, this customer, or employee, or she only said she saw one and left it where it was?" "I don't know. I only heard her. I'm almost sure she said it. Try the office there." "I was going to. Thanks." I go to the office and say to the only person in it, the same woman from before, "Excuse me. But one of your cashiers says she thinks someone found my cap, or just saw it—the cap I spoke to you about before," and she says, "I haven't heard of it, and no one's turned in anything since you were last here." "And not before then, of course—you already told me that," and she says, "That is correct." "Do you think I can leave my name and phone number and email address with you in case anything does turn up? The people who clean up at night, for instance, might come across it. Because now I'm almost positive I lost it somewhere in the store." "I don't see why not," she says. "Can I have a piece of paper to write on?" I say. "Oh, don't bother. I have a pen and I can tear a page out of my memobook." I take the memobook out of my back pants pocket, tear a page out, flatten the paper against the booth wall and write my name, phone number and email address on it, and underneath those: "Missing baseball cap's a dark blue, somewhere between a navy and baby blue. It has this insignia above the peak," and I draw the Wooden Boat insignia as close as I can get to it. "The insignia's white," I write. I hand the paper to her. She looks at it. "If I find a cap that fits this description, I'll be sure to contact you, Mr. Epstein." "Contact me if you find any kind of baseball cap," I say, "and not just today but in the next few days or weeks. So keep the paper up there. You never know. There's always the chance the cap that's found in your store is mine."

I walk through the store again. Keeping my eyes open, as Doris, the cashier, said in a different way, for a place I might have missed. Then head for the exit. On the newspaper rack on the inside of the door I see my cap on a top of a number of *Washington Posts*. "My cap," I say. I was excited and didn't mean to say it so loud, and a cashier—the one who said she heard a woman say she found a hat—says from her station, "Great. You got it. The long-lost cap. I knew a lady said she saw one. And now I remember where. In the parking lot, she said, on the ground, so she must have brought it inside." "But how could me and you and Doris"—the other cashier I spoke to; her checkout stand's closed, so she must be through for the day or on a break—"not have seen it till now? Think that woman walked around with it?" "Where'd you find it?" she says, and I say, "In the newspaper rack," and she says, "Then that's why. This lady must not have known what to do with it and was in a big rush to get her shopping done and so she got rid of it fast as she could and that's where she left it. At the door.

She probably thought, if you were still in the store, you'd see it on your way out." "You could be right. I'm so happy," I say. "Silly as this has to sound to you, this cap means a lot to me. I mean, I don't go to sleep in it, but I'm happy I found it and also that my persistence in looking for it paid off. Doesn't happen every time." "Good. I'm glad for you." She looks at the next customer in line, who just finished putting the contents of her shopping cart onto the counter and seems impatient to be rung up, and says, "Sorry, ma'am. Big important matter," and the customer smiles and she says, "So I understand." I go back to the office, say to the woman there, "Excuse me. Excuse me. I found my cap. You can tear up the paper I gave you." "Will do," she says.

I leave the store, put on my cap the moment I get outside, and go to my car. That's all there is to it. Or all—I was going to say "all I've got," but I don't know how much sense that would make. Not much of a story. Probably not even a story. Probably just an example of how tenacious I can be sometimes. But why does it have to be anything? Well, if it's going to be a story? Then no story. Settle on that. Just a long glimpse—no, another phrase, because that one would be an oxymoron, I think, a word I don't ever remember being part of my vocabulary. Funny how some words just pop out of your head after being stored there unused for God knows how long, and by "your head" I mean mine, any adult's, and in this case fifty to sixty years. Possible that long? Possible. What about this, then—this piece here—being just an account of something out of the norm that happened to me in my mostly solitary and uneventful humdrum life? Too strong and a bit self-pitying? Probably, but I can be that way too, less so now than I think I've ever been, though for now, because I want to finish this, and I'll have to do something about that awkward-sounding double-now, that reasoning will have to do. And so by showing, if you're still with me, all the places I went back to in my search for the cap, I was saying something about my present life. Maybe that comes closest to what I was trying to do with this and sort of justifies my writing this. I would have liked to include in my search for the cap my bank (M&T, Ruxton branch, account number 99-2462-7224—only kidding, and that isn't my account number; just numbers that came into my head; I've no idea what the real number is), which is a few steps away from the dry cleaners and pharmacy. Also to have included the wine shop, which is owned by the owners of the market and is in the same building but has a separate entrance, but I didn't go to either of them today so I couldn't have lost my cap in them. I suppose, though—no supposing: I brought up those other places to get them into this piece. Why? To give a complete picture of all the places I go to in my village, and I think I can call it that. It's not a town, and because it has definite boundaries, not just a community or neighborhood. I go to these other places—wine shop, bank and a Mobil gas station, which is across a sidestreet from the bank, about once every other week. There is another gas station I go to, a Citgo, which is about half a mile away from the Mobil station. It's always a few cents more a gallon of gas than the Mobil, but I sometimes prefer getting my gas there because they put detergent in the window-cleaning tanks at the pumps while the Mobil only puts clear water in and often lets them run dry. There's one more store I used to go to in the shopping area—a flower shop—but I haven't been there since my wife died. Anyway, it was just five to six places I went to in search of my cap: market, post office, farmstand, dry cleaners, pharmacy, market again. I leave one out? I don't think so. There are, I haven't mentioned, four other stores in this shopping area, all between the wine shop and bank. One for women's casual clothes, another for jewelry, a third for women's accessories, nightclothes and lingerie, and a fourth, from what I can tell from the store window, just for crocheting and knitting. I've never been in any of them in my twenty-one years here, not even when my wife was alive. What a dull life. I wish it were more, but I do little to make it such, so I guess I'm stuck with it. No guessing there, either. I'm stuck.

I drive home, back up into the carport, unlock the door to the kitchen—the front door to the house, you can say, but I might have already said that—and go inside and put the cap on the dryer there. Oops, left the bag of medicine on the front passenger seat, but I can get it tomorrow morning or if I go outside again today. No, get it now. Why wait? I get the medicine, put away all the groceries and things I bought at the market and farmstand, then make a gin and tonic with lots of ice and a slice of lemon because I forgot to buy limes, though it had been on my mind, too, before I went shopping. I sit with my drink in the easy chair in the living room and read the front page of today's *New York Times*. So, I think while sitting there, newspaper now folded in half on my lap, gin and tonic on the side table to my right by the chair, is it a story? Going to go over that again? Then what is it, if it's not a story, and I'm not saying it isn't: a recounting through an isolated simple incident of some aspect of my life today, or an exercise, as I said before, and a little of its history, in perseverance to show the kind of person I am? I'm not sure of any of that, and surely I could have said that last sentence much simpler. Okay, then answer this: is this piece worth working on starting tomorrow morning and continuing working on the two to three weeks after that as a story? Because that's all I do. Otherwise, the whole thing will have to be put away and probably eventually discarded, or thrown out in the next few days. Might be. A new kind of story, maybe, at least for me. We'll see.

4

Mora

THE PHONE'S RINGING. I first hear it in my dream. A woman comes into the room I'm in and the phone's ringing and she says, "Why don't you answer it?" and the dream ends. I wake up and the phone's still ringing. It's late and I should probably get up to answer it. It could be my daughter with something alarming to tell me. Or my sister or one of her children with something alarming to tell me about her. I stay in bed. Covers are over me, room's dark. Five rings, six, seven. And the three or four when I thought they were part of my dream. So about ten rings total. Who was that woman in my dream? I didn't recognize her, can't place her now. Then the ringing stops. Twelve rings, thirteen? An awful lot anytime, but more so for someone calling so late. And I know who it is. I don't have to answer it. I don't want to talk to her. I don't want to hear her voice. Nor what she has to say about herself. Maybe that she only recently found out my wife died five years ago and is calling with much belated condolences. Mora Stone. That's who it is. Calling from BWI airport. On her way to Italy with her partner, she'll call him. Been together for a year and a half now and it's as unrocky a relationship as she's ever had. "In a way, he's much like you," she'll say. "He's Jewish. That's not why, though I'm sure it has something to do with it. He's serious and artistic. Thinks constantly about his craft and is always working on something, when he isn't scrounging around for money to do it. Also like you, he's produced an enormous body of work. A documentary filmmaker. Seven films already and he's working on his eighth: a full-length feature on me. That's how we met. He came to my studio to speak to me about a possible film on my life and we immediately flashed on each other and hooked up the next day and have been together since. But tell me how you are. It's been so long. We're on our way to Florence for a wedding there and have an unscheduled three-hour layover in Baltimore. I know it's late. Though not that late, I don't think." "What time is it?" I'll say. "A little past ten. Why, were you asleep? You sound tired. We're still on California time." "I wasn't asleep," I'll say. "I was reading in bed." "So we thought, or I did since I haven't seen you in what must be more than thirty years, you might want to come to the airport and you and I and Harrison—that's my partner's name—can have a drink together before our flight takes off." "I can't," I'll say. "I don't much like driving at night. My eyes. They're getting a little old. I'm wearing trifocals now, while when I knew you, it was single lenses in my glasses, just for reading." "You should get special glasses for night-driving," she'll say. "Are there any for what I have?" I'll say. "I don't know what you have. It's probably glaucoma, from what you're saying. Then an operation, with lasers, I think. One eye at a time, simple and quick and ninety-nine point nine percent effective. But tell me; are you still writing? I don't see you ever stopping, but I'm asking anyway." "Sure I'm writing," I'll say. "Much as ever. It's what gives me—far as my work's concerned—my greatest pleasure and occupies enough time of my day to…well, you know. I haven't changed on that." "Same with me," she'll say. "My sculpturing goes well, too, and never stops exciting me. I do it all the time. I go into my beautiful studio, which I had built to my specifications about ten years ago, and sculpt and draw and assemble and plan my work all day. From nine to nine most times, weekends included, and sometimes that's nine p.m. to nine a.m. if I'm really deep into a piece and don't want to let go of it or can't. I never get tired doing my art. Collages and Matisse-like cutouts too. I don't only do one thing. I've had some success too, just not in New York yet, but my agent and I are working on it. Just as I suppose you've had your fair share of success, though I'll be honest with you and say I don't keep up with your books. I hear they're around but I don't see them or look for them. Have you had anything out recently?" "Several books," I'll say. "Maybe four in the last eight years, two of them long ones." "How long?" and I'll say, "One was six-hundred-plus pages and the other seven-hundred and forty-nine." "Too long for me," she'll say. "I like my books short, or much shorter than those. Each of them would take me half a year to read. And how is your cat?" and I'll say, "My cat? I have a new one, if getting a cat five years ago can be considered a new one." "Derek told me you had one, that's how I knew. Black, like mine." "How are Derek and Lindsey?" and she'll say, "You must know. He says you exchange letters, not emails." "Twice a year at the most," I'll say. "He never told me about your wife till a month ago," she'll say. "I don't know why. It could be he doesn't like to convey bad news. I'm sorry for you, Charles. So sorry," and I'll say, "Thank you." "Have you been in a serious relationship since?" and I'll say, "No. Nothing at all." "You will," she'll say. "Yours must have been, and I can hear it in your voice, a very strong and loving marriage, and I admire that. So, my dear, you won't come to the airport? It would be so nice. And you'd be surprised how I look. I might be seventy-two— you're seventy-eight; I even remember your birthdate—but I look nothing like it, everyone says. It must be a combination of things I do and don't do. I work out daily on my exercise machines in my house and eat well and drink sparingly and haven't touched a cigarette or joint in twenty years. I also swim and jog a mile on alternate days and even play one-on-one basketball with Anthony a couple of times a week on the backboard and hoop by my garage. You know who Anthony is." "Your son," I'll say; "what do you think? Come on, I lived with you for four years and was the kid's surrogate father for all that time."

"Four years?" she'll say. "I think it was three. By the way, I told Harrison all about you. He'd like to talk to you." "If you mean now, I don't know," I'll say and she'll say, "He's very nice. You'd like him. Here, speak to him. He knows everything about us. My getting knocked up. You wanting the child and to marry me and I didn't want to ever get married again or have a second child and for certain not with someone who at the time had to work at three different jobs at once to make a half-decent living." "I tried," I'll say, "and I really don't want to speak to your partner." "Are you being cynical or sarcastic with that last remark—your emphasis on 'partner'?" and I'll say, "No. That's what you called him." "I also called him 'Harrison.' All right. And he just doesn't want to say hello. He wants to ask you something, which he was going to do if you came to the airport. But I don't want to force you to do anything. You don't want to speak to him, you don't have to," and I'll say, "Put him on. It's okay," and I'll hear her say away from the phone, "Here," and Harrison will get on and say, "Hello, Charles. 'Charlie? Charles'?" and I'll say, "Just Charles." "It's nice to finally have the opportunity to speak to you. I've heard a lot about you, of course. You were a very important person in Mora's life, and Anthony's too." "Well, we lived together for three years, and it wasn't easy then. We didn't have much money and jobs were tough to get for both of us, even menial ones. I'm glad that struggle—the money part—is over, it seems, for all of us. According to Derek, whom I'm sure you know, even Anthony is doing well. But Mora said you have something to ask me," and he'll say, "I do. She told you I'm making a film about her. Her life, her art. Particularly, California in the sixties. People she knew. Poets, composers, other artists, dancers, fiction writers, gurus. The drugs and all that. The mind opening to totally different experiences. And she was right at the center of it. So I wonder if you'd allow me to take a day or day and a half out of your life to interview you for this film. I'd fly in from San Francisco, book a room at a Baltimore hotel for two nights. That's how long it'd take. One day for me to prepare for the shoot, the second day to interview you. Two days total, I figure, and I'd take care of all the logistics of hiring a sound man and lighting man from your neck of the woods. All the TV work done there, they have some very good ones. It's going to be a great film. She's a magnificent subject and presence and she has a great biographical story to tell and is a dream in front of the camera. Looks great; terrific poise; talks great. Funny, sharp, intelligent. Everything, and not an actress. Pure naturelle. I joke with her that she'll be the darling of documentarians after the film is shown and the value of her artwork will zoom. But I don't see how the film can be complete without an appearance from you, and I'm willing to go to the expense of getting it. Sixty-three to sixty-eight. Those, I feel, were the daring years. Though much of what I'll be depicting will have happened before you came onto the scene. Do I sound like a salesman? I guess that's what I also have to be to make a film. So what do you say, Charles? Mora and I will fly in together but I only want to shoot you and then perhaps a handshake and hug and even a big kiss between you and Mora on camera after I'm done interviewing you. I already have other former lovers of hers and housemates and her ex-husband and of course Anthony and her brother, and now what I need is you. And when I say 'at your convenience,' I hope it can be done in the next two months after we get back from Italy. I've had a little success making documentaries—" and Mora will say away from the phone, "Don't listen to him, Charles. He's had a tremendous amount of success. Nominated for an Academy Award. Almost all his films have been screened at Telluride and Sundance and the Toronto Film Festival and longlisted for Cannes." "What's Telluride?" I'll say and he'll say, "Not important." "And 'longlisted'? A word I never heard before," and he'll say, "The same. Also not important. As you can see, I leave all my boasting to Mora. She's a great press agent. So have I convinced you about an interview?" and I'll say, "I'll think about it." "Good. Think hard. Think positively. The ayes will have it. And it'll be fun for you too. And I'm sure you're an old hand at being interviewed, so a snap." "Now I should get back to sleep," I'll say and he'll say, "I'm sorry. You were sleeping when we called?" "I meant I'm a bit tired because it's been a long day and I'm sleepy now and want to get to bed and maybe read a little more and then get to sleep." "I'll give the phone back to Mora—I'm sure she'll want to say goodbye," and I'll say "You needn't. It's fine as it is. We sort of said goodbye. Have a wonderful stay in Florence." "Did I say Florence?" and I'll say,

"I think Mora did." "Bologna," he'll say. "Then after the wedding, we'll go to Florence. My best friend's daughter is getting married." "Sounds nice. Have fun," and he'll say, "I'll be in contact with you, Charles," and I'll say, "If you want," and hang up and he'll hang up and Mora will say to him, "He didn't sound like the old Charles. His voice. It's softened, as if something's wrong with his vocal cords. At times I couldn't make out or even hear what he was saying." "I didn't have any trouble," he'll say and she'll say, "I'm worried about him. He used to have such a strong voice. Great projection, like a professional actor's. Without him shouting, you could hear him from twice the distance you could hear other people from far away. It's the Parkinson's, I bet. Derek told me a few years ago he had it but I didn't want to bring it up. And he wasn't as quick with his mind as he used to be." "Well, that can come with age. I'll probably get there in ten years, but you probably never will." "I hope not," she'll say. "And I'm almost sure he didn't remember who Anthony was when I first mentioned his name. Took him awhile. Then he covered himself up fast enough. He's changed so much. You still think he'll be an asset to the film? I don't want him embarrassing me. He used to embarrass me a lot. He drank too much. Two vodka or gin drinks every night and then wine. Maybe that was what made him slow tonight. I don't see him ever stopping drinking. And when he smoked pot, which Derek says he gave up thirty years ago, maybe longer, he used to get wilder and more talkative and sometimes obnoxiously talkative than almost anybody I knew who smoked it. No, he didn't sound good. That's what I got from this call." "Don't worry," he'll say. "If he consents to the interview and I do it, I won't let anything he says on camera make you look bad. I just won't use it. No reason to. Nor will I let what he says about himself make him look bad, I promise, because I know you wouldn't want that too." "It would've been nice if he came to the airport," she'll say. "It only would have been an hour, at most. I'm curious what he looks like. If he got heavier or stayed slim. Slim, I bet, as he was always extremely conscious of his weight and looking trim, and I'm sure that's stuck. I frequently saw him pinch his waist to see if there was any extra flesh there. Sounds bizarre, but that's what he did. And I wanted him to see me too, for old time sake or something, at least once more before we both start to fade. Though from this call, I think he'll be fading a lot faster than I will, and not only because he's got those six years on me. Although I will say, outside of his drinking, he did take good care of himself when we lived together. We used to—Anthony and I—call him Mr. Natural because of what he ate and cooked for us—he was the chef six days out of seven—and his daily workouts and runs. Even then I hated cooking and had no imagination or tolerance for it, so don't think I developed that attitude when you and I met." "I don't," he'll say. "But I think he was just sleepy and that softened his voice, if sleeping does that, and possibly slowed down his brain. No one's their best when they're sleepy or very tired or just woke up. But you may be right." "On my medical report?" she'll say. "Oh, I'm right, all right. He isn't what he used to be and he probably tried to hide it, and I can understand that. But I'm afraid he's in such bad shape that one reason he didn't want to come to the airport was because he didn't want me to see how weak and feeble and old he looks. I don't think he should be in the documentary. It will bring the whole project down and depress anyone who sees him, especially if you're going to run photos of Charles and me together from the sixties." "If that's what you want or don't want," he'll say, "then that's what we'll do," and she'll say, "That's what I want and don't want, you silly boy," and she'll ruffle his hair, like she used to ruffle mine, and kiss him on the lips and then say, "So. We have nearly three hours to kill. Let's get a drink at a sit-down place and maybe a hamburger or some good bar food. Crab cakes. Lobster rolls. Fried oysters. Baltimore's known for its seafood, right? There must be a couple of places still open in this vast terminal that also serve wine and beer." "That's okay with me," he'll say, and they'll go looking for a restaurant or bar.

5

The Rest of the Day

I GO TO THE BATHROOM. I go for a run. I go to my desk in my bedroom to write. I go to the kitchen for a snack. I go to the Y. I go to the pharmacy. I go home. I go to bed to rest. I go to the market. I go home. I go to the phone on my dresser. I call my daughter in New York. I leave a message. "Hi. It's Dad. Not that you don't know my voice by now. Just checking in, seeing how you are. Much love to you." I think if there's anyone else to call. There isn't. I spoke to my sister yesterday and there's no reason to speak to her again today. I go to my bedroom. I sit down at my desk. I lie on my bed. I nap for half an hour. I didn't plan on doing anything on the bed but lie on my back and rest for a few minutes. That seems the best way to get rid of or reduce the pain in my lower back that was hurting me so much I couldn't stand straight. I dreamed during the nap. In it my wife and I and our daughter who looks to be around three go to my wife's parents' apartment in New York. Her father offers me a drink. I say, "It's not even noon yet, Victor." "So what's wrong with having a little Schnapps before noon?" he says. "It's the weekend." "Papa," my wife says, "let Charles be. He doesn't want to drink, don't force him. He probably wants to keep a clear head for more writing this afternoon." "Who's forcing?" he says. "I'm offering." "And I truly thank you for that," I say to him. "You're always so generous and kind." I go to the bathroom in the dream. I sit on the toilet. Our cat is lying on top of the toilet tank, staring at me. "How did you get there?" I say. "You're supposed to be at home." That's when the dream ended. I get up and call my daughter. We usually speak to each other every day. Either she calls me or I call her. "I've designated myself to check up on you daily," she said a few days ago, "so let's not let a day go by." "Dad?" she says before she even hears my voice. Probably my name or phone number came up on her phone's screen. "Good, you're there," I say. "How are you?" "I'm fine," she says. "And you?" "Couldn't be better. It's a beautiful day. Perfect temperature, low humidity, soft sun and light breeze. I love it." "Same here in New York," she says. "How's your day been so far?" "Busy," I say. "Very busy. Lots of different things. Too numerous to mention everything. Wrote, went to the Y, shopped, stopped off at the Falls Road Atwater's for soup and coffee and a small loaf of their flax seed bread. Wrote some more. Story's going well. Took a walk around the neighborhood, ran earlier in the day. Read. Played with the cat. Did some clipping around the house. Napped. Had a few nice short dreams." "Really sounds busy-like," she says. "And I'm glad your work's going well. I know how good that makes you feel." "Well, it makes me feel I'm doing something valuable to me during the day, or gives me the illusion I am. And you, my darling? What have you done today? Are you outside now?" "No, home. And my day's been nothing as busy as yours. Saw a couple of patients I couldn't see yesterday. Working now on a paper I'm giving at a psychoanalytical conference in December. I went for a walk and had a mug of tea and apple tart at my favorite Brooklyn place. And I'm meeting Richard for dinner and a movie tonight." "I'm glad things are going well for you," I say. "And I should go now so you can get back to your paper." "No, I can talk." "But I've run out of things to say," I say, "and also to ask. You know me. Phone isn't my forte. Speak to you tomorrow?" "Tomorrow," she says. "I love you." "Love you too," I say. I go into the kitchen to take two pills. Stomach growls and I say, "I'm hungry," and eat a slice of Swiss cheese and half a raw carrot. I think of preparing tonight's dinner for myself but don't know what I want to eat. I know I have to eat, but I can skip one dinner. Maybe just another slice of cheese and the rest of the carrot. I look at the stove clock and wonder what I'm going to do the rest of the day. I've been to the Y. I've tried writing the first draft of a new story twice. No, three times. I've checked my emails since this morning, haven't I? I haven't. I go to what was my wife's study for many years and turn on her old computer. My daughter said it wouldn't last this long, but I use it so little, maybe that's why it has. I check for emails. Nothing's come since the last time I looked. Actually, nothing new in two days. I go to the *New York Times* site. Lots of news. Nothing that interests me. Dow's up, which I guess is good for me, but what do I know? Something else to get anxious about. I think of my wife. I'd be nice if she were around. "Nice?" Find a better word. "Great. Stupendous. A miracle come true." All fall short. "My dear," I say, "if only you were around. If only you were round. If only you were here—round, slim, but alive and miraculous and real and talking to me and asking me things and I asking you things and so on and on and on and we'd talk about our lovely daughter and I'd say, 'I love you,' and kiss you and hug you and so on again and more of it and do everything like that. 'Let's take a walk,' I'd say. Or 'Let's go out for dinner at a good place tonight, no matter what the cost'—Dow's up; that must be good for us—and order a great bottle of wine and I might have a cocktail before and eat and hold hands and I'd kiss your hands and you'd squeeze mine and we'd stare at each other's eyes without saying anything and we might even kiss in this restaurant. A quick kiss. We don't want to be ostentatious—would that be the word for what we wouldn't want to be? And then go home after dinner and make love." "Let's make love," I have her say in my head. "Let's go into the bedroom and make it right now." I shut off the computer, or do I "shut the computer off"? I go to the Y. Second time today. I've never done that before, or maybe done it once. Maybe even three times before, meaning I went to the Y twice in one day three times, but that's in the last ten years. I work out on fifteen weight machines there. Always fifteen. And not the same fifteen each time I work out there, though there are eight I always work out on each time. Next I ride an exercise bike for thirty minutes. Always an exercise bike to end my workouts and always for thirty minutes exactly, and then shower at the Y, second shower today. I rarely do that too. Well, on very sticky summer days I've sometimes showered three to four times at home in one day. Or one at the Y and the others at home in one day. I get in my car and go home. But stop off and pick up some prepared food at either of the two markets I like going to near my house. For one reason this time, to stay out a little longer. I buy some prepared food at the market closest to my house. Chose that one because I stopped at the other market yesterday. If I hadn't, I might just as well have chosen it today, since the prepared foods at both markets are about equal in quality, variety and price. At home I don't feel like eating this food now and I don't think I'll want to heat it up later and eat it. In fact, I know I won't. I freeze the prepared food. In the freezer are two or three other containers of prepared food, and now there'll be three or four. I should use them all before I buy more prepared food. Or just toss them out, newest one included, because why am I keeping them if I'm not going to eat them? They're all different kinds of cooked chicken and I don't want to eat any more chicken, and my daughter, who comes down for a visit every six weeks or so, has been a vegetarian for about twenty years. I slice a bagel in half and then those halves in half, toast the four halves, two together in each toaster slot, smear the untoasted sides with Dijon mustard, put a slice each of Swiss cheese and tomato and a little lettuce on each of them and eat all four while standing up by the sink, and that'll be tonight's dinner. I wash the plate and knife. An idea for a short story comes into my head and I go into my room and write the first draft of it in half an hour. I title it "Thirteen" at the top of the first page and also today's date: "9/19/2014." In it an elderly man—I picture him to be around my age—looks back to when he recently turned thirteen and had the best three months straight in his life. Everything seemed to work out for him. First, he's bar mitzvahed in an Orthodox synagogue. The chief rabbi, who up till then was very stern and hadn't said a word to him, says he never heard the haftorah read so well and sung so beautifully by a bar mitzvah boy and in such flawless Hebrew. "Take my advice. If your voice holds, become a cantor." Gets into the two elite public high schools he took exams for and chooses Brooklyn Tech over Bronx Science because his ambition the last few years is to be an architect. Gets the leading role in the eighth-grade musical and is made valedictorian of his class and at graduation reads the speech he wrote for it. The principal, handing him his diploma, says, "To be honest, usually the valedictory address puts me to sleep, but yours was truly inspiring. I want a copy of it to show all future valedictorians." At sleepaway that summer he gets the best male athlete and all-around camper awards. "A first in thirty years," the head counselor announces at the awards ceremony, "just so you all know what an achievement it is." Also at camp he has his first serious girlfriend, Janet Tannenbaum, who's a year older than him. On the last night before camp ends she lets him feel her breasts through her shirt and touches his penis through his jeans several times before resting her hand there. He flunks out of high school at the end of the first term. The technical courses are too hard for him. Transfers to a regular public high school near his home and is robbed of his wallet and sweater his second week there by two boys with zip guns. His best friends from grade school have either moved to another part of the city with their families or joined tough gangs in his new high school and he no longer wants to be friends with them. His voice changes for the worse, not that he ever thought of becoming a professional singer or cantor. He was once a good-looking kid and now his face is puffed up and full of pimples and he thinks he's beginning to lose his hair. Janet's father won't let him come to Forest Hills to see her and won't even let her talk to him on the phone. "You're both too young for that. Call her when you reach sixteen." In other words, the best three months of his life are followed by the worst three. More than three. More like six or nine or twelve. In other words, everything's changed and gone wrong. He's lonely. He sometimes feels suicidal. His parents tell him to cheer up. His sister, whom he's always been close to, and she's a couple of years older, says he's become too gloomy and depressing to hang around with anymore. The story stinks. I don't like the style or content. It's like something I wrote fifty-five years ago when I first started writing fiction and didn't know better. The point to it is too easy or simplistic or something, but nothing good. No matter how hard and long I'd work on it, I know it could never be a story I'd like and would want to send out. A story for me has to be interesting and exciting and new or a different take on something I already wrote and have a self-generating energy that takes over the writing of it, and this one doesn't do anything like that. Do I know what I'm saying? I'm not sure I do. But I won't put this first draft into my "Unfinished Stories" box. I've done that with lots of first drafts. Kept them in the box for six months to a year or at the most two, and about a quarter of them, maybe less than that, I went back to—well, I eventually went back to all of them or at least reread them or started to—but these I turned into finished stories that were pretty good but none among my best. But all the first drafts I put into the box showed potential. This one, like about fifty before it the last thirty years, doesn't. How do I know? I know. It's more than "something tells me." The only thing to do with a first draft like that is throw it out. Kill it, in other words. Anything less would be wasting my time. So that's what I do with this one. I tear it up and dump the pieces into the tall shopping bag of recyclable paper in the kitchen. The bag, once it's full, will join two or three other bags in the carport and probably one more after this one, and on Sunday I'll carry them all to the end of my driveway for Monday's pickup. I make myself a drink: half a juice glass of rum with orange juice and seltzer and no ice because there's no room for even a single cube. I sip the top of the glass so nothing spills while I carry it, and sit in the easy chair in the living room and drink the drink down. I get a carrot and pickle out of the refrigerator, slice both into coins, I think the word for it is, and eat them. I slap cream cheese on the two heels of a loaf of rye bread I bought a few days ago, stuff them into my mouth, and after a couple of bites but no swallows, spit it all out into the kitchen trash can. I'm not really hungry. It's all compulsive eating. I'll just get paunchy if I continue to eat like this and, eventually, heavy, and then it'll take me months to lose all that uncomfortable extra weight, if I'm ever able to do it. I put the loaf of bread into the freezer. When my daughter next visits me, I'll take it out for her. I open a good bottle of wine and pour out a glass. I sit on the patio with it and drink and read an article in a magazine. I get another glass of wine and sit in the easy chair with the magazine, but just drink. I feel tired. Of course it's the rum and wine and probably also that it's late afternoon and maybe also that I have nothing I really want to do. I go to my bedroom, kick off my sneakers, lie on the bed with all my clothes on and shut my eyes. My wife, without my doing anything to get her there, appears in my head. She's sitting in her wheelchair at her computer, asking me to help her with it, which she did a lot: it's frozen, which happened a lot. I tell her anything I can do for her, I will. She smiles and the image of her disappears. I try to get it back, but can't. I fall asleep and dream of my wife. She's in her mobility scooter, which she got around in for several years before she was unable to operate it. I can hear it moving behind me. It sounds like a tank. I turn around and she's holding on to the handlebar with one hand and waving to me with the other as she passes. I wave back. "Where you going?" I say. She shakes her head. "You can't speak and steer at the same time?" She hunches her shoulders as if she doesn't know the answer to that or how to word it. Then she speeds up the scooter and it's way in front of me and she makes a right at the next city cross street and disappears. When I get to that street and look in the direction she went, there's nobody there as far as I can see. I wake up and wonder what the dream could mean. I can't figure it out. Just right now, anyway. I like dreaming about my wife—long dreams, short dreams—especially when she's healthy in them and affectionate to me. In this one, she was on a mobility scooter but looked good. It's still sunny out. I shut my eyes and hope I can go back to sleep for another nap and dream some more about her, maybe even continue the last dream. I fall asleep and dream. In it I go into a room where there are a number of people. My wife's sitting on a couch with another woman and I go over to her and without saying anything give her a quick kiss on the lips. She's a little startled and I say, "Do you mind my kissing you like this in front of other people?" It was just a quick kiss on the lips. What I'd do with my mother if she were in a room with other people that I just walked in to and I hadn't seen her in a while, but I'd kiss her on the cheek. "I didn't mind," she says, "and it'd be a rare time I would." I wake up. It's still sunny out. I look at my watch on the night table. Where it always is—I never wear it unless I'm on a trip out of town—and see only twenty-five minutes have passed since I poured myself a second glass of wine in the kitchen. I'd like a third glass. I almost never drink so much before six o'clock, but I feel like it today. I don't know why. Or I do know why and I don't want to think of it. So what if it makes me tired—where am I going? I've gone to all the places I could go to today. I guess I could do a little yardwork, but I don't feel like it. So if I go to sleep earlier than usual today, I'll get up earlier than usual tomorrow. Amounts to the same thing, especially when I have nothing to do in the house for the rest of the day. I get the wine, sit in the easy chair with it—patio or easy chair? I thought. Easy chair, because it's more comfortable than the metal folding chairs outside—and start reading a story from an anthology called *The World's Best Short Stories, 2014.* I bought it a week ago. An arm gets amputated in a logging accident on the first page of the story, and that quickly turned me off it. Too graphic and gruesome. Next it'll be something horrible done to someone's eyes or lips or toes. So far I haven't liked any of the stories in the book—the one I stopped reading is from Holland, an odd place to take down a 200-foot tree, I'd think—and I've read about half of the twenty in it. So why'd I buy it? Good question. Oh, I remember. It was recommended to me by a former colleague at the university department I used to teach at, whose opinions on literature and contemporary fiction in particular I respect. I said to her when I bumped into her at a farmers market that I haven't anything to read and that I haven't liked anything I've read for about a year. Maybe two years, I said, except for some novels by a Hungarian writer I reread. She emailed me the titles and authors of ten books, with comments on all of them. For this one, she wrote something like "What a rich period for the short story we're living in. This book also shows that putting together an anthology of stories or poems can be an art form itself comparable of the art being anthologized." I thought that was ridiculous, but only wrote back my thanks for her going to so much trouble for me.

I went to my local bookstore the next day—actually, the only good bookstore in the city—and this book was the only one it had from her list. "Quite the esoteric assemblage you have there," the store's one salesperson said. But stop stalling. Get through all the stories in the anthology. If only to have an informed opinion about the entire book in case I bump into my former colleague again, and surely there'll be one or two stories in it I'll like. It'd seem impossible that all of them could be bad. And maybe the one I stopped reading will get better and also explain what a 200-foot tree is doing in Holland. I bet there aren't any there. I bet there aren't any in Netherlands—I should call it "the Netherlands"? Just "Netherlands"? It sounds awkward without the article—that are even 150 feet—and that also there'll be no more gruesome scenes. Sure enough, two pages later, a woman attacks the narrator with a serrated knife. It had to be serrated, just to make it more gruesome. He's in his car, waiting for the traffic light to turn green. The back seat is bloody because the injured logger was taken to the hospital in it. The woman comes to his window and motions for him to roll it down—she has something important to tell him about his car. He thinks, "One of my tires? Damn, what a day." Right after he rolls down his window, she starts slashing away at his face. "That's it," I say. "I don't care if you cost me fifteen bucks and change—you stink," and I throw the book across the room. I've heard of people doing that with books they didn't like, but never did it myself. At most I just dropped the book to the floor, though there have been books I disliked a lot more than this one. Now I'm sorry I threw it. The book split in two when it hit the wall. I could have given it to Vietnam Vets or Goodwill or some organization like that. About five of them call me once a month or so to see if I have anything to give away. Then I shut my eyes, lean my head back, and next thing I know—I don't remember ever dropping off so fast in a chair—I'm waking up from a long nap. I didn't dream or don't remember dreaming if I did. I must have napped for an hour or so, because it's getting dark out. Time for bed. Early, I know, but I'll be safest there. I'm feeling a bit woozy—all that alcohol and not much to eat, it must be—and I might fall if I stay up and move around. I have fallen some nights when I drank too much, and one time I had a hard time getting up and making it to my bed. I don't think I stood up again that time and I had to crawl from the living room to the bedroom and then lift myself up from the floor to the bed. Slept on top of the covers with my clothes on that night, or the first few hours of sleep. I also remember wetting the bed but not changing it till the morning. Too tired too. Maybe even afraid to, that I'd fall again. I did manage to get my pants and undershorts off. I stand up, test myself by walking a few steps—I'm all right; not going to fall—and pick up the broken book and drop it in the bag of recyclable paper in the kitchen. I lock the kitchen and porch doors and turn off the living room lights. The cat. Where is it? In? Out? I forget. Oh, jeez, I hope it's not out. "Huey? I say. "Huey, you here?" He runs into the living room from the back of the house. "Where you been, my friend? What's your secret hiding place these days? Come on, let's go to bed." I start for the bedroom. The cat runs ahead of me and I hear it jump onto the bed. The hallway is dark and I have to feel my way in it to the bedroom. I turn on my bedlamp, take off my clothes, pee, brush my teeth, think I'll floss and then think I'll skip it. I get in bed and look at the night table for a book to read. There are two stacks of them, but nothing that interests me. A few have been there for several years and I'd no doubt have to dust them with a paper towel before I could open them. I was in the middle of rereading one of the Hungarian's novels before I started reading the anthology, but I forget where I put it and anyhow don't want to get up to look. It could even be in my gym bag in the car. I'll find something tomorrow. Either that one, which I think is my third reading of it, or something else. Maybe one of the two or three novels I haven't read by my wife's favorite contemporary fiction writer, a Russian, although she said none of her books have been translated well. "Maybe you ought to do one," I said then. "Maybe I will," she said. And tomorrow I have to start a new story. Write the first draft of one. It'll probably have a dream or two in it. Almost everything I write the last few months seems to. But what am I going on about? I'm too tired to read now. I turn off the light. The room's dark. No moon and no streetlight near my house and the house is surrounded by tall trees and the leaves haven't started to fall. I turn over on my side. Handkerchief. I have to have one near me before I go to sleep. I turn on the light, get up and get the handkerchief out of my pants pocket on the chair. But get a clean one if you're going to stick it under your pillow; the one from your pants you've been using all day. I get a handkerchief out of the dresser, shove it under the pillow I'll be sleeping on, pick up the cat and set it down on the other side of the bed—the side I won't initially be sleeping on—so I can stretch out my legs. If I don't, they'll cramp. I get back in bed, turn off the light and pull the covers up to my neck. The pillow is just right, doesn't have to be adjusted to my head, and I fall asleep almost immediately and start dreaming. I'm sitting on a couch somewhere with my wife and I ask her to marry me. "Why would I want to?" she says. "It's time. We've been together so long." "A better reason." "Because you love me," I say. "Who said so?" "You did." "I don't." "That's a lie." "All right, I do." "Tomorrow?" I say. "Shouldn't we wait a few days? There are legal procedures to go through. You need to get a license. I mean, we do. We'll go down there together. In fact, we have to go together. And I want my parents to be at the ceremony, and you'll want your mother there too." "Fine by me. So it's done?" "Done," she says. "Except perhaps for a wedding reception—something simple for a few people in a modest Russian restaurant. I'll do the preordering. And the two days after the wedding at a rustic inn in rural Connecticut, just to make it official. Though won't we also need to take some kind of genetic testing before we can get married? Sachs-Tay? Tay-Sachs? We're Ashkenazic Jews." "No, we're good." "One more thing," she says, "and then I'll stop. Won't this marriage make us bigamists and land us in jail?" "Not if we're marrying the person we're married to. But no more stalling. We're getting married. I'm adamant on this." I wake up. Should I write the dream in my dreambook? Why not? If I don't, I'll forget it, even if I now think I won't, and it's a good one. I turn on the light, get my dreambook and a pen out of the night table drawer and write the dream down in it, date it, as I date all my dreams I write down, and put the book back in the drawer, leave the pen on the night table and turn off the light. I want to turn over to my right side but that cat's there. Leave it. He seems to be sleeping and I've disturbed him enough tonight. Wake him and he might get angry. "Good friend, great cat,"

I say, and touch his back. "That's all I'm going to do. I won't bother you. But what would I do without you? Sleep well. Have good dreams. And don't ever get hurt. Be extra careful when you're outside. Cars. Foxes. Feral cats. Remember to stay clear of them, and come in every night before it gets dark." It doesn't stir or open its eyes. I stretch out my legs, rest my head back on the pillow. Again, it fits perfectly and I don't have to adjust it to the pillow or the pillow to my head. Usually I do.

6

Sunday, Around 3

"SO YOU'RE GOING to New Zealand," I say. "We are," and she points to the man on the other side of her, who's busy looking at a travel book on New Zealand. "It's a long trip," I say, and she says, "yes," and turns away from me and writes "January 10" in the notebook open on the counter in front of her and then looks at the man. "Go on," she says to him. "I'm ready." That's it for any further conversation with her. I butter my bread and look around. Don McClendon is still here on a stool five stools away from the man. He's looking at me when I look at him, and he waves and I wave back. I saw him when I first sat down and he waved then and I waved back. Sooner or later he's going to come over to me and say hello and hold his hand out for a few seconds before he shakes my hand. Who's Don McClendon? Who's the young couple sitting on stools to my right? First, Don. He's a kid…not a kid. He must be in his mid- to late twenties.

Went to the college I taught at in this city for twenty-seven years, but I don't know him from there. I know him from here. And what's that? A restaurant. Soup, salad, sandwich and coffee place I go to every Sunday, always around three. Why always around the same time? Less crowded then. Easier to get service and coffee refills. Also easier to get an end stool at a counter, which I prefer to the other stools. And if all the end stools are taken, and there are eight of them because there are four separate counters in this restaurant, then if possible a stool with an empty stool on either side of it. I like to have room for my food and book and *Sunday New York Times* book review section if I bring it with me. There are plenty of tables and chairs there, but I don't like taking one if I'm alone. It also has for very young children a long table about a foot shorter than the others with crayons and drawing paper on it, although I don't recall ever seeing a kid sitting at it. But why Sunday? It just seems like the right day to go if I'm going to take myself out for a treat once a week, which is all I do. To take myself out more would be excessive, I'd think. Or perhaps just lessen the pleasure and expectation—can I call it?—of a once-a-week treat. Also, weekdays are too crowded and it's tough finding a parking space in the restaurant's lot. That means I'd have to park at a meter on the street. Saturdays are also pretty crowded and a meter day—only Sunday isn't. And I come here every Sunday? Every. Even when my daughter's in town. Then we go together, maybe around one or two— I try to avoid noon, which is when it's most crowded here all the time—and sit at a table, even if we have to wait for one and there are two empty stools next to each other at one of the counters. She loves the place. Her favorite informal restaurant in Baltimore, she's said, and maybe anywhere. "Food's so good and fairly priced," she's said, "and always great coffee and all the refills you want, and they don't charge you extra for soy milk with it." In fact, she was the one who introduced me to the place. Took me out for lunch on Father's Day a couple of years ago. Probably more crowded than usual that day. So coming here on Sunday has become my weekly ritual, obviously. Just as going to the Y for my workouts is my daily ritual. On Sundays I work out later than I do the rest of the week so I can drive from the Y to the restaurant. Main reason being the trip here from the Y is half the distance than it is from my house. But Don McClendon? How do I know him? About three months ago, while I was sitting at the counter, he tapped me on the shoulder and said, "You're the writer, right?" "I'm a writer, that's true," I said. "Fiction. Solamente fiction, this newspaper article I read about you said and how I recognized you. The photo. Like me, I've noticed, you lunch here every Sunday at this time." "I wouldn't say 'at.' 'Around,' yeah." "Around, then," he said. "Correcting me like my English teachers used to. It fits. And I don't mind. After all, you were an English teacher, while I, you can say, am still a student, even if I graduated college some years ago." "I taught writing, not English." "I stand corrected again. But this article. It struck a chord. The things you said. I read it several times. It was on your retirement from teaching after a zillion years and a new novel of yours coming out." "You've got a good memory," I said. "And also a good one for faces." "Because I knew who you were from the start and saw you here so much. Solamente Sundays. Do you know how to say 'Sundays' in Italian?" "No." "I thought you would. You're an educated man. Must speak many languages." "I'm not that educated. Mostly self-taught. Barely got my B.A. And English is my only language." "Just like me in both those last categories. So we have much in common. Which is what I'm getting at and why I came over to say hello. Not only our barely achieved baccalaureates, if I can believe you, and that we're here every Sunday around this time and we're originally New Yorkers who now live in Baltimore. And that we both write, though of course what I put out, so relatively new am I at it, can't be compared to your professional work. Am I holding you from your food?" "It's okay. It's a cold soup. So what's up?" "My writing," he said. "I've led a very interesting life. Seen and gone through things you would find hard to believe for someone my age. I've many stories to write about it and have tried doing so a lot, but can't seem to get much down of any worth." "If you're looking for someone to write them for you, count me out." "No, just to look at what I've written so far and give me good feedback whether I'm on the right track and also advice where to take it from there." "That too. I've retired from everything but my own stuff." "Not even a few pages?" "Not even." "I like you," he said. "Straightforward. No beating around the bush or bullcrap. A necessary posture for a serious writer, I suppose. Time spent on my writing is time not spent on yours. But you wouldn't reconsider? Two pages, let's say?" "No page." "So I'll see you again here, I'm sure. Don McClendon." He stuck out his hand to shake and I shook it. Every Sunday since then he comes over to me—I make a point of not sitting near him, even if the only available end stool is there, but he always sees me—and says his full name as if I've forgotten it and holds up his opened hand a second or two and then shoots it to me to shake. A few times he brought up the subject of his writing again and said, "You haven't changed your mind about looking at some of it?" and I either said no or shook my head. The last time, he said, "I thought both of us being Jewish would help change your mind," and I said, "You're Jewish? With that surname? So just your mother?" "Both parents, and no conversions. That's only one of the strange and I think interesting stories I have to tell." "Still, the answer's no," I said. And the place all this is at? The largest and I think the first of the five Atwater's restaurants in the Baltimore area, in what's called Belvedere Square, which is just south of the Baltimore County line. There's Baltimore County and there's Baltimore, but Baltimore isn't in the county. I always have one of the four soups they always have on the menu. A cup, never a bowl. If they run out of one of the four, they scratch it off the menu and write in a soup of the same category: vegetarian or meat. The meat can be shrimp, chicken or beef. The vegetarian can be vegan. I always have one of the two vegetarian soups—I don't like meat in my soup and I've gotten stomach poisoning from shrimp three times in my adult life and have stayed away from it since the last time I got sick from it about thirty years ago. I'll also have coffee, of course, and sometimes a side salad. Today, no salad. If the side salad on today's menu had been the one I like best—mixed field greens with roasted cauliflower florets and pecans and marinated black olives—I would have got it, even though I wasn't that hungry. But the side salad they offered was the one I like the least: bibb lettuce and sliced tomatoes. I had it once and found it so bland and the lettuce a little sandy that I told myself never to order it again. I always ask for a pad of butter for the slice of very good bread that comes with the soup. Bread and soup are the restaurant's specialties and probably what made the place so popular. Unless you ask for butter, you won't get it with the bread. A few times I asked for the heel of bread instead of a regular slice—I love crust—but didn't get it and have given up asking for it. About half the times the butter didn't come with the soup after I asked for it and I had to ask for it again, saying something like, "I hate to have you go back to the kitchen for such a small matter, but I do like a little butter with my bread." And the woman sitting next to me? Young—mid-twenties, I'd say—pretty, an intelligent face, stack of books in front of her on the counter, although at the time I didn't know they were all on traveling to New Zealand, but none of that was why I sat down beside her. That end stool was one of the two available in the restaurant—I did a quick walkaround when I came in. The other was next to this big heavyset guy with a long, to me ugly logger's beard whom I didn't feel like sitting beside. He also had—I assume they were his; who else's could they be?—a baseball cap and City Paper on the empty stool and I didn't want to ask him to remove them. My gut feeling was that he might be unpleasant about it. While I'm eating my soup the server comes up to me and says, "How is everything?" meaning the soup and coffee and I guess also the bread. Or maybe she's asking how I am, since I have sat at her station a couple of times before, so as server and customer we sort of know each other. She's the only person I've spoken to here today other than the young woman beside me. In fact, only the third person I spoke to all day, if I can call saying "Hello" and "Good morning" and "See ya" and "Have a nice rest of the day" speaking to someone. That was with Caroline, at the entry desk at the Y this morning, when I swiped my member key in front of a scanner, and after I worked out and showered and was leaving the Y to go home and she was still sitting behind the desk at the entrance to the Y, making sure the faces on the monitor beside her matched the ones of the people swiping their member keys to get in. Oh, what am I doing with all this? I had nothing to write, I felt I had to write something, I covered my typewriter, drove to the restaurant, got the idea there while sitting at the counter and after I'd ordered my food that if I just write the most insignificant and minute details of my day it'd be some kind of new story, where you get to know the narrator by all the little things he sees, thinks and does, because I'm always interested in writing a new kind of story in a new way, doing what isn't typically done in a story, taking it where I think it hasn't been or not quite in this way, or just writing a different kind of story in an original way, and that it'd work and be complete, but it didn't and wasn't and won't, even if I include a lot more minor and inconsequential details that I was thinking of putting in that again wouldn't normally be included in a story. But look at me. I can't even get the explanation of it right of what I wanted to do, of what I'm doing and now trying to explain. The server, for instance. Not the one that gave me the menu and took my order and brought first the coffee and then the food over and later asked me how everything was, and I'm sure she meant the food and coffee, but another server. The one I look for and have seen here almost every Sunday for months and who looks like a young Audrey Hepburn—almost the spitting image—especially in the movie *Roman Holiday*. Hair, shape of face, big eyes, swan-like neck, I have to say, even if it is a descriptive cliché, slim dancer's body, solid bulging behind, long legs, small breasts. She must be a dancer. Ballet. Student of or just out of work. She's glanced at me a number of times as if she thinks she might know me from someplace other than this restaurant. She couldn't be a friend of my daughter because my daughter is probably seven to eight years older than her. Anyway, she would have said. I've said hello to her a few times and she's said hello back to me those times, though she's never initiated a hello when I looked at her and hadn't yet said anything to her, so her hello always came after mine. She's given me a menu and served me a couple of times when I sat at her station at one of the counters, but I've stopped sitting at any station I saw when I came into the restaurant that she was the server at. Even if the only available end stool was at her station and there was no big beefy somewhat angry-looking guy, and the guy that time did look a little angry, sitting next to it. I didn't want her to think I'd chosen her station to sit at because she was the server there and I wanted to look at her and say hello and get a hello back and give my order and later ask for a refill of coffee—I always asked for one, no matter who was the server—or just to top it off or that I was in any way interested in her beyond giving my order and getting my food and that refill or top-off. I know I didn't explain that well but I'll continue. I didn't want to make her feel awkward by my presence. "Awkward" isn't the word. "Self-conscious" is more like it. When I was around nineteen I thought Audrey Hepburn was the most beautiful and desirable woman I've ever seen, despite her being so thin. That didn't put me off. Those legs, that face, her expressions, that derriere I'll call it so as not to sound crude; her voice. Maybe I was sixteen or seventeen, but I knew then what I liked. So maybe that's it, or something like it, because I'm not sure how to explain it. I wish I were fifty to fifty-five years younger than I am, meaning around the same age or a few years older than this young woman. The most ridiculous thought I think I ever had, this wish to be that much younger than I am, but there it is. Is something wrong with me for thinking it? Tell it to your therapist. No, I don't want to tell her any of this. I'd be too embarrassed to: the old idiot desiring the impossible and meaning it. But that's all. Or enough. No story here. I'll have to start a new one in a day or so. If I don't have something to write, and I know I've written this before a number of times, just that I've used that phrase if it's a phrase "or something like it," I don't know what to do with myself once I've done all the mundane things. Because if I'm not writing, to put it another way, what else do I do but the mundane? I wake up. I wash and dress and go for a short run. I have breakfast while reading the front page of the *New York Times*. I go to the Y. I usually have a bowl of soup and slice of buttered toast or instead of the toast, half a bagel with mustard and a piece of cheese on it for lunch. I go to one of two liquor stores for wine and booze just about every other week. I shop for a few foods at a time at one of four markets I go to almost every weekday. I go to one of three Starbucks near me for a cappuccino or some other coffee drink, but never just a mug of coffee, about once a month. I go to the drugstore once a month to pick up the three renewals of medicine I've called in and the over-the-counter medicine I take every night to prevent acid reflux. I go to Target around once every three months to stock up on toilet paper and paper towels and a ream of computer paper I use as typing paper and once every other time or so, trash and leaf bags. I go to this restaurant every

Sunday afternoon. I take a long walk every afternoon around five if the weather permits it and my back holds up. I finish reading the *Times* in the evening while I have a sandwich or frittata or some prepared food I bought that day at one of the four markets I go to and a glass of wine and rum and seltzer or vodka and grapefruit juice, and usually a couple of glasses of those: wine and either vodka or rum. I have lunch in a restaurant about once a month with my best friends here, a married couple, and am invited to a dinner party at their home about every other month and, with my daughter, always for Thanksgiving and the first Passover seder. I see my therapist every Tuesday at ten. I see my dentist and dermatologist and general physician every six months. Every other Thursday, the cleaning woman comes. I leave the house for most of the four hours she's there, taking my time at the Y and sometimes going to the bookstore I like to see if anything new has come in I might want to buy and going someplace for coffee and sound and once every three months getting the car serviced and, if I still have time, doing a food shop. I type a letter every other week or so to an English professor in Minnesota I've been exchanging letters with for more than thirty years and whom I've never met or talked to on the phone. I watch a movie or just the beginning of one if it looks as if it's going to be too violent for me, on my wife's old computer I'd say about five times a year. I don't like watching movies alone and I never go to a movie theater or play or concert or opera by myself. I never turn on my flat-screen TV and don't even think I'd know how to work it. My daughter bought it for me three years ago when I was convalescing at home after a serious operation. I think the only time I've seen anything on it was the day she brought it home and installed it in my bedroom and turned it on. Some PBS World War I drama that takes place in London and the English countryside and the battle of the Somme. We sat there for a while watching it and she said, "You don't like it," and I said, "I don't," and she said, "There'll be better things on it—is it all right?" and I said, "yes," and she turned it off. I don't like watching TV alone, either. I read books and take one with me just about wherever I go: at the Starbucks while I'm having a coffee drink, at the Y while I'm on a stationary bike, at a restaurant if I have to wait for my friends to arrive, while I'm waiting to see the dental hygienist and dentist and dermatologist and general physician and also the ophthalmologist every other year, at that Atwater's on Sunday afternoon, at night in my armchair after I finish the *Times*, and later in bed for about half an hour before I go to sleep, and sometimes in the middle of the night when I wake up and can't get back to sleep. Right now I'm reading the fifth and final volume of Michael Reynolds' biography of Hemingway. I'm drawn to the last years of famous fiction writers, except the ones who died very young. I forgot to say I often take a book with me when I go for a long walk. I like to stop off at a bench along the way and read a few pages and maybe jot down my thoughts or some ideas for short stories in progress or new ones in the future that came to me while I walked. But what else do I do? Lots of other little things. I talk to my daughter on the phone almost every day. I clean my linens and clothes in my washing machine every other week. I do yardwork several times a week for about half an hour if the weather's good. I mow what little grass I have. I collect twigs and broken branches and use them in the fireplace as kindling and firewood when it gets cold. In the fall I mulch the leaves around my house with my rechargeable lawn mower. In the spring my daughter makes a special trip down here so we can put in a vegetable and herb garden. I play with the cat. I let the cat in and out of the house, in and out, maybe ten times a day. I wake up early. I go to bed early almost every night. I put my eyeglasses into the night table drawer so the cat won't knock them to the floor. I shut off the light. I get up to pee two to three times a night. I dream. I dream. I dream.

7

Once More

HE SAID HE'D never write about her again. Told others, told himself. Began saying that after he finished his last book, which he could say was all about her and his missing her and his memories of her since the first time they met. It was at a party in Greenwich Village. First Saturday after Thanksgiving Day. Light snow falling. But he's written about all that. Goes to the front door as she's about to leave. He'd been looking at her, following her around the party for the last hour. From a distance looking at her. Feeling nervous—not "nervous." That's not the right word for it. Something else. It'll come to him. Maybe it was nervousness. Certainly his stomach was acting up. But for about an hour he just kept his eyes on her, didn't go up to her. Then, a short time after she disappeared from his sight—it was a crowded party in several rooms—he saw her heading to the front door with her coat on and gloves and scarf in her hand, and he told himself, "Better do it now," and made his move to her. "You probably won't want to talk to me," which she told him later—days later, in their first arranged meeting—was an odd line, or "approach," he thinks she said, to open with. "First funny line"…he means "Funny first line to start off a conversation," is what she said. But it worked out. They spoke for a few minutes—How does she know the host? How does he? And so on—and he got her phone number. They met for coffee a few days later—their "first arranged meeting." Beer at a college bar and then dinner the same night at an Indian restaurant, both near her building, a few days after that. Went to bed together in her apartment after their next dinner date a week or so after that. A fish place, again near her building. Began seeing each other several times a week shortly after that. Married three years later. Daughter, seven months after the wedding. But what about his telling himself or his promise or whatever he wants to or should call it to never again write about her? Especially not about the party they first met at, which he's done about half a dozen times. Once, even, the party took up almost half a long novel. Since he finished his last book five months ago, which took three years to write and is an interlinked story collection of their lives together from the first time they met at a party given by a woman friend of both of them, he's written seven stories and not one has her in it or is in any way, at least that he can see, about them together. He finished the seventh story yesterday around noon. Hour or so later, after he decided there was nothing he wanted to change in the story, he drove to the copy place he always goes to after he finishes a story, though not always the same day, and made four copies of it. One he always puts in a cardboard box in the trunk of his car with all the other stories that haven't been published in a book of his. Does that in case he loses the original and three other copies of it, though he knows the chances of that happening are nearly impossible. This morning, while he was having breakfast and reading the Week in Review section of last Sunday's *New York Times*, he got the idea to write about them again, starting from the first night they met at a party. He doesn't know what will come of it but thinks something new will in content or style or both. Why does he think that? Just a feeling. And the feeling was strong, which was usually the greatest impetus, he thinks he could say, if he's using that word right, to write a first draft of a short story. That's all. So where does he go from here? The story.

He meets her at a party. I meet her at a party. They meet at a party. He sees her at a party. He thinks she's about to leave the party they're at. He looked at her a lot the past hour since he first saw her at the party. She caught him looking at her a few times and immediately turned away. He thinks he caught her looking at him a couple of times when he turned to her, or at least was looking in his direction. Then she's heading for the front door with her coat on. Nobody's with her. "Better hustle if you're going to say something," he tells himself, and goes to the door. She's already opened it and is about to step into—onto?—the top-floor landing of this four-story rowhouse facing Washington Square Park. That its name? Been so long since he thought of it. He always knew what it was called and now he forgets it or isn't sure. No, Washington Square Park sounds right. What else could it be? Thinks. Comes up with nothing. It's what he first said it was. "You probably won't want to speak to me," he says. "Now that has to be the strangest thing—certainly one of," she says, "any man has ever said to me when it's the first thing he says." That clear, or clear enough, and what a woman with her intelligence and poise would say? Sounds okay, but again, he can always fix it up later. Just stop stopping the flow. Important thing now is to get down in one sitting, which is how he always does it, the first draft of a short story so he'll have something to start working on tomorrow morning. "Why wouldn't I—" No. "I am sort of in a rush, but why do you think I wouldn't want to talk to you? So long as it doesn't go on too long." "That's what I meant," he says, "but it didn't come out well. That you're obviously in a hurry to get someplace and don't have time to talk. Nothing critical about myself. To be honest, that's not what I meant. That business, I mean, about my knowing you're not having the time to talk. I know I'm killing this more than helping it, but you must have noticed me looking at you at the party. Almost spying on you, really. I didn't mean to. I intended at one point or another to come over to you and introduce myself. In other words, when the moment was right for it. But there were always a few people with you and I never know how to bust into a group like that when it's already formed and I know no one in it." He asks her name. Or gives his first. "By the way, I'm Charles Epsteen. Nice to meet you. And you're?" He forgets who gave their name first. Doesn't matter. She could have said—she was always very polite; had much better manners than he; he learned a lot from her about how to behave with people—"Long as we're talking, I'm Eleanor Adler, friend of Arlene's. And you…?" Then they say how they know the host. She asks what discipline, she calls it, he pursued, she says, at Yaddo. "I could have guessed it. Arlene is fascinated by writers." He asks what she got her doctorate in at Columbia and if she's teaching now. She answers and looks at her watch. "I'm sorry I have to cut this short," she says, but she's meeting someone at Lincoln Center and she has the tickets and it's getting late. He asks if she thinks he could have her phone number so he could call her to meet for coffee one day, if that's possible. "Sure," she says, if the place they meet at isn't too far from her home. "I've a deskful of final exams to correct in the next two weeks and my own scholarly paper to finish up." He writes her name and phone number in his memo book. "So perhaps I'll hear from you, Charles," and he says, "You definitely will." She sticks out her hand to shake and starts for the stairs. "Why don't you take the elevator? It might be faster." "It's so small, old and noisy. And the truth is, I don't trust it. Arlene told me she got stuck in it once for an hour, or a visitor of hers had. But thanks for thinking of it," all this said while walking, and then she's around the stairwell and on the third floor. Standing on the landing—"still standing"—he raises his hands and clenches them into fists and shakes them triumphantly and says out loud but low enough so she wouldn't hear, "I can't believe it. I'm going to have coffee with her. And to think I didn't want to go to the party and almost didn't come. What a doll."

Stayed at the party another hour. Talked to no one. Either stood against a wall or sat in a chair and drank and had some food and watched the other guests talking, drinking, eating, doing what they do at big parties. Maybe half an hour. He knows he got self-conscious about being by himself and not talking to anyone and left without saying goodbye to Arlene. He'll send her one of his Van Gogh picture postcards, thanking her for inviting him and hoping they could get together for lunch one day soon. Nothing about Eleanor in it, though. Walks all the way home to West 75th Street between Columbus Avenue and Central Park West. Just "West 75th Street." Stops at a bar on Sixth or Seventh Avenue for a beer but mainly to check the Manhattan phone directory there to see if she's in it with the number she gave. One Eleanor Adler in the book—several "E. Adler" listings—with the number she gave, at 425 Riverside Drive. Writes "425 RSD" next to her name and phone number in his memo book. It's in the Columbia University area—he knows because he went to a Christmas party last year at 405. Got off the subway at 116th Street and walked two blocks south on Broadway and then down to the Drive. But did she say she lived in Manhattan and that's why he looked in that directory? Just assumed. Or he could work it into the conversation they had at the door. "If the place we meet at isn't too far from my apartment in the Morningside Heights area." So what's he getting at with all this? Going on eight pages and he isn't sure. But he has to have some idea. He's just bringing it back because he likes bringing it back, that's about all. Especially the first night they met. The night they first met. And maybe also that it's almost six years since she died and he can't stop writing about her, though he's tried, and that's the story. He saw her leaving and sort of half ran to the door to catch her. What she wore, what she said, what she looked like—her hair in a bun at the back of her head, some kind of hair holder sticking out of it. Even her shoes. Brown and maybe one-inch heels; no more than that. No makeup, or as far as he could tell. For sure no lipstick or anything around the eyes. Blue-green eyes, or a little yellow in them. But a healthy yellow. He once said to her, "Your eyes are the color of spring." "Oh, please," she said to that, "though it's nice of you to say so." Blond hair. Ear studs that sparkled, or were they pearls? White blouse. Looked like silk. "How do you wash silk?" he once asked her. "Can it even be dry-cleaned?" What'd she say? Forgets. Beautiful smile. Beautiful voice. She used the word "propitious," but he can't recall about what. Remembers he thought, on his way home, her use of it impressed him. Also "aforementioned." Again, forgets about what. He asked her what she got her doctorate in. Or did he ask her that when they met for coffee the first time? "Babel's Red Calvary stories, ten of them, with an emphasis on their endings." "One of my favorite writers of any era and one of the world's great story collections." "That's good to hear for a change. Most people I tell that to have never heard of him, so I don't usually like the question because my answer is lost on them. 'Babel, who?' But you're a writer, you say. You must know what Hemingway said of him, or is supposed to have." "No," and she told him and he tries now to remember what it was but can't come up with it. Something about a spoon stirring the clotted cream. But to get back to her voice. On their second or third date—he thinks it was when they were making out on the couch the first time she invited him up to her apartment—he said something like, "Your voice is so soft and your speech so articulate. Every single word is clear. Do you also sing?" and she said, "Terribly. My speaking voice is a misleader." "Is that a pun?" and she said "I didn't intend it as one. But I see what you mean, and because I'm not normally a funny person, I'll take total credit for it." He also stops off at a bar on Columbus and 72nd Street. "Ruppert's" he thinks it was called then, or maybe it was still "O'Neal Bros." Or even earlier: "Kelly's Bar & Grill." He hopes his friend Dennis is there. He is, sitting where he always sits, if it's not taken: on the bar stool nearest the door, an arm's length from the wall pay phone, where he sometimes receives calls. He sits beside Dennis and says, "I think tonight I'm going to have a glass of their best brandy—I feel that good," and orders a brandy, not the best, it turns out, because it's too expensive, but a good French one. He starts to tell him about the woman he met at a party not even two hours ago. Dennis cuts him off. "A party? How come you didn't take me along?" "You wouldn't have liked it. All literary people and academics. Most of the talk was incomprehensible to me or just boring, except for this woman's." "Good stuff to eat and drink?" and he says, "Great stuff. Everything catered. There was even a bartender." "So why do you say I wouldn't have liked it?" Sitting there with Dennis, he thinks he thought if things go well with this woman, it'll be a long time before he introduces her to him. He doubts she'll like him. Too crude. His clothes. He smokes too much. His hair is never combed. He only reads newspapers. Maybe one novel a year, and a short one: Camus's *The Stranger*. Chekhov's (at his recommendation) *The Steppe*. Ones that take him several months to finish—he's said he sometimes reads only one page a day—and which he thinks he could turn into a salable screenplay. Curses a lot. But the worst curse words: "Cunt. Motherfucker. Cocksucker." In front of anybody. He just can't help himself. Gets loaded about once a week and half the week looks like he has a hangover. But is funny. The funniest guy he knows, but he doesn't think she'd like his humor. But he's getting off-track. And the right name of the bar on Columbus will come to him. He goes on about this woman to Dennis. Attractive. Intelligent. Obviously very cultured. One could pick that up in a minute. His guess is her folks come from Europe. She probably speaks three or four languages. Blond. These incredible eyes. Beautiful speaking voice. Good figure. Has a Ph.D. Teaches at Columbia. She gave him her phone number. Seemed interested, "or I can hope so," and he's going to call her tomorrow. "I don't know why— Yes I do. In that short time I was with her—five, ten minutes at the most—I felt she was perfect for me, although she might eventually think I'm too old for her." "How old is she?" and he says, "She looks to be around thirty." "Ten years' difference is nothing. A few years over that, I'd say forget it; too big a divide." He finishes his brandy and orders a beer and buys one for Dennis. Watches the end of a basketball game on the TV above the bar and goes home—"Let me know what happens with your blond chickie," Dennis says. Too much on Dennis. He'll cut a lot of it out, but keep almost all the stuff in about Eleanor. At home, he decides to call her the day after tomorrow. Maybe two days after. No, one's okay, but he doesn't want her to think he's in that big a hurry to see her. So two days. Calls her the next day. They meet for coffee. Meet a few days after that, or it could have been a week after, for lunch, he now remembers, not dinner. Their first dinner together was a few days or a week after they met for lunch. He asked to see her sooner but she said she was busy but didn't say with what. Another guy? He wanted to ask but didn't. At their first dinner he asked if she was seeing anyone—"Just trying to protect myself you understand"—and she said, "Not seriously. For the time being, let's leave it at that." Few weeks later she got a call and spoke for a few minutes and told him it was the man she saw, whenever he was in New York, about once a month, but had stopped seeing this fellow soon after she started seeing him. How can he make that clearer? She said, "But I stopped seeing him soon after I started seeing you." After their first dinner at a restaurant, she invites him up to her apartment for a drink and introduces him to her cats, Lucy and Maria. He sits down beside her on the couch, which is actually a Hollywood bed made up to look like a couch. Indian bedspread and lots of couch pillows in embroidered Russian pillowslips she bought in the Soviet Union. A couple of them are still on the sofa in his house. They kiss a few times and share a glass of stout. He gets his hand under her shirt in back and keeps it there. Wants to move his hand down or around but doesn't think she's ready for that yet. Then after another kiss, she says, "I think that should be enough for tonight, do you mind? Don't think I'm not enjoying it, but you should leave before things get too serious." "Okay with me," he says. "We'll see each other again. Can I kiss you, though, one more time at the door?" and she says yes, and that's their longest kiss. A minute. Two. Really. Very long. He just kept his lips there and with his tongue got her mouth open and she didn't move her lips away or shut her mouth. After it, she says she "saw stars with that one," and he says, "Coincidence, or something. Because I saw the first few seconds of the creation of the world, or it looked like that. Big explosion, lots of lights." At the door, his coat on, he says, "One more before I leave? I'll try to make it quicker." "You needn't rush if you don't want." No open mouth this time or anytime after, he thinks, or not intentionally, because she says she only likes kissing when it's just lips on lips. "With the soul kiss, it's like my tongue's drowning in your spit." Or maybe she told him this the next time he was at her apartment and they started kissing. Anyway, at the door, another long one—minute or so—and after it he says, "So what'd you see this time? Anything?" and she says, "Oh, more of the same. It was good. I liked it. It made me dizzy. Now go."

And after? He walks to the bus stop on Broadway, thinking next time they'll probably make love, or get very close to it. Then for sure, the time after that. As he's said, he's written about most of this before. First, in a novel started soon after they met and published almost thirty years ago. Lousy reviews. The publisher dropped him. Second time, soon after that, in a short story. Then another story a few years ago. Changed things around a little to a lot. The spit but not the soul kissing is new. Stout this time instead of the two of them in the novel clicking and then sipping from small snifters Israeli brandy her father had brought back from Israel that year. Another time, in one of the stories, only he having half a juice glass of Armagnac. "I ought to get brandy snifters for such high quality stuff," she said. And then, when she was in the bathroom, he shot the rest of the drink down and poured another half glass of it without telling her or asking if he could, hoping she'd think, after he drank most of it before she came out, it was the original drink she's got for him. Her last boyfriend, the one she saw about once a month, had given her this expensive brandy as a Hanukkah gift, although that wasn't his holiday. Some months later she told him this fellow was the only man she'd ever made love with who had a foreskin. "I didn't like it," she said. Many things in common between them from the start. The Russian writers. They both subscribed to *The Nation*. Spent half a year in Paris ten years apart but only she became fluent in French. Classical music of all kinds. Baroque. Scarlatti's piano sonatas. Pachelbel's Canon in D, he thinks it is, played any which way, and he always seems to get the letter wrong. Not "letter," but right now he forgets what it's called. Beckett's recent short plays, which she saw at Lincoln Center the summer before they met and he couldn't get a ticket to: sold out. "Note," that's what it is. How could he have forgotten something so simple as that? Their first date for dinner. Coffee, lunch, they've done. Asking him up after. Introduces him to the doorman: "Sergei, this is my friend Charles." Her apartment's view of the Hudson and Riverside Park streetlamps and lights of New Jersey at night. Thought: What a great place for something romantic to happen. Her two Siamese. "If you don't want them on your lap, just lift them to the floor; don't push them." Several tall bookcases she built from scratch and hundreds of books, half of them in Russian, it seemed, in every room including the kitchen and boxes of unpacked books in her bedroom. He's mixed up the tenses, which he'll fix up later if he's still interested in this. "If you want, I'll help you put up the rest of the bookcases," and she said,

"Thank you, but I like doing it myself and don't need any help." What they said about the kisses. The first time they made love. They sit on the couch together and kiss and hug. Or at least, in two to three separate stories and the novel, end up on the couch together, she first, he first, and the other joined. "Why don't you sit here?" "Mind if I sit next to you?" Felt her breast under her bra. She felt his thigh through his pants. In one of them, she put her hand on his pants where his penis was and said, "Oops, I didn't mean that," and moved her hand away and said, "It was so hard. We should probably move this to the bedroom, but finish your drink first." "It's all right, I've had plenty," and put his glass down on the coffee table in front of them, and then said, "Actually, maybe I should. It's so good. Too good to waste," and drank it down. The bedroom was cold in all accounts of that night; the living room not as much. "It's a terrific building," she says, "—doorman, elevator, laundry room, lobby and landing mopped every day—but the real estate outfit that owns it is stingy with the heat. Ten p.m., which I think is when the city says the landlords can do this, the heat's shut off till six. I should seal the windows so it doesn't get so cold at night, something I'm always saying I'll get around to doing but I never do." "I can do it for you," he says. "I'll get insulation strips and window putty and seal up all the openings and cracks. I've done it with mine. Your windows are very old and you should get your landlord to replace them." "Maybe one day. For now, br-r-r, it's cold, so let's just get under the covers, though take off our clothes first, of course. Want to use the bathroom before I do?" They see each other almost every day after that, spend the next July and August in the cottage in Maine she's rented the last three summers. Go to Europe their second June together. Besides Russian and Polish, she speaks French and Italian and can get by in German. Or just France in one story—mostly Provence—and only Paris and Chartres in another. What else? Lots. They get engaged a little more than two years after they meet, hold the wedding ceremony and reception in her apartment a couple of months later. Coldest January 17th on record in New York, or was it the 19th? Another thing he often gets mixed up. Knows it was on Chekhov's birthday, which is how he makes sure what day they got married: Googles

"Chekhov" on her old computer. Gets a teaching job in Baltimore and they move there but keep her New York apartment. He was publishing a book almost every year by then. Their daughter's born seven months after they marry and his wife's diagnosed with her disease about three years after that. She has to use a cane for a while and then a walker and then a walker with wheels and then some contraption made in Sweden she can push like she did her wheeled walker and also sit on its attached fold-up seat when she wants to. Then she gets pneumonia. "You're looking very strangely at me. Like you don't know me. Is anything wrong?" "Yeah. Who are you? I know I know you. But you don't look like yourself. You should see a doctor." "Something's definitely wrong. I think I have to take you to the hospital." "Why? I'm all right. It's you who has a problem. You want me out of here so you can carry on." The doctors in ICU say she has a two-to-three-percent chance of surviving. Then pneumonia again a year later and same odds of surviving. Then pneumonia again a half year later—their daughter's twenty-five or -six by now—and she says in the hospital once she's able to talk again after she's extubated, if that's the right word—he'll look it up; he knows intubated is the right word for inserting the breathing tube down her throat—"This is the last time I'm going through this. Next time I get this bad a case of pneumonia, and please, for God's sake, don't tell me there won't be a next time, I want you to help me die." "No, no. Don't think like that. You always get better, always," and she says, "Listen. I'm talking. Don't argue with me. You can't know what I've gone through, so you have to do what I ask. You don't, I'll find some other way." She gets pneumonia a couple of months after that. A month. A few weeks. The doctors in ICU, after trying the strongest antibiotics on her, give her no chance of surviving and want to transfer her to hospice. She says, "I only want to die in my own bed, even if it's a hospital one on loan." "You still can be very witty," he says, and she says, "I'm not laughing." An ambulette takes her home. She refuses all nourishment, liquid, medicine and oxygen. "I'm comfortable. No pain. Just keep the morphine handy and plentiful for when things change, which I hear they will." She goes into a coma in four days and dies eleven days after that. The hospice nurse, who came every day for around fifteen minutes to check up on her and replenish the morphine supply, says, "It took much longer than I thought it would. Usually I can tell from the start how long they'll live. Now I think we should all pray," and he says, "We don't pray in this house, never have, but thank you for the thought." "That's okay. You're entitled," and she takes his daughter's hand, bows her head—his daughter's stays upright—mumbles what he supposes is a prayer and which he can't make out a word of, then asks for the morphine tablets or capsules he didn't use—he forgets what form they were in that he used to put under her tongue—and destroys them.

And after? This had all been prearranged. After the nurse leaves, he calls the funeral home and says his wife died an hour ago and will be ready to be transported to NIH in half an hour. "Time is of the essence they told me." His daughter and he clean her up and brush her hair and tie it into a ponytail and get her in a new pad and an extra-large long-sleeve T-shirt of his and the hearse comes and she's zipped up in a black body bag and the cat sniffs at the gurney's wheels and her body's driven to NIH near D.C., or maybe it's in D.C., so certain parts of her body—her brain and spinal cord particularly—can be dissected and examined to help the researchers know more about her disease. It was what she wanted to be done and only then her body cremated. "But no urn. Too macabre and a ridiculous waste of money. Just spoon a few spoonfuls of my ashes into the ground somewhere around the house—under the star magnolia tree where we put my parents' ashes—and that'd be the end of it." "Let's not talk about it, all right?" "I understand. I'm only trying to be thorough to save you the trouble of figuring out what to do when you might be too upset to." "Thank you," he thinks he said. "I mean it. Thank you."

So what happens next? The hearse picks up the body at NIH two days later and takes it to the funeral home. And then? He gets a phone call. He was expecting it but not what the funeral director said. Does he want to have a last look at his wife before she's cremated? "After what the pathologists at NIH must have done to her? No. I couldn't see her like that." "I didn't think so, but it's what we're required by law to ask." He's done this, all of it, several times, even the gurney and cat. Changes here and there but always her starving herself for four days till she goes into a coma and a total of fifteen days in the hospital bed in their home till she dies. Written about it, he means, in his last novel and a number of stories. His daughter and his wife's best friend wouldn't read any of it and he doesn't tell them anymore when a story of his with his wife's last days in it is in a magazine. She also refused to have a feeding tube put in her stomach the last two times she was in the hospital, but he could always work that in. Also, she didn't want to go to the hospital that last time. Well, she never wanted to go, but she was adamant about it this time. Did he include that in anything he's written about her so far? Thinks so, but not exactly what she said. "I'm not going. You can't force me. I'm staying here, and that's final." He had to call her best friend to help persuade her. She came right over, shut the door—"You wait outside the room; we ladies have to have a private talk"—and convinced her she had to go to the hospital and promised they'd take her home anytime she wanted to once she got there. "I don't believe any of you," her friend told him his wife said. "You're all liars, but for now you've got me beat."

His daughter's now thirty-one, same age his wife was when he first met her. So? Why'd he put that in? Thought it'd be interesting. She'll probably marry the man she's involved with for more than a year. That too. Doesn't really belong. What also doesn't belong but is interesting is that this man's the same age he was—forty-two—when he first met his wife. So why'd he write it? He's just fishing for a way to end this. As he's said, he's written about this, and again, all of it—her death, how they met, his grief, those last three weeks, kiss that made her see stars or took her breath away, he's now not sure which; first time they made love, though he wishes he could remember more of the details of that last one—two to three times at least. Party they first met at? He'd say a half dozen times, and always at the same place: an old rowhouse across from Washington Square in New York. Does he think anyone would be interested in a seventh time, let's say? He doesn't. But he had nothing to write today—something he's also said. He'd finished, as he thinks he said, story number eight or nine in this new collection he's writing. Yesterday he had nothing to write, as he's almost sure he said in this one, and he always likes to have something to work on, as he knows he's said. So after a short slow jog and breakfast this morning and after being up half the night worrying that for a second straight day he won't have anything to write when he gets up, he went to the typewriter in his bedroom and wrote this. Let's face it: he likes bringing her back in his fiction. Of course loves dreaming about her too. It's been almost six years since he pleaded with her to eat and drink and take the medications and not die. He cried and she cried and she said, "My poor sweetie. This is best for us both. And you'll be all right. You'll find someone else." "Mommy," their daughter said, "don't say things like that." "Why not? Your father knows what I mean. He needs to be with a woman. So I'm only saying it'll take time and it'll be with someone he doesn't have to take care of for twenty years." "Never," he said. "You're the only woman for me. Please stay alive." "Nonsense," she said. He broke down again and said, "Excuse me for a few minutes"—she was in bed; she never left it once the ambulette people put her there—and left the house and went for a walk and cried during it and came back maybe an hour later—he also sat for a while on a bench in front of the church across the street from their house—and their daughter met him at the door and very somberly said, "Mommy's resting now," and he said, "She died?" "No, Dad. She fell asleep right after you left and is sleeping peacefully. And please listen to me. I've thought about this hard and concluded we have to let her go and not give her any reason to hang on. It's what she wants. She feels she's suffered more than anyone deserves and doesn't want to suffer anymore." "I can't stand it," and he headed for her room. "Daddy. Don't disturb her. I said she's sleeping peacefully." "I won't. I just want to kiss her. Who knows? It could be my last chance to while she's alive." He went into her room and kissed her forehead as softly as he could, but she still opened her eyes—she was lying on her back—and smiled at him and said, "It's so nice to be home and to wake up to you." "I'm sorry if I woke you. Our dear daughter warned me not to." "It's okay. It's not hard for me to go back to sleep. Just remember the morphine if I show serious distress," and her eyes closed and she fell asleep almost immediately, it seemed—the blank expression, or something like that, after her smile faded—and two days later she fell asleep and went into a coma she never came out of.

That's all. They buried her ashes, or what the funeral home gave them of her—"Two scoopfuls; enough to fill up the small container"— in the front yard under the star magnolia her closest friend had driven down from New York more than fifteen years ago and which they had a tree service plant so it would take. "You once said it was one of your favorite trees and is native to Maryland, so I got it for you. Not too big? It was the smallest the nursery had, but it still hung out the rear of the hatchback the whole trip and I thought I'd lose it. It would have been sad if I had." He surrounded the spot where the canister of her ashes was buried with three concentric circles of polished stones his wife and daughter and he had collected on beaches in Maine the thirty or so summers before she died. The last twenty years, he'll say, she never went down to the beach for the stones but sat in her wheelchair and watched them. He's written about all that a few times too. He'll probably never be able to stop writing about her, repeating himself in what he writes. Going over, which is the same thing, many of the same things of their life together and with their daughter. Does he think he can turn what he wrote today, and it's a lot—twenty-eight pages—into a short story? In other words, does he think it'd be worth working on? He kind of doubts it. Long as it is, and it'll only get longer as he writes it, he doesn't think there's enough in it for a story. Tomorrow he'll read what he wrote today, and he'll see. At least he got something in today. That's always important. To never let a day go by, as he did yesterday, without writing something, if he can help it.

8

Time

HE'S WRITTEN ABOUT THIS TOO. He's almost sure of it. Or at least thought seriously of writing about it a number of times and jotted the incident down in his notebook as an idea for a story. That every time he sits down at his typewriter for the first time that day, or almost every time—six times out of seven, he'd say—he thinks about his wife. But not just thinks of her but of the same scene of her shouting to him from their bedroom window on the second floor of the cottage they rented in Maine that summer that she has great news for him—sometimes "the most wonderful news." That someone from *Time* magazine called and said they're going to run a review of his new book next week and are sending up a photographer from Portland to take pictures of him to go with the review.

It's always right after he gets out of their car. The Chevrolet Citation, the one with the rear-wheel lockup problem that spun around on them on ice a couple of times and was finally recalled and fixed. She must have heard him—he never asked her if this was it—drive down their road and park on the grass in front of the cottage. In the image he has of her she always, as he's getting out of the car or just after he gets out of it, cranks open the window, if it isn't already open, or cranks it open all the way and raises the window screen as far as it can go so she can stick her head out, and shouts, "Charles, Charles"—always twice and always excitedly—"I have great news for you" or "the most wonderful news. Someone from *Time* magazine called and said they're going to run a review of your book *Endings*" or just "they're going to review *Endings* in next week's issue and they're sending up a photographer from Portland to take pictures of you to go with the review."

Sometimes when she tells him this he's with their daughter, who was how old at the time? The book was published in June or July, 1985, and she was born in late September, '82, so she was almost three. The way he remembers it, when he's with their daughter, he yells up to his wife, "That's great; that's fantastic. *Time* magazine. Jesus Christ," or something like that, and then gets their daughter out of the car seat and picks her up and says, "Did you hear? *Time* magazine. A very big important magazine. Is going to write about Daddy's new book and is sending a man with a camera to take pictures of me to go with the story the magazine is writing about my book. Probably pictures of me at the beach behind our cottage, or at my typewriter. And there's a good chance this person, a photographer, will want to shoot pictures of you and Mommy too." "I don't want anyone to shoot me and Mommy and you," and he says, "Don't worry, my darling, he won't. It's with a camera, I said. And if it's a lady photographer, she won't too."

If it's his daughter he's with when he comes back to the cottage and his wife shouts to him from the upstairs bedroom window, then they've just returned from getting her an ice cream and to pick up a *New York Times* and a few necessary items at the general store in town four miles away. But if it's his mother he's with, who visited them for a week every summer for about fifteen years, it's because he's taken her, and probably also his daughter, to lunch in town or to another lunch place a few miles from it, and maybe for a drive someplace his mother would be interested in—an antique store or two; a beach with a beautiful view; a larger market in a much larger town about twenty miles from the cottage. In other words: to be out of the house for a few hours with his daughter alone or mother alone or with both of them so his wife could get some work in without being interrupted by any of them. Her mother also used to spend a week with them every summer, but always in late August, and the review was in July. So it definitely wasn't her mother he was with when he drove up to the cottage and learned about the *Time* review. And her father only visited them in Maine once, the first summer they were there together, and then swore off it because of the mosquitoes and deer flies and black flies and some other biting insect so small you could barely see it but which drew blood. "I'll see you when you get back," her father used to say the day they picked up her parents' two Siamese cats and drove to Maine with their two cats and her parents' cats and their daughter.

Or he drives up to the cottage alone. His daughter's napping in the cottage. Their mothers are in New York. His wife's working at her electric typewriter in the upstairs bedroom when she hears their car coming down the private road. Or just "a car"—she doesn't know for sure yet that it's theirs. She gets up, looks out the window, sees their car, opens the window all the way—"I was so excited and happy for you," she later said—raises the window screen and when he gets out of the car—he might have gone to town to get the *Times* and a few other things at the general store and maybe also gone to the well-stocked library there if it was open that day—she sticks her head out the window, holds the windowsill with her hands and shouts, "Charles, Charles. I have some great news" or "terrific news" or "the most wonderful news for you. You got a call from someone named Elizabeth Green at *Time* magazine. I have it all written down here. They're going to do a review of *Endings* next week and are sending up a photographer from Portland to take pictures of you to go with the review. They need to get the pictures in right away, so she said is tomorrow okay and I said yes. Was that all right?" He remembers saying something like, "For a review in *Time* magazine? Any day.

Any hour. They can come at midnight if they like. Oh, this is incredible. For a book by a small publisher to get a review in a major magazine? And for a collection of stories, no less? What could be better?" "I'll be right down," she says, and he hears her running down the staircase and she comes outside and they hug. If he's with his daughter, he says, "Let me get the kid out of her car seat." If he's with his mother, he says "Did you hear, Mom?" and she'd say something like "*Time* magazine. My, my. You're becoming a big man," which she said twice before when he told her about something good that happened to one of his books, and he didn't know either time, because of the way she looked at him and said it, if she was complimenting him or being sarcastic.

His father, he should probably mention, died six years before he met his wife and he doesn't think he's ever been to Maine. He asked his mother about it once and she said—they were having lunch in the Maine cottage at the time, so this would also be in the early eighties—"Not with me. And prior to my meeting your father, and we're going back here now more than fifty years—getting to Maine, even the southern tip of it—Kittery; those places; where the vice president has a summer home—if you didn't go by a large passenger boat, I was told, it took three days by car, if you were lucky, and wasn't an easy journey. So nobody went except the very rich, by boat, and their staff." "Had you been to Maine before you started coming up to see us?" and she said, "I don't believe so, but you know my memory."

But he's gotten away from what he first started thinking about. That almost every time—and this has gone on since a few months after his wife died and he started writing again. When he sits in front of his typewriter in the morning, and it's always in the morning. It never seems to happen if the first time he sits at his typewriter that day is around noon or any time past that. He pictures his wife at the upstairs bedroom window of the cottage they rented in Maine their first six summers there together, excitedly telling him about the *Time* magazine book review. Always just before or right after he takes the dust cover off the typewriter and also before he puts the paper into the typewriter and certainly before he start typing. Opening the window all the way. Raising the window screen as high as it'll go. Leaning out the window while holding on to the windowsill. Probably right after he gets out of the car. If their daughter's with him, then while he's preparing to take her out of her car seat. If his mother's with him, then while he's opening the front passenger door and about to help her unhitch her seat belt, which she always had trouble doing herself. If both his mother and daughter are with him, then tending to his mother first. Shouting his name twice and that she has great news for him. Terrific news. The most wonderful news. "I'm almost too excited to speak." "What is it?" he could have said. "I love it when people tell me they have good news for me." "*Time* magazine called when you were out. Someone by the name of Elizabeth Green. I have her phone number. They're going to review your new book in the next issue next week." "That's fantastic," he said. Or something like it. "'Incredible.' 'Unbelievable.' For a story collection from a small publisher? I'm really surprised." "That's not all. They're sending up a photographer from Portland tomorrow to take pictures of you to go with the review." "Even better. To get such attention for the book? I wouldn't even care if it was a bad review, though I doubt they'd be doing it if the reviewer didn't like some of it. But please don't fall out of the window," he might have said. That'd be just like him. "Get inside and pull down the screen. The mosquitoes will get in the house. Enough do, then good news and all and maybe at dinner a bottle of champagne to celebrate it with, we'll still never get to sleep tonight." "Meet you downstairs," he thinks she said, and a few seconds later—thirty; maybe a minute—she was outside. If it was his mother with him, he would have said, "Mom, did you hear?" If just his daughter: "Do you know what Mommy just said?" If both were with him, he might have said, "We better get in the house before the mosquitoes find us," and gotten his mother out of her seat belt and then his daughter out of her car seat.

9

A Very Short One

MAKE IT SHORT. He has a headache and his back hurts. He slipped on ice this morning on his way to get the mail in his mailbox and fell on his back and head. For some reason, his head bounced, so it hit the ground twice, the second time as hard as the first. But he has a story to write, or one he's going to try to, or he should say the first draft of one. And he knows he won't be able to sit at the typewriter for very long. His back and head need to rest. He wants to finish this fast, take two Tylenols, and lie on his back on his bed and maybe nap.

So the story. He had lunch this week with a former graduate student of his and a fellow who now teaches in the same department he retired from seven years ago. The former grad student, "June," also now teaches in the writing department. The fellow, "Tom," he'd only met once, and briefly, at a Christmas party the department gave a year ago. June and Tom seem to be good friends. The way they kid each other and say good things about the other's work. He doesn't think they're lovers. Nothing that goes on between them even hints at that, and they're both married for a second time and from what they say, and with June he's seen when she's with her husband, their marriages seem to be smooth ones. That doesn't make the sense he intended it to, but go on. So. June had called him to have lunch. "We haven't got together in a long time," she said, "and I miss our talks." He said fine, he'd love it, and they set a date and decided on a place. Then she emailed him that when Tom heard she was meeting him for lunch, he wanted to join them. Would that be all right? "He thinks very highly of your work and wants to get to know you better." "Why not?" he wrote back. "Short time I was with him, he seemed like a nice bright guy. And we can always have lunch, just the two of us, some other time." Is he romantically interested in June? But that—the way he said it—can be confusing. Is he talking here, the reader could wonder, of Tom or himself? More himself than Tom, it sounds like, but it's still open to misinterpretation. He thinks he started off on the wrong foot, doing this in third. If he had said, "Am I romantically interested in June?" there'd be no mistaking whom he was referring to. Maybe he should start again, using first this time, and try to make it shorter than what he wrote before, as his back and head, and now his neck a little, hurt even worse than when he first started this.

I had lunch with June, a former grad student of mine, and Tom, also a writer, who teaches in the same department she does and which I retired from seven years ago. The conversation was good. Books, writers, movies, gossip and news about former grad students of mine who were in her graduating class and some of my former colleagues. And they're both bright, funny, lively and candid, so I had a good time with them, the first time I'd been out of the house for lunch or anything, really, with anybody for weeks. They did most of the talking, which was all right with me. I'd become kind of quiet the last year or so and didn't feel I had much to say about anything. Anyway, the check came and I grabbed it off the table. "No, this has to be my treat," June said, trying to pull the check out of my hand. "I was the one who invited you to lunch." "Then it should be my treat," Tom said, "since I forced my way into this lunch." "Please, both of you, it's mine, tip included," I said. "I'm June's ex-writing coach. And as for you," I said to Tom, "I have no excuse for picking up the check other than I'm around thirty years older than you and it's the norm for the older guy, if he's that much older and not broke, to pick up the check. And my only child's out of the house and doing pretty well on her own, so I've only myself to feed, while you have two young kids." "And a wife who works and makes more money than me," Tom said, "so that blows that part of your argument. But if you insist. Next time, and I hope there'll be a next time, the check's mine." "And what about me?" June said. "Don't I ever get a chance to pay it? Charles has snatched the check away our last two lunches and now here." "We'll split it then," Tom said. "And if there's a third lunch with the three of us, which I hope for also, you and I will split that one too." But I like it better in third person. I'm not sure why. Distance, of course, but it just sounds and reads better. And I'll work out that "romantically interested" line, which seems to have been the only one I had trouble with in third.

After he paid, they all stood up and Tom looked at him in a way that seemed he didn't think he looked well. No, it has to be in first. He's running in to too many problems in third. And remember to tighten it and keep it short.

I paid the check, we were all standing by now and about to say our goodbyes, when Tom's expression suddenly changed and he looked at me in a way that seemed he didn't think I looked well. That I'd gotten much older and a bit sickly looking since he last saw me at that Christmas party a year ago, and maybe even worse: that I was ailing with something serious and possibly on my last legs. That's what I caught in his look before it changed back to the normal friendly unalarmed look, I guess I can say, he had through lunch. We had been sitting next to each other at the rather cramped table, across from June—a table that was better suited for just two people. What I'm saying is he hadn't till now had a chance to get a clear look at my face because of our seating positions. That's also a little confusing and not quite what I wanted to say, but get on with this: you can mess with what you've written later. They were going to the parking lot to their cars. I said, "I'm not leaving just yet. I don't have anyplace important to go to and I want to look around the place"—there were several food shops and restaurants in this big enclosed space. "Buy a loaf of bread at the bakery here and maybe something at the smoked-fish shop: salmon or whitefish or trout, which I loved smoked, all three, whitefish the best, and can't get anywhere else that's as good. Can't get anywhere else in Baltimore, period. One smoke-fish shop! You'd think with all the fish and shellfish eaten in this city, there'd be more. Also a poppyseed bar at the bakery, if they have it. They have all the other times I've been here. I love poppyseed in any form, but especially in the poppyseed bar they make. But here I am, blathering on about food I'm going to buy, when I said almost nothing at lunch." "You said plenty," Tom said, "and all of it very interesting." "Oh, yeah," I said. "But thanks. So. It's been great seeing you." "Same here," they both said. I shook Tom's hand, kissed June's cheek and watched them leave till they were outside. For some reason—maybe a good one—I thought Tom would turn around and look back. If he had, I would have waved. If both had looked back: same wave.

I bought an olive bread and two poppyseed bars. I nixed the smoked fish: not good for me. I've been on an almost salt-free diet since my last checkup, to bring my blood pressure down. Tom's look right after we got up from the table still bothered me. I imagined what they said when they walked to their cars and maybe stood beside one before they kissed or hugged like two friends would and then one of them got in the car. "He doesn't look good": Tom. June: "You think so?" Tom: "He was so healthy-looking the last time I saw him at the department's Christmas party a year ago. Strong, vigorous, energetic. You would never have been able to guess his age. He also seems to have lost considerable weight." June: "That's what Richard said the last time we saw him. No pep to his walk, and he'd sort of shriveled a little and you could barely hear him speak. It was at a Whole Foods, only a few months ago. I guess I put it out of my head because I didn't want to think anything was wrong. Well, he's getting up there. People his age lose weight without trying to. Seventy-four? Seventy-five?" Tom: "Seventy-eight. Either when I Googled him or from the copyright page of a book of his. 1936. He's slowing down. He also might be ill with something and didn't want to tell us." June:

"Oh, I hope not. Could be all it is is a pulled muscle someplace: his shoulder or back. That would account for the way he slumps. Let's hope it's no worse than that or just part of the slow gradual decline a very older person goes through."

He's standing in front of the Korean noodle shop in this hall... I'm standing next to the noodle shop next to the bakery... I'm standing in front of the noodle shop next to the bakery, thinking if I should get one of its noodle dishes to take home. Nah, I've got plenty of food for tonight and my dinner's already prepared: same things I had the last two nights and which I like: tuna melts on sliced everything bagels, ready to go into the oven for half an hour, and a salad and kosher pickle and now one of the poppyseed bars. Then I think: Do I look that much worse than I thought I did? I probably do. No, I know I do. I also don't speak and certainly don't stand up and walk and even just stand as well as I used to. And when I do speak—or at least most of the time—it's not with the force and clarity and confidence that I used to. I don't project. I don't seem to be able to, and sometimes I can't even be heard. I take over-the-counter pills for whatever it is that's wrong with my esophagus and vocal cords. I think they're for that. But there's an example. I'm not thinking right. I don't know what the hell's happened to me. Yes, I do. I've gotten old. I should get out of here. This place, I mean. I didn't want to have lunch with them. I told June I wasn't feeling that sociable. But if she insisted, I'd go. So I sort of let her pressure me into it, if I'm remembering right. No, I told her I wanted to see her. That it had been too long. I love her in a way, and being with her always made me feel good. She's so peppy and happy and funny and bright. I don't have to lie to her; I really like her work. But just with her, not with Tom, though none of that is what I told her. So what made me not say no to having Tom join us? I forget. I usually go along with what the other person wants. I'm getting what I felt then all mixed up. Maybe I didn't feel that hesitant about meeting them. Certainly I wanted to see June. You said get out of here, so get.

When I get home around two hours later—I went from lunch to the Y to work out and then took a wonderful shower there, letting the warm water run down my neck and back for a few minutes (jeez, that felt good) and for about a minute, the hottest water I could take directly on my lower back—there is an email from June. "Thank you for lunch. You're always so generous. It was an absolute delight seeing you again, and Tom enjoyed it too. Thanks for letting him have lunch with us. He thinks the world of you. We have to do it again soon. This time, I pay. Remember that, mister: I PAY. Or Tom and I split it, if he comes along, because I know he'd want to pick up the check—he told me he wanted to for today's lunch but you were too fast for him—and would give me an argument over it. But we have to, as I said, do lunch again and not wait untold months to. XXX"

I write back: "It was wonderful seeing you too. But tell me. There was a look on Tom's face when we were saying our shaloms, and I think on your face, too, that I didn't look well. Am I reading it right? The way you were both looking at me, or Tom definitely, you maybe, was kind of spooky. As if you were seeing something in me you just noticed and which startled you: an illness you thought I had. Not an illness, or possibly one, but you know what I mean. I hope you do, because I'm not putting it well." She writes back: "Not at all. Nothing of the kind. You looked chipper, healthy and strong. You never seem to age. Maybe you need a new prescription for your glasses. I'm just kidding. I'm sure your eyesight is eagle-sharp too." I write back: "I doubt I looked healthy and strong and the other one you said. Perhaps for someone my age I do, which means I look as if I'm 75 rather than three years older than that." She writes back: "You're 78? Actually, I knew that, but it's still hard to believe. If I didn't know you, I'd say 65 at most." I write back: "I didn't want to write back. I know you have lots else to do other than answer me: kids, school, work, family life, your writing. But I will, just to say you're very sweet and kind. See you soon, I hope, or better put: when you have the time."

That night, in the middle of the night, he has to get up to pee. He sits off the side of the bed—this is what his physical therapist told him to do before he gets off the bed—he's been going to one twice a week for his back—then slowly raises himself up on the balls of his feet—"Don't forget to tighten your abdominals," she says every time he sees her—and stands, and falls. He can't get up. Tries many times. I think I've had a stroke, he thinks. Or something. He has to pee and he can't hold it any longer and he pees on the floor. He isn't wearing undershorts. The cat comes in and sniffs at the pee and lies alongside him. He pets him. I said this would be a short one. "Nice cat," he says. "Good friend. What a pal you are. If only you could help me get up." And then he can't speak. He tried and no words come out and maybe they didn't when he thought he spoke just now. He wants to say, "What are you going to do now? And look at the mess you made. Who's going to clean it up? If the carpet's not washed down, it'll stink of piss. It's obvious I won't be able to, or not right away. Maybe I can." He crawls to the toilet a few feet away. The cover's up, which is how he always leaves it in this bathroom. He grabs a towel off the towel rack and dips it into the toilet, which is fresh water—he flushed the toilet the last time he used it—and crawls back to where he peed and rubs the carpet with the wet towel. The cat gets out of his way and leaves the room. He throws the towel into the bathroom and tries to lift himself onto the mattress, but can't. I don't know what happened, he thinks. And if it was a stroke, I wouldn't have been able to crawl to the bathroom or even throw the towel into it, would I? I doubt it. Maybe I should crawl to the dresser and get on my knees and reach for the phone on it or pull it off the dresser by the cord, and call 911. But I don't want to go to the hospital. It's flu season, plus icy driveways and streets, so Emergency will be jammed. I also probably don't need to go. My mind's fine. And my voice: "Tra-la-la," he says. It's fine too. I probably should just stay here on the carpet and fall asleep if I can, and when I wake up I might be able to lift myself onto the bed. But what happened? In the order that they happened, as sort of a test. I was in bed. I had to pee. I stood up the way the physical therapist told me to when I want to get off the bed—tightened my abdominals—when suddenly my left leg collapsed from under me and I was on the floor, lucky not to have hit my head on anything on my way down—night table, radio, lamp—and couldn't get up and peed on the floor. Then the cat came in, put its nose close to the pee, lay down beside me, I petted him and said what a good cat he is. Good. You got everything in order. "Tra-la-la," he says. Good. Rest. Sleep.

He lies on his side of the floor. It's cold. He pulls the covers off the bed and gets them on top of him. Reaches for a pillow but his hand can't get that far. Gets a book off the night table, puts his head on top of it and falls asleep.

He wakes up when it's light out. This is supposed to be short. Manages to get back on the bed. It's a struggle but he makes it. Pulls the covers back onto the bed, gets under them and lies on his side and closes his eyes. I'm much better, he thinks. I'm almost well. This pillow feels so good. I should email June today to tell her she and Tom were right in what he thinks they saw in him at lunch yesterday. I'm sure I didn't look well, he'll say, and I turned out not to be well later. I don't know what it was, he'll say—a 24-hour flu, maybe, and if that was it, I hope neither of you caught it—but I'm all right now. I feel so good now, he'll say, that I'm not going to worry about it or see my doctor about it. If you can, let's meet for lunch next Friday or the Friday after that, same place and time, which seems to be a good hour and day for you, and if not then, then any time and day you want. I'm usually free, he'll say, so I'll leave the logistics up to you, and if you'd like Tom to join us again, that's okay by me. But I have to get out of the house more. I've become such a loner, he'll say, and I seem to be only getting worse.

He falls asleep. Before he does, he thinks don't send June the email you contemplated sending. Give her some room. Don't make her think you need her company or want her sympathy. Don't write her for at least a week, maybe two. And call your doctor tomorrow. Or call him Monday. He gets in at seven, so call him then, to make sure of getting an appointment that day. Tell him about the fall—or email him all this—and your inability to get off the floor for hours, and maybe he'll know the reason. Could be it's a simple explanation and he can prescribe a medication to prevent it from happening again. It isn't easy living alone in a house at his age. If he had a companion, it'd be easier. She'd see to him. She'd help him get back on the bed. She'd call 911, if it had to come to that, just as he'd do the same for her, as he did for his wife, and stay in her hospital room all day with her till she was discharged. But nothing he can do about getting a companion now. And probably nothing he can do about it in the future. No, definitely nothing. It doesn't seem he'll ever be with a woman again. He knows he'll never go out of his way or make an effort to. What's he supposed to do, sign up with some matching service, or whatever they're called? No chance. It's not him. He'll just have to stay healthy. And when he's really feeling better, call or email June and arrange to meet for lunch again. Say: If Tom wants to join them or she'd like Tom to, that'd be fine with him. "He's a likeable guy," say or write. Write. It's simpler. "I enjoyed his company. And he certainly—you both do—picks up the conversational slack where I let off." Does that sound right? Doesn't. So say it a different way and nothing about slack. So: a short story he has here, but not short enough. What's he mean by that? He means—counting the pages he's written—it needs to be cut in half if not down to a third, to make it a very short one, which is all it's worth. There for sure isn't enough here to warrant a story this long.

He calls his doctor at seven o'clock sharp on Monday, sees him a few hours later. Doctor checks him out, puts him through a number of procedures and tests. Urine. Blood. A cardiogram. Says: "Let me see your two forefingers touch. Now touch my forefinger with yours. Walk to the door and back a couple of times," and so on. "I'll call you tomorrow with the tests' results, but I'm sure they won't show anything. All my 78-year-old patients should be as healthy as you and their bodies in such good shape. Even my 70-year-old patients. Your left knee went temporarily. That's what accounts for the fall. You heard as well as I did, when I was examining you, your bones cracking there. Don't use the leg press at the Y anymore. And get a kneepad for both knees. That can't hurt. If you insist on cortisone shots, we'll do that. But you know me. I always take the conservative approach, so I suggest you stay away from shots of any kind for as long as you can. You're fine. And no more deep knee bends if you still do them in your spare time. I'm telling you. You're fine."

10

Another Breakup

THIS IS ANOTHER ONE he keeps going back to. They'd spent
the summer in Maine. It was less than a year since they first met:
November 28th to the end of August. They drove back from Maine
in her car. She double-parked in front of his building. He got out
with his typewriter and two boat bags with his clothes and books and
manuscripts and writing supplies in them and said, "So I'll see you
tomorrow, okay? Tonight we both should get a good sleep. It's been
a long trip. I know I'm tired. See you, cats," and he waved to her two
Siamese cats in their carrier on the back seat. She said, "Charles?"
He said, "What?" "Charles, I have to tell you something." "Uh-oh, it
sounds bad." "What I'm trying to say is it's not working. We're not.
I'm breaking up with you." "You're kidding." "I'm not." "But why?
I can't believe this." "I knew you'd say that. No, that's not nice of me.
I know this comes as a surprise, but I didn't think it'd be that much

of one. It's not working. I said that, didn't I. Anyway, it's not working and it won't work and we should end it and I'm ending it and that's all I can say for now. All I can say, period. I'm sorry." "Okay," he said. "But listen, and I don't say this out of anger or in any way getting even with you or anything like that. I say it out of self-protection, probably, or I don't know what. I'm totally confused. But don't call or write or contact me in any way unless you think you want to try getting back together, though I doubt you ever will, try or want to." "Don't worry, and I'm not being sarcastic; I won't." "Good. Because I'm not going to let this bother me, is what I'm saying. It's always been like this. A woman I love and have been seeing a while—one, Donna, for more than three years. But suddenly, out of nowhere, or I was just too stupid not to see it coming, breaking it off with me. It's happened too often, and my misery after, is the reason I'm not going to let it bother me this time. Not 'bother,' but disturb and sadden me and so forth. That misery. Ruin my life for weeks. You say we're done; okay, we're done. Good life to you. I mean that. I wish you all the happiness and good fortune in the world. What drivel I'm talking. Yeah, I feel hurt, but the hell with it," and he turned around and picked up his boat bags and the typewriter by its case handle and went down the steps to his brownstone building. Didn't look back. He knew her car was still there because he didn't hear it start up and drive off. She was probably looking at him, thinking he doesn't know what, or maybe just dealing with something entirely unrelated to him: making sure she has her apartment keys, seeing that the cats were all right. He heard her car go while he was getting the boat bags and typewriter into his building's vestibule. He felt lousy. Stomachache. Sweat. The works. He bet she felt lousy too, for him, and because of his last remarks and angry way he said them. He looked in his mailbox. It seemed stuffed. He'll open it later. Fuck the mail. He wasn't expecting anything and he didn't care about anything. He unlocked the door to the ground floor hallway and started up the stairs with the typewriter and boat bags to his apartment on the third floor.

He thought of her a lot the next few weeks. Didn't think she'd call, but just about every time his phone rang he hoped it was her. Thought, despite what he told her in front of his building, she might send him a letter explaining why she broke up with him, and saying she hopes it hasn't made him...made him what? Not sad. Not disgusted with her. Something. Bitter, maybe. No, she wouldn't worry about that either. But she had to have felt a little bad about the breakup and that he was probably taking it badly—she knew how he felt about her—but nothing more than that. Nothing to bring her back. Anyway, no letter or phone call. He thought a few times: What would he do if she did call? Don't even think about it, he then thought, because she's not going to, but what would he do if she did? He'd listen to her say why she called and he wouldn't say anything till she finished. But what she said from the car while the front passenger window was all the way down and he was standing on the sidewalk, was final. Not only in what she said, but her determined look of finality, he supposes he could call it, for want—wont?—of anything else right now. Face it. He's seen the last of her, unless he bumps into her one day, and then what would he say? "Hi, goodbye," or "Hi, how are you? Nice to see you," and "Goodbye." No, not so fast. They'd talk. Catch up. But if she was with some guy, he'd make it as fast as he said. It's too bad. He thought he might end up marrying her. Before she broke up with him, he'd been thinking it's what he wanted. They never talked about it—too early in their relationship: just nine months—but things were going so well, it seemed, she must have thought about it too. He even thought of their having a child soon after they married—he was 43, she was 32. She said plenty of times she loved him, and whenever he told her he loved her, she said, "I'm glad," and would give him a kiss. They were so right for each other: intellectually, emotionally, even the same religion, which was a first for him in around twenty years, not that it played a big part in it, and their likes and dislikes. Sexually, there was never anyone better. She never said the same about him, though she may have thought it. Anyway, right for each other all ways. Everything. He couldn't rule out one. Maybe their age difference, but she never said it was a problem. Everyone they knew seemed to think they were a perfect pair. Even her parents, she said, "and they're not easy to please when it comes to me. I've brought in boyfriends before and there wasn't one they really liked, especially not the one I married." His mother? "I love her as I would my own daughter, and

I've never seen you so happy. This is the one. Don't lose her." Two months after the breakup, when he was thinking of her he thought she probably has a new boyfriend by now. Word would have got out that this great catch was unattached again. She was so gentle and beautiful, kind and smart. Men flocked to her. He saw it at parties and readings and lectures they went to. Her body. Long real blond hair and that Madonna-like smile, or whatever it could be compared to. Soft voice, angelic face. You name it, she had it. A good teaching job at Columbia for two more years and good prospects for more. That great apartment on Riverside Drive, facing the Hudson, on the seventh floor, so no trees blocking its view. That really impressed him, and at such low rent. Also her poetry. He loved what she let him read of it. No fakery in her at all. Positive, positive, positive. Early in the breakup he thought once or twice of writing her, asking for an explanation—one better than she gave him from the car, though he wouldn't say that; he'd just say he was still mystified—why she broke up with him, but then thought it the wrong move and it went against what he said when he was standing on the sidewalk: "And don't worry. I'll never try to get in contact with you again. This has been hard enough. I don't want to make it worse for myself." If she was going to come back to him, which is what he wanted, it would be because he did nothing: no letter or phone call. No gift of a book or two he thought she might like, which he'd mail or drop off with her doorman. That's what he did with two other women who broke off with him, and he felt lucky to get a brief written thank-you note from one. With the other, he left the package of books under the mailboxes in her building's vestibule, so who knows if she even got it? He never found out. But she'd have to be the one to write or call. And the longer they were split up, the less chance there'd be of their getting together. She might even think he'd gotten a new girlfriend by now. That he would have called or written her, despite what he said that day, if he hadn't hooked up with someone else. She knew his need to be with a woman he liked and have sex with and do a little traveling with and so on. Didn't they talk this summer about going to France for a month next year? That is, he remembers saying, if he can come up with his share of the money for the trip. She spoke

French fluently, another thing he loved about her. "I speak it a little," he said, "so you'll be my translator and book all the hotels and trains."

Two months after she broke up with him, maybe three—he used to say three; she, two—she called him. By this time he didn't think anymore it could be her. It wasn't that he'd stopped thinking of her. He still did, but a lot less. Still dreamed of her, too, though down to about twice a week, when at the beginning it was almost every night and sometimes two and three times a night and a few times they were sequential dreams, or what is he trying to say? Dreams told in continuing order. No, that still doesn't sound right. In a few of the dreams he's had with her since she broke up with him, they were making love. In one, just a few days ago, she was pregnant, maybe five to six months pregnant, judging by the distention of her belly—now there's a word he never used before, in speech or his writing, and he's not even sure he's got the meaning right here. He said, putting his hand on her belly and feeling the baby kicking, "Is she mine?" and she said, "Who else could she be from? You're the only one I've slept with the last year." In one dream, maybe a week after the breakup, he was on top and came in her, a first for his entire dream life. At least he doesn't remember it happening before, and it felt like the real thing. But she called. "Hi, Charles," after he said hello, "it's Eleanor." "I recognized your voice. It hasn't been that long. Three months?" "More like two." "You're probably right." "How are you? How's your work going?" she said. "If you mean my writing, good as can be expected. You know me. Finish a story, start a story." "And your writing classes at NYU? You were anxious about teaching adults for the first time." "It's just continuing ed. Very little money for lots of work, but no grades or office hours. It's not like teaching undergrads at Columbia. And I'm perfectly lousy at it. I'm sure they won't rehire me next term." "Of course they will. All your publications? They're getting a bargain. And I know you're undervaluing your teaching skills." "Thanks. But I'm not. I have to read their manuscripts three times before I understand them. And when I give them a story by a professional writer to read—you know, to show how it's done—I get tongue-tied and unintelligible and sound like an idiot, as if I forgot to read the story myself. I'm hopeless. It's hopeless. But look. I'm happy to hear from you, but what's this all about? Do I owe you something from last summer's cottage bill?" "You sound angry," she said. "Did I get you at a bad time? Or you don't want to talk to me?" "No, just asking. Really. And I did think maybe I owed you some money from the summer." "No, you don't. I called to find out how you've been doing. To say I've been thinking of you." "And I've been thinking of you. For one thing, what I'd say if you did call." "And?" "What I'm saying, I guess. What's the reason for your calling, and so on. That I've thought of you now and then, and so on." "Nice thoughts, I hope." "Well, everything till you showed me the door. That came pretty abruptly. Good thing I had this lousy teaching job to prepare for and go to three times a week, and my writing." "That is a good thing. Did you get a story out of it?" "Again, you know me. Felt I had to get it out of my system some way and also make a good thing out of a bad one. But you're totally unrecognizable in it. Brown hair, hazel eyes, and you're a Gentile, or she is. Never had a woman character with hazel eyes and bangs, though plenty of Gentiles. I'm not even sure I know exactly what color hazel is. Dumb of me, right? I'm a writer and I could have looked it up. But I got lazy. What about you? Good stuff, I hope." "You mean thinking of you? For the most part, yes." "And what's going on with you now? Have you started seeing somebody?" "Where'd that come from?" she said. "No. And you, if I may bounce the question back to you?" "The same. Not much desire to, and no opportunity to, also. After all, you broke up with me. Nah, I don't know what I'm saying." "As for me, I just didn't want to. Too soon after you." "Yeah, that's closer to what I was feeling than what I said. Skip the opportunity business." "So, I was thinking, Charles. We're having a pleasant conversation now, which I had hoped we would. No anger, no blame. So like to meet for coffee one day and talk some more? If you didn't want to, I'd understand." "No, I'd like to." "Meet?" "Yes." "I'm glad."

They meet for coffee that same week. She seemed happy to see him. He was nervous about seeing her. Walked the entire forty-one blocks and three sidestreets to the coffee shop she suggested they meet at. "It's only five minutes from my last class that day, so I'm being selfish dragging you up here. But I know I'll be tired after two classes that day and couldn't shlep myself much further." "It's okay, and you know me. I love walking up upper Broadway. So much to see." She was sitting at a small table when he walked in, reading a book. He said, "Hi" and extended his hand to shake. She said, "Don't be silly. When was the last time we shook hands, when we were saying goodbye after the first time we met?" and she offered her cheek to be kissed. They talked they laughed. After about an hour, when she stood up to leave, she said, "This has been fun. Like to do it again?" "Sure, yes. What about for dinner?" They meet for dinner the next week. "I'd make it sooner," she said, "but I'm up to my ears in school work. In other words—" "You don't have to go any further. I mean, I didn't mean to cut you off. But it makes sense, what you say. And just to know I'll be seeing you again, makes me feel good." "Me too, with you." "Well, great."

She invited him to her apartment after dinner. During dinner he wanted to ask her what was the reason—"The main reason," he was going to say, "or main two or three, if there were more than one"—she broke up with him this past summer, but never found a good time to ask it. The conversation was good and never stopped. Again, they laughed a lot. At one point near the end of dinner, when their dishes had been cleared and they were finishing their second glass of wine, he took her hand in his over the table and then let it go after a few seconds and said, "Sorry." "No need to be," she said. "I didn't mind. It felt nice. Comfortable." "That's good. But I wasn't thinking, really. Just did it instinctually. Instinctively?" "Both. I prefer the latter. I like the sound of it better. But use whichever you want." They walked to her building a few blocks away. Didn't hold hands, which he wanted to. Just walked side by side at a good clip because it was a bit chilly and she wasn't dressed for it. Again he wanted to ask what was the reason or maybe even reasons she broke up with him this past summer, but then thought let's just get inside first. And don't spoil it. So far it's going well. "Hi, Alex," he said to the overnight doorman of her building. "How you doing, Charles? Long time no see. Oops, did I say the wrong thing?" "No, it's fine. Good to see ya." "All I have is brandy," she said in the elevator. "Brandy's fine," he said. "Just the right thing to drink on a cold night." "I don't even have a bottle of wine to open. I wasn't prepared for your coming here. No beer, either." "Beer I wouldn't want unless it was the only thing you had to drink. I don't know why but I've lost my taste for it. Though beer's what we drank—actually, Bass Ale, remember? On our first real date after our afternoon coffee date." "I don't." "At the West End." "I forget that too. How do you remember everything?" "Place is the same," she said, unlocking her door, "except for the enormous bookcase I built. All by myself, too. I'm sure you'll be impressed. Watch out for the cats." He sat down beside her on the couch. "All right?" "Sure. Why do you think I'm sitting here?" They started kissing. He said, "I love this but I should put my glass down before I make a mess." More kissing before she said, "I think we should move this to the bedroom." She invited him for dinner the night after the next. "You take care of the bread, dessert and red wine, and anything else you want to drink. But a special dessert. Not just a Danish." During dinner, while she was chewing her food, he said, "There's one thing I've been meaning to ask you. It's been so long, you might not remember. I know I don't have the answer. And if you don't want to go in to it now, or anytime, for whatever reason, don't. I won't push it. I'm curious, though." "Come on, come on; what is it?" "Why'd you break up with me after we got back from Maine? I never understood why. We were in your car. Or you were, and I was on the sidewalk in front of my building." "The car I no longer have." "Oh, yes? You got rid of it?" "I had help. Some crazy uninsured bastard drove into it and totally destroyed it and then backed up and drove away dragging his front fender. Head-on. The front of my car like the proverbial accordion. Thank God for air bags. I was lucky someone witnessing it took down his license plate number, though of course luckier I wasn't killed." "I'm so sorry. I didn't know. But you weren't hurt?" "Just some soreness from the air bag and a few facial cuts from the broken windshield. This scar here." "Jesus. The windshield too? I'm so glad it wasn't worse. Forget my question. It seems so small, after what you said happened to you." "I'm not sure I could answer it anyway. My memory for those kind of things is nowhere near as good as yours. So. You done with your plate? I didn't do half badly for a first time with that dish, did I? Now help me clear the table and we'll take a peek at what you brought for dessert. It must be good. The box says 'patisserie,' and anything from a fancy French patisserie in New York has to be delicious. You must have made a special trip to the East Side to get it, unless they delivered, and I can't see them doing that for one small box. You didn't have to, but I know I'll be glad you did. And perhaps one day it'll all come back to me. If it does and you're not with me at that moment, I'll write it down and tell you it later. The answer to your question about our breakup, I'm saying. So we'll save it for then, if it happens, all right?" "Of course. And we don't even have to put it on hold. It really isn't important."

That was it. It never came up again and he never asked her about it again. He thought to a few times for about a year, and then thought what would be the point? They're happy together. Let it go. Then, twenty-nine years after that dinner, when he was slightly unhinged by what was going on with her, he asked it. Then quickly retracted the question by saying he was only kidding. She was in a coma. Had been in one for more than a week. Many years after she was first diagnosed with her disease. Twenty-four, to be exact. The visiting hospice nurse that morning had given her one or two more days. "I wouldn't be surprised if it was today." She was in a hospital bed at home. She wanted to die there rather than in a hospice. In the hospital she'd said she wanted to be with her family in a place she knows. "I want to be with our dear cat." Once she was home from the hospital, she said she would refuse all food and drink and life support. "Not even ice chips unless I seem to be suffering so much from thirst that I need something to dampen," she said, "dampen my lips and tongue. And morphine as a last resort, of course, which wouldn't qualify as anything keeping me alive." She was on her back. Had been in almost the same position since she went into the coma. "No need to worry about bed sores now," the visiting nurse had said. Pillow under her head, another one under her knees. He'd just changed her, though there hadn't been much need to change her the last two days. "Everything's shutting down," the visiting nurse had said the day before. It was around ten a.m. Their daughter was still sleeping—she had sat almost the entire night with her mother—and the same nurse had been there for about fifteen minutes and just left.

He was going to read his wife some poetry, which he and their daughter had been doing on and off since she went into a coma. "Are those for you or her?" the nurse had said a few days ago, pointing to a stack of poetry books on the side table by the hospital bed. "Her," he said. "You know, there's still a chance she can hear you—we've spoken of the last of the five senses to go—but a very small one at the stage she's in. Can't hurt, though, if she likes your voice and poetry." "She does—poetry—but I'm not sure about my voice. She used to say it was a little rough." So where was he? He got the idea—he doesn't know where it came from—to ask her about the breakup. Knew it was pointless—ridiculous; worse than that—but he was, as he said, slightly to maybe even deeply unhinged by her dying by now. He put his mouth close to her ear, almost to where his lips were touching it, and said softly, "One thing I'm still curious about…remember? Well, how could you? But 'curious' is what I said the last time we spoke about this thirty years ago right after we got back together and you invited me to dinner at your apartment. It's about the time we'd driven back from Maine our first summer there. You were sitting in the driver's seat of your car—the one that was totaled a short time later. I was standing on the sidewalk in front of my building with my typewriter and summer things. You'd just dropped me off. Your car was double-parked. I thought everything was hunky-dory with us and that we'd see each other the next day. But now both of us were very tired from the long trip, and before that, cleaning up the cottage we'd rented for two months. When all of a sudden—out of the proverbial blue, I'll unoriginally say—you said you were breaking up with me. You didn't say why. Neither then or the next time we briefly spoke about it at that dinner at your apartment a few months later. We started talking about something else—your car totaled and I was very distressed to hear you were almost seriously hurt and maybe even almost killed. So I wonder if you could tell me now the reason for your breaking up with me then. Only kidding, my dear one. And I apologize if this conversation—the question—bothers you in any way. I know you can't hear me, or the great possibility of that. Or maybe you can, but you can't—or most likely, can't—understand what I'm saying, and you certainly can't answer me. Give me a blink that you can, my darling. Oh, what am I doing here? I don't mean my life, I mean this, this. Better I do what I intended to before I started on all this and that's reading you some poetry I think you'll like." He sat back in the chair and got off the top of the stack of books on the side table an anthology of three thousand years of Chinese poetry. It was one of her favorite books, one she kept on her night table in their bedroom for about twenty years. He brought it in here after she came home from the hospital this time. Unwieldy as it was—it's a hardcover and more than 600 pages—she would read in bed, when she was still sleeping in their bedroom, a poem or two almost every night and then start reading another book or was too sleepy to read anymore and would kiss him goodnight or say, "A kiss; I'm going to sleep," and he'd kiss her and then lean over her and shut off her light. He checked the table of contents and opened the book to the poet she once said she liked better than any of the others in the book and maybe better than any poet but Whitman, Blake and Yeats. He turned to what he remembered her saying was one of her favorite poems by this poet and moved closer to her but not up to her ear. "'Daybreak,'" he said. "A poem by a Chinese poet of the twelfth century whose name I'm unable to pronounce right so I won't even try."

11

Good News

HIS DAUGHTER CALLS and says, "I've good news. I got into the Stanford Ph.D. program in English literature, the one that was my top choice to go to."

"Oh, I'm so happy for you," he says. "You couldn't have made me happier today."

"And listen to this. It's with complete tuition waiver and an eighteen thousand dollar stipend."

"That's amazing. The good news gets better and better."

"The big drawback, of course—the only one—is that I'll be so far away from you for the next four years. I'll fly in whenever I can and you'll have to come out to see me too."

"I'll take care of your air transportation. And if you need a car out there—if a bike won't do—I'll help in that too. And your rent there and anything you want. You know my money is really Mommy's and mine, so it's as much yours too."

"Thank you, Daddy. You've been so generous. I'll try to live frugally, be not such an expense on you. And maybe in a year or two I can get a teaching assistantship or an expository writing class to teach and that'll give me even more money and I won't need your help at all."

"Don't live too frugally. It's not necessary to. As for coming out to see you, I don't think there's much chance of that. So it seems we'll have to see each other less while you're there."

"We'll Skype."

"I don't Skype," he says. "One's face gets all distorted in them, and I don't know how."

"We'll work it out. I probably won't see you as much as when I live in Brooklyn, but I'll see you, as I said, as much as I can."

"You're very sweet. And I'm tearing up. At the good news and what you just said. That you'll see me as much as you can."

"I will."

"But I can't talk anymore. Congratulations, my dear sweetheart."

"Where are you, by the way?"

"At the Y," he says. "That's the noise you hear, I guess. I forgot to leave the cellphone in the car. So when I heard it ringing—it's a popular ringtone; lots of people seem to have it—I looked around to see where it was coming from and then realized it was in my pants pocket. We'll speak tonight, all right? I'll be more composed then."

"You're such a good father."

"Don't say anymore or I'll start crying again. Talk to you later."

"Bye. I love you."

"Love you too."

All this time he continued pedaling on the exercise bike. He didn't know he was. He put the phone back into his pants pocket. The Y's crowded. All the bikes are taken. The biker on his left has heavily padded headphones on, so most likely hadn't heard him talking. "Excuse me," he says to the woman on the bike to his right.

"For what?" she says, looking up from her book.

"For receiving a call on my cellphone and maybe talking too loud."

"I didn't hear anything."

"Must be a good book, then, to drown out everything but it."

"It's okay."

"What's the title and who's it by?" He's wiping his face with a paper towel.

"Caught something in your eye?"

"You mean my wiping? No. My daughter. That's who called me. I don't like taking calls when I'm around other people, you know—restaurants, the Y here. But this one I'm glad I did. It was one of the happiest I ever got."

"Oh, yes?"

"But I don't want to bother you with it."

"No, go on. We can still continue exercising."

"She called to say she got into a great Ph.D. program in English literature and it includes complete tuition waiver and a sizable stipend."

"What's a stipend?"

"Sort of like a salary. Except she won't be working. Just studying, attending classes, writing papers, and such. So it's to help her live without going broke and getting too deep in debt."

"Sounds like a good deal. What school?"

"Stanford."

"In Connecticut? So it's at least not too far away."

"That's Stamford. Her school's in California. Stanford University."

"That's too bad. It's so far away. Is that where she is now?"

"She's in Brooklyn, New York. I know, and it bothers me. If she knew how much it bothers me—I tried to hide it on the phone—she'd probably turn the program down. Maybe not go that far, but I'm sure she'd think it. She's my only child. We're very close."

"It's tough, but she's got to do what she's got to do. And what do you mean by 'program'?"

"A curriculum. Course of academic study. Four to five years of it. The Ph.D. program."

"I'm sorry for so many questions, which might seem ignorant of me. But as long as I have you here, what does Ph.D. stand for? I've always wondered. It's big and it takes lots of time, that I'm aware of. It doesn't come easy."

"Doctor of Philosophy. In Latin, I think—Philosophiae Doctor, though I don't think I'm pronouncing 'Philosophiae' correctly."

"That's okay. I understand. But I thought you said she got into an English program."

"She did. Don't ask me why it isn't called Doctor of English or whatever 'English' is in Latin, 'Doctor,' but it's called Ph.D."

"That's the top one, am I right?"

"I'm not sure what you mean," he says.

"The top scholarly peak, I'll put it. Regular B.A., master's and then doctor's."

"That's the order."

"And it makes you so happy. No wonder you were wiping your eyes. She got what she most wanted and you're proud. That's only natural, you being her father. And her mother? Does she know?"

"Her mother's dead. That's what makes it an even more moving event for me, the news. That her mother—my wife—isn't here to hear it."

"That is sad. I'm very sorry, for you and your daughter. Was it recent?"

"Six years ago."

"That's recent. She would have been thrilled to hear the news, I'm sure. And you have no other children, you say."

"Just this one."

"So of course, even worse that she'll be so far away. I have four kids and they all live around here, married, children of their own, except for one of them, who just got married. My husband and I are very lucky. But it's not unusual for Baltimore, as you probably know, the children sticking around or not moving too far away. Mine don't have the great brains your daughter must, going so far in her college work. But they're all terrific people, and their spouses, and good in what they do."

"'Four kids.' We wanted two and even talked about having three, but could only have that one. Miscarriages, twice. Before our daughter was born and again two years after. We decided to give up trying to have a second child when my wife was diagnosed and we were told a pregnancy would make her condition worse. My daughter was wonderful with her mother, helped me to take care of her for years. Went to college in Baltimore just to stay close to home and help out with her mother. After her mother died she settled in New York and worked there in publishing, till she decided to apply to graduate school. She took it very hard, the death. I took it badly, too, but she took it worse. Which is why I'm so pleased for her now and would never suggest she not go so far away for her Ph.D. I mean, just because it would be so much nicer having her closer geographically, where she could just zip down and back by train or bus."

"Trains have gotten so expensive," she says.

"They have, but I don't mind paying her fare. It's not as if she commutes. And half the time she takes the bus. What do your children do for a living?"

"Not English literature, I can assure you. The oldest—a girl—is a state trooper, one of the few of her gender. Her sister closest in age to her is a physical therapist. Our son's a salesman—always on the road—for an educational publisher. His job comes closest to literature, you can say, although like his sisters, he isn't much of a reader. And our youngest daughter is a homemaker, as they used to say. She had triplets. Just a year and a half old."

"A full-time job."

"And then some. And me? I'm retired, as my husband is. We enjoy life to the fullest, and that includes but doesn't exclude being with our grandkids. And they are grand kids. I suspect they won't be scholars or bookworms, either, but you never know how far the apple falls from the tree."

"And what are you reading there? I'm interested in books."

"Are you a teacher?"

"Was. College. I'm also a writer."

"Of books?"

"Yes. A lot of them."

"How interesting." She shows him the cover of her book. "It's trash, but easy on the brain to read when I'm on this recumbent bike. Not good at all on those Nordic, whatever you call them, ski machines."

"As long as you keep reading, no matter what it is, I think it's okay."

"Nah. It's trash. I don't challenge myself enough. But I wouldn't enjoy reading if I had to read anything deeper and harder than this book and others like it. And there are others like it. Tons. The author of this book alone has written more than forty others and I've read most of them."

"So you're a reader. Good. That's all I'm saying. Well, nice talking to you."

"Nice talking to you too. It's been very interesting. And next time you speak to your daughter, tell her the lady who heard the good news beside you while you were on your bike here said congratulations to her too."

"I will. Thank you."

She resumes reading. He opens his book to where he closed it on its bookmark when he got the call and starts reading. A minute later, he looks up from it. He's so happy, he thinks. Happy for her. More than anybody he knows, she could use such good news. Acceptance into the program. Stipend. Complete tuition waiver. Maybe even more. Palo Alto. The beautiful weather in that part of California. He's lived there. All the nice smart people she'll meet and become friends with. Four to five years there, maybe longer. Good chance she'll become close with a fellow grad student or an assistant professor or somebody there and marry and have a child or two. People from the Northeast who study and work there awhile often stay there. He won't be able to visit her. Has trouble getting on a train to New York, what makes him think he could make it out to California? Tries to stay in shape but his legs and lower back are very bad and seem to be getting worse no matter what he does for them. Prostate too. Makes it tough to travel long distances. Also, he doesn't like to be away from home for more than a day. His work and his cat are here. But he'll see her. She'll fly in now and then. She has good friends here and in New York she'll want to see too. And this woman. She's absorbed in her book. He said he's a writer and of lots of books, and she doesn't ask what kind? Fiction? Nonfiction? Not interested. It's true. Unless you're a star, people couldn't care less what you write or that you're a writer. He said he taught at a university once—maybe he said "college"—and she doesn't ask what he taught and what school? Questions he'd ask if someone told him any of that. He told her so much of his life he normally wouldn't tell anyone he doesn't know. His wife. Daughter. Death. Sadness. Crying. These are deep things. He should have kept them in. God knows why he felt he had to get them out. Not so much that he had to but just that he did. She was pleasant enough, though. Not over-nosy. And she didn't continue gabbing after she saw he was through. But the bike. And she gave him the name of it too: recumbent. He forgot that's what it's also called and what the trainers here always call it. After he finishes, and his thirty minutes on it are coming up, he should do some stretching on one of the mats here, if one of them's free, to lessen the chances later of his lower back aching. And then maybe work out on the resistance machines and with the weights a little more and then go home. No, go to the wine store on the way home and buy a bottle of moderately priced Champagne and uncork it tonight with whatever he has for dinner, even if it's just a sandwich and carrot and celery sticks, and drink to his daughter. Tell her tonight, if he speaks to her before he has dinner, he's going to do that. Or tell her tomorrow if he doesn't speak to her tonight. They usually only talk to each other on the phone once a day. It'll make her happy. It'll be like he's telling her he's not sad about her going to California for her Ph.D. And when he gets home, email his sister and the woman who was his wife's best friend since their first year in college and tell them the good news he got today. It'll make them happy too.

12

Carla Jean

"WHY ARE YOU asking me so many questions?"

"For one thing, I want to know if I have another first cousin."

"I told you. As far as I know, Margot's my only child. As for Carla Jean, it's never been proven through DNA or blood tests, if they're not the same thing, that she's my biological daughter. Her mother said she was. The man she always called her father said she was. And when she became fourteen or fifteen, her mother—her father had died the year before; motorcycle accident—told her she was. And after that, she started saying she was to me. I have letters from her. Or had them. You know me. I throw out everything but manuscripts that haven't been published in book form and this year's receipts for proof of income tax deductions, and the three letters I have from Eleanor before we were married."

Let's get back to when and where you first met Sylvia."

"In 1965. Her name was Daisy then. Her maiden name was Robertson. Her married name was Dash. Daisy Dash. You can see why she hated it. She once said to me, 'What could my parents have been thinking of to name me Daisy? And with the name Daisy, what could I have been thinking of to marry a man with the surname Dash?' Soon after her husband died she changed her name to Sylvia. And then, a couple of years later, her surname back to Robertson. But your question. I met her at a party in New York. She drove in from Milwaukee, where she lived with her husband, to stay with her best friend for a week. Her two-year-old son was with her. Marcel. I was attracted to her and introduced myself and we got along well from the start. We talked a lot about books and classical music, especially her favorite composer at the time, Prokofiev. She even brought to New York recordings of his third piano concerto and second violin concerto so she could listen to them while she was there. We arranged to meet the next day. Her friend would look after Marcel. She was the kid's godmother. We had lunch at the Central Park Zoo. Hotdogs, I remember, and probably their cole slaw, which I'd had a few times there and really liked. Sat on the restaurant's patio. I was smitten and she seemed taken with me. She liked that I was a writer, laughed at all my dumb jokes. She let me hold her hand. Apparently, things weren't going too well with her husband, or her boyfriend."

"She also had a boyfriend at the time?"

"We can talk about him later. But it's why she decided to take a break from them and drive to New York. This is all, in a variety of ways, in a few of my short stories and couple of my novels."

"Which ones?"

"I don't know. I have so many. Definitely the last novel last year— the Los Angeles parts."

"I have some of your books—I know I don't have the new one— and have read lots of your short stories in them. So far, nothing about Sylvia or Carla Jean. My mother bought them for me. Or you gave her them and she passed them on to me. Some are inscribed to her, and one was dedicated to her. 'To Darlene Rabinowitz,' it says, 'for her support.' What support did she give you?"

"She bought my books. Sometimes, five at a time, and at bookstores, not online. To give to friends and clients. And I guess to you too. That's what I call support. I don't think she's read any but the first two or three. Too much of the family in them. An interesting but too often a tragic family, or tragic circumstances, and I can get pretty close. Our parents, brother, sister. All ridiculous deaths or from a rare disease. I don't blame her for staying away from them."

"It's true. She's spoken about it to me."

"What'd she say?"

"Well, you know. Just what you said. I think, for the same reasons, everyone in the family's stayed away from your work. But back to Sylvia and that time with you in New York before she returned to Milwaukee. I'm assuming she returned."

"Oh, yeah. I wanted to drive back with her. Maybe get let off at the bus station in Milwaukee before she drove home. I wanted that much to be with her a little longer. I told her we could take our time. Do it in three to four days. See some sights and museums along the way, and for her kid, a zoo or two. She thought it a dumb idea. Besides, she needed to get back to work and do the trip in a single day. But she knew we'd see each other again. This wasn't just a fling. I told her I loved her. She never said she loved me, but she acted like she did."

"Okay. That first date."

"Skip the last what–I–said about love. We had fun. I don't know if I talked about love. I think I took that out of one of my stories about her. I sometimes get things like that mixed up."

"Got ya."

"I mean that one of my made-up stories actually happened, or taken-from-life stories happened exactly the way I wrote it, when it didn't."

"I think I understand. But that first date. If it's all right for me to ask—say no if it isn't—did you two sleep together that day?"

"She came to my apartment after we strolled around a little in Central Park after lunch. The original reason for meeting up was to go to the Metropolitan Museum, but we never made it. The zoo restaurant was only ten blocks from my place on West 74th Street. I probably planned it that way. No, I had to have planned it. That's what I was like then—a lot more conniving or devious or whatever you want to call it, than I am today."

"Okay. This is what I'm getting at with this. Was Carla Jean conceived during your time with Sylvia in New York? Because she also had a husband in Milwaukee she was going to see in a few days and most likely sleep with."

"Also the lover there. The boyfriend."

"That's right. I forgot him."

"He was her husband's best friend from med school. Lived with them, split the rent, had his own room, which she used to pay him a visit in, as she put it, every now and then. Okay with her husband. He had his girlfriends too. One he even shared with his best friend. See how crazy things were then? That time—1965 and adjacent years—hasn't been exaggerated. And, although both men were doing complicated brain research at a prestigious Milwaukee institute of some sort, deep into hallucinogens at home and other drugs."

"What's that got to do with it?"

"Judgment. Being medical men and scientists, you'd think they'd be wary of the dangers of the drugs and lay off them."

"Maybe. But all that's what made you think Carla Jean might not be your kid? Even if her parents and probably also the boyfriend said she was?"

"I don't know what the boyfriend thought, but there was never any scientific proof she was mine. I asked for it—was willing to cough up the dough for DNA, or blood tests, for all of us, boyfriend included—but Sylvia refused. She said—and now that I think of it, two doctors could have got their tests for almost nothing—it would be physically painful and emotionally traumatizing for Carla Jean at such a young age. Her husband—Glen was his name, with two n's or one—agreed to be tested. I'm sure the boyfriend too. Glen was sure the child was mine and gung-ho—again, in Sylvia's words—to share some of the paternal responsibilities and expenses with me. He even said the kid looked like me, when she didn't and like no one in my family. For that matter, she didn't resemble Glen or Sylvia either, except for her blond hair. Sylvia's was almost white it was so light."

"And the boyfriend?"

"I've never seen a photo of him. But according to Sylvia, when I questioned her in a letter, Carla Jean looked less like him than she did the rest of us. He was swarthy and had a large aquiline nose and black hair, and a multitude of other non-resemblances, she said. As for Glen, I met him once. They came in from Nashville, where they were living now, for some scientific conference and to take in the city, and I went to their hotel. Carla Jean was around two, then. Their son was five. First time I saw the girl. Anyway, she started screaming hysterically about something, and Glen said to me, 'Take care of your kid, Daddy.' Good-humoredly. He seemed like a nice-enough guy. Handsome, intelligent, a little wild. And I now remember it was a motorcycle he was killed on and that he might have been high on something when he crashed, or did I already tell you that?"

"You might have. So, you and Sylvia made love, had sex, whatever you want to call it, that night in your apartment on your first date."

"Probably not night. She had to be back to her son. To get him dinner, or just look after him, or something. We'd met in front of the Plaza Hotel around noon, had lunch at the zoo, were in bed a couple of hours later. Frankfurters on our breath. I don't know why I remember the franks so well. I had really fallen for her that day. A feeling which had started at the party the previous afternoon. She was so blond, so pretty, so comfortable to be with, so serious and smart."

"Do you have any contact with her now?"

"She's dead. I thought you knew that."

"I'm sorry. I meant, of course, Carla Jean."

"About every three years or so I get a letter from her."

"Not email?"

"I never gave her my email address. I don't even know if I was using the damn machine the last time I heard from her. But she liked writing letters to me. Said I was the only person she corresponded with that way. Last she wrote, and she said she'd had the job for a while, she was the top chef of a fancy fish restaurant in Portland."

"Maine?"

"If it were Maine I would have stopped to see her on my way up or back from the summer cottage I used to rent for a month, three hours north of Portland. And before that, in the same area and if she were working in Portland then, the farmhouse Eleanor and I used to rent for the entire summer. Oh boy, those were the days. But I haven't seen Carla Jean since 1995."

"When you were on a book tour in California. I know. I was there. You took us out to dinner before the reading. In Palo Alto. The restaurant was next door to the bookstore."

"I thought it was in Menlo Park I read. The Peninsula Bookshop."

"You got the name right. What a memory you have. It's been twenty years. But Palo Alto. I should know. I lived there before I moved to Sunnyvale. Carla Jean drove over Skyline Drive from Half Moon Bay. She must have really wanted to see you. It's a good hour's drive, and at night, on her drive back, it can get pretty perilous. Well, it was the first time you saw each other in a long time, am I right?"

"Yes. More than twenty-five years, not that she would have remembered me."

"You gave us each a copy of the book you read from. *Biways and Other Stories*, though it was a novel. The first chapter was so sad I could never get any further into it. You bought them from the store and refused the author's discount they offered. Very generous of you, I thought, and Carla Jean did too."

"So that's one your mother didn't have to give to you."

"No. Or maybe she did and I ended up with two copies. I think she once said she has no room in her tiny apartment for more than ten books. So what month did you meet Sylvia?"

"July. Week after the Fourth. You don't have to tell me. I know where you're going. Carla Jean was born on April 13th. And there was no delay in the birth, Sylvia said, and the baby wasn't premature. Took two hours. Less. She said Carla Jean was emerging by the time they got to the hospital. Sylvia drove back to Milwaukee about five days after we met. We saw each other every day till then, and for most of the day, and no doubt made love every day too. Am I on the right track? Every morning after nine or so, after our first date, I'd go to her friend's apartment she was staying at, but after her friend had left for work. Ten Downing Street in the Village. I remember the address because it's such a famous one in London. Since Sylvia had to look after her son those weekdays—the party was Saturday, the zoo lunch

Sunday—we'd make a fairly quick go at it, I guess, before the kid woke up in the guest room. No more leisurely sex in my apartment. In fact, the first had to be the last where we took our time, if I remember. And probably no more comfortable sex either, since we had to use the living room couch. I don't know why we didn't go into her friend's bedroom and put a towel on the bed, but we didn't. Sylvia must not have wanted us to. Even with a towel, our possibly messing up the bed. I can see her point, if that's what she thought."

"Okay. So I'll ask this again. If Sylvia went back to Milwaukee within a week and I suppose made up with her husband and slept with him the night she got back, or day, or night or day close to her getting back, why were she and her husband so certain the baby was yours?"

"Maybe they didn't sleep together so soon. I don't know. It's a good question."

"Then before she drove to New York."

"She said they hadn't made love for a week before she took off. At least that's what she said later, when she wrote me that she was definitely pregnant."

"Her boyfriend?"

"Again. No. She only slept with him about once a month, and when I brought that up, she said it had been a while. She said it could only have been that first time with me in my apartment. You see, she hadn't brought her diaphragm to New York with her. Didn't think she'd need it. And I didn't have a condom. Hadn't had to use one since I was maybe sixteen and with my friends went to a whore. Women always had diaphragms or were on the pill or the intra-, or inter-... What is it?"

"The device? Intrauterine."

"Right. So she said, after we played around with each other a while and had all our clothes off and were ready to go, did I have a condom? No. Then did I want to run down the block to a drugstore and buy a pack? I said I didn't. Getting dressed. Going to the store. It would stop everything. Then did I think I could pull out in time? I said I could. I had good control. But, according to her, I didn't have as good control as I'd thought and a little of me must have leaked into her before I pulled out completely. She was also at her most fertile period when we made love that first time. Which was another reason—the main one, she said—she was so sure I was the one who had made her pregnant, though the other reasons helped."

"Her husband? The boyfriend? No sex with them during her most fertile period?"

"Yes. One of the last things she said to me before she drove back to Milwaukee was that if I made her pregnant—and we used condoms all those other times, the three or four, and, I remember, some kind of spermicide she also had me buy at the drugstore—she'd have the child. She wanted to get having her second and last child over with, and based on everything I said about my family and me and my health, I seemed to have good genes. Better than her husband's, anyway."

"And the boyfriend?"

"Much better than his. What can I say? That's what she said, or most of it. That I was tall, lean, still had most of my hair then. My looks and intellect, and so on. That my mother had been a beauty queen. My father a professional boxer for a few years. I don't know. I'm just making them up. That I was Jewish. That she really said. She liked Jews. Jews and Armenians she admired most and liked best, she said. And that I was an artist. By that she meant 'a serious writer.' So she was sure almost from day one. I was never sure."

"Did you see her again—after you met them at their hotel in New York?"

"Oh, yeah. She drove up from Nashville to see me. Or maybe it was Shreveport or Baton Rouge. I know it was some Southern city with a big university and medical center. Later, they moved to Berkeley and I never saw her again after that. But from Nashville, we'll say, she drove up a couple of times when Carla Jean was three or four. With both kids. They stayed in my small apartment, which was basically one room and a kitchenette. The kids slept in the bed, Sylvia and I on the floor. She brought an air mattress with her and her diaphragm. But I shouldn't joke. She used to say Carla Jean looked most like your mother. I'd shown her a photograph of Darlene. She said that because Carla Jean looked nothing like me, or her, except for her blond hair, and Darlene and me looked nothing like each other. I didn't see the resemblance between Darlene and Carla Jean, but maybe there was one.

What she was trying to say was that Carla Jean looked more like my family than hers or Glen's. I know I'm not being very clear here."

"It's all right. I can put it together. Tell me, and only if you want to, did Carla Jean ever ask you for some kind of financial support?"

"Why would she?"

"Well, she thought you were her biological father. And once Glen was gone, you were all there was for, I suppose you can call it, paternal support? And you said she had a tough life. After Glen died, they lived in a trailer."

"I told you that?"

"Then my mother did."

"Anyway, the trailer was years after Glen died. I offered. And remember, Carla Jean…I mean, Sylvia, disappeared with her kids for about ten years after Glen died. That was before the trailer park. Lived in Indonesia. For a while in Thailand. Teaching English in both countries. When she finally wrote me after my not hearing from her for about ten years—I was with Eleanor by then—I sent her checks. Not much and not often. Maybe twice. I never made much till I got the college job when I was forty-four, but she sent them back. Or saying—that's what it was—in a note that she'd torn them up. 'We don't need your guilt money,' or something. No, she would never be that curt. She was really quite wonderful. More like, she said, 'We're doing fine and don't need your help. But thanks.'"

"Why'd you send the money, then?"

"Because of something she may have said in a previous letter where I thought she could use some. And the second time, because I thought she might have changed her mind, and as I said, it wasn't for much. As for Carla Jean, she never asked for money either and I never on my own sent any. Paper trail. That it could be used in the future against me and, if I wasn't still around, my kid. That I was her bio dad and she should have part of my vast estate. Not a nice thought, but I thought it. You know, you ask a lot of questions I can't answer. And to tell you the truth, they're beginning to tire me. I don't say that hostilely. Just, I think I've said more than enough for now about everything we've been talking about, and I'm still not sure what you want to know. Why you're asking them. That."

"I told you. To find out whether I have another first cousin. I'm big on family. More so than you are. And that she lives near me in California also has something to do with it, while the rest of them are in Massachusetts and New York. That, actually, has little to do with it. Or maybe it does. And her age. We're close in it. A year. But just as important, I've always been curious of your relationship with Sylvia and the possible offspring from it. It's a great story."

"Story?"

"It's intriguing, then. Interesting. Complicated. I've always thought so."

"So you've known about Carla Jean and this offspring business for a long time?"

"Much longer than before your book reading in Palo Alto. I didn't just think then, like you told me, you invited her because she was the daughter of good friends. My mother told me when I was thirteen. 'Here's a bar mitzvah present for you' she said, 'now that you've gone through the ceremony and are considered a man. You have another cousin, or there's a good chance you do. Uncle Charles most likely fathered a daughter more than fifteen years before Margot was born.' No, she couldn't have said exactly that. Doing quick mental calculations, Margot wasn't born yet and I don't even know if you knew Eleanor at the time. But you get my point. And she did tell me soon after I was bar mitzvahed."

"I went to it. I hate bar mitzvahs. Mine. Everybody's. Though yours was done simply and was unusually low-keyed and didn't go on too long and you read and sang your haphtarah very well."

"Thanks."

"But the 'Uncle Charles.' It sounds so funny, so long after, that all you kids called me that."

"I'm not sure about the 'Uncle Charles.' I just threw that in."

"Another thing. What took you this long to ask me about it? I mean, you're close to fifty and we've had dozens of conversations."

"I guess it never came up or I thought talking about it might upset you, something you didn't want to hear. Today was different. No real reason. Maybe because I am almost fifty. Next November. One thing, though, I was glad of when you invited me and Carla Jean for dinner twenty years ago was that I knew almost for certain that she was my first cousin. Because she was so bright and attractive, and that hair. And that she was a serious bodybuilder and dancer and hang-glider and was thinking of joining the Army, and things like that. I said 'bright,' right? And full of personality. If I hadn't known we were possibly related, I could have gone for her. And maybe she for me too. Nah. She knew, or had it in her mind we were definitely related. She would have done or said something to cut off my interest, if I had shown any, and, between you and me, I would have. So we were safe. Now, if I hadn't known and things went the way I just said they could have because she let them despite knowing how I was related to you and her paternal bloodline turned out to be, you know, what we spoke about, that could have been a big mess, true?"

"I'm not sure if I got everything you just said. But to answer your question, it wouldn't have been good. Though I once read some scientific study of it that the danger of such unions—cousins—and we're only talking about having babies, is vastly overstated. Anyway, you could have got out of it long before it reached that stage. See ya, pal."

"Bye-bye, Charles. Stay well. We'll talk again soon."

The phone rings about ten minutes later.

"Oh, no, not you again."

"One more question, and I swear, I'll make it short. First off—"

"You said 'one.'"

"Give me two. I'm your nephew. First, you wouldn't have liked my getting involved, and of course we're talking romantically and sexually here, with someone who believes deep down she's your biological daughter."

"That's a question? To get it over with, let's say it is. At the time—twenty years ago—probably. Now, I couldn't care. And your second?"

"Suppose Carla Jean got a court order against you that you have to by law submit to a DNA test? The idea behind it being that if you are her biological father, as the tests could show, she's entitled to half your estate instead of you leaving it all to Margot, which I assume you will."

"She wouldn't do that. She's like her mother; I just know it. But I wouldn't submit to any test like that, and not just because I wouldn't want to jeopardize whatever the heck it is I'm going to leave to Margot.

Not that there would be such a court order, and one issued in California for someone in New York. But for argument's sake, if there was they're not going to force a 78-year-old man, and one not in the best of health, and if I had to I could probably fake it where I seem even worse, to a test like that."

"I see. But just one further question."

"That's it, Nat. I don't want to talk about it anymore. I'm sick of the subject. I'm also tired of talking on the phone. Not just my stamina. My vocal cords. You hear how my voice had gradually softened during this call. It's part of the disease. And if your question was going to be have I written Carla Jean into my will—"

"It's true. How'd you know? No, of course not. Not even close. And I was hearing you fine."

"Well, if it were, I'll put it, the answer would have been yes, but not much. Just as I haven't directed much of my vast estate to you. And I do have a will. I'd be a fool not to, and wrong because of the hassles, without one, I'd be putting Margot through. So, a little to you, a little to your mom, a little to Carla Jean—I think, all equal amounts—and a little to my indigent writer friend, Ferdinand, who's been a big booster of my work and a great help in getting me a couple of publishers, and who needs the money more than any of you. And a little to the classical music radio station in Baltimore, and I think that's all. Oh, yeah. A woman I was engaged to when we were both twenty-four and who I've been in touch with and who's had a hard time the last ten years. And the rest—the ninety percent of it—to Margot."

"All that seems fair enough and more than generous of you. As for me, you don't have to leave me anything. I'm good. But I appreciate you thinking of me that way."

"So that's it then, okay? I hate to be rude, but I'm hanging up and I don't expect you to call back again today."

"Don't worry. You're my favorite uncle. I don't take it personally. Speak to ya."

13

Try

I GO OUT for a jog and come back with an opening line. "I try to get up but I can't. 'Try. Try.'" Or three lines, if "Try. Try," can be considered lines. Can they? I don't know. Or I'm not sure. No, I don't know. I really don't. I don't know a lot of things one would think I do or should. Been writing for fifty years now—serious writing. I wrote for about five years before those fifty, but I wasn't serious or I just wasn't good. Not that I'm good now. But I am better than I was when I started writing fiction fifty-five years ago. I was a reporter in Washington, D.C., and worked all day and had nothing to do at night and nobody to do anything with so I started to write. Paragraphs, dialog, stories. I am so ignorant, I can say. That's really what I meant when I said, "No, I don't know." I read a lot of serious stuff—in books, newspapers, magazines—but forget almost everything I read. And it was a slog I went out for and which I came back from with that line or lines or whatever "Try. Try," should be called: a slow jog. Whenever I call it that, and I've called it that many times, people usually laugh, think it clever or funny or pretend they do. I probably won't call it that again to anyone but myself because I've already said it to people too much. "Too often?" I'm not a very funny person. Maybe no longer funny at all. And though I like to make people laugh—I used to do that a lot when I was a much funnier guy than I am now—I have few things to say to make them laugh. My wife used to say her mother told her that her sense of humor had greatly improved since she met me. My wife's sense of humor. I don't think that's true. I even think my mother-in-law said it to put my wife down a little. Why she'd do that, I don't know. I never told my wife why I thought her mother said it, and she said her mother said it several times. I didn't want to hurt her or belittle her mother, because that would hurt her too. My wife had a terrific sense of humor from the time I first knew her. Right from our first date. It was at a bar in her neighborhood. We'd arranged on the phone to meet there because it was convenient for both of us. I was going to be in her neighborhood—that's right: to pick up some books I ordered from an academic bookstore up there, the only place in the city I could get them—and, of course, she lived in the neighborhood. The West End. The name of the bar. One mostly college students went to—the minimum drinking age then was eighteen—and my wife at the time was on a post-doctoral fellowship at Columbia. She said things there, on our first date, that made me laugh out loud. I wasn't putting it on, either. Especially something about her two Siamese cats and beer, although I forget exactly what it was. And her imitation of the cats lapping up the spilled beer when she had no idea they liked it. Last night, or early this morning—it was still dark out—I had maybe the best dream I ever had of my wife. I don't know why I just don't call her Eleanor, but I started with "my wife," so I'll stick to it. I can always change it later. But the dream. Why'd I bring it up? I don't know, but it was what I'd call a perfect dream. No, a perfect dream is one I've never had of her. Meaning, I've never had a perfect dream of her, or what I'd consider perfect. That would be where we kiss for a long time—deep kisses, like the one we had in this dream—but then, after the kisses or kiss, we make love, and it really feels like making love, and I ejaculate in her. In the dream I had we kissed for what was two minutes straight. Meaning, one kiss that lasted for two minutes. In the dream I'm sitting at the right end of a couch. My wife is sitting beside me, back of her body against my shoulder and chest. Then with my right hand—and she looks healthy in this dream, age around thirty-five—I move her head to the right till it's facing my face and we kiss, without coming up for air, as they say, or used to, for two minutes straight. Did I time it? No. It just seemed to be around two minutes. It's the longest kiss I've ever had in a dream. I think it is, anyway, and maybe in real life too. I can't remember a dream or time when I kissed someone longer than that. Then I woke up. But I really didn't wake up, or only woke up in a dream rather than from it, because we were still seated on the couch, but a different couch—one I didn't recognize—than the one in my house, back of her body still pressed against my shoulder and chest, but we were no longer kissing. We were just sort of staring out into space, my left arm around her shoulder. Then I really woke up and I thought about the dream or dreams I just had and how wonderful and, in a way, fulfilling it was. "Fulfilling" might not be the right word. Now I'm on the floor in my bedroom and I can't get up. It's the same day, maybe two or three hours after I woke up from that dream or those dreams. What happened was that after I woke up and made my bed and brushed my teeth and shaved and had breakfast and read the newspaper for a while, I went out for a short jog—my slog—and came back and was starting to undress for a shower—had only kicked off my running shoes and taken off my T-shirt and was about to sit on the bed and take off my socks—when I fell to the floor—"collapsed" would be more like it; my legs just folded under me and I landed on my back. After wondering for a few seconds what had happened, I tried to turn over on my stomach and couldn't. Then I tried to stand but couldn't. Did I have a stroke? I didn't think so. I don't know why I didn't think so—I know nothing about strokes other than that sometimes they kill you right away and sometimes you don't know you've had one till a doctor examines you. Is there anyone here to help me? My daughter's in New York and my wife's been dead for six years and I live alone in this house. Am I able to call for help on my telephone or cellphone? Not this moment. Both are on top of the dresser and I'm not only unable to get up but unable to crawl, and certainly not on my back. How do you know? Have you tried? No. I just think so. So, try. Try. Maybe that's why I think I didn't have a stroke. My head's clear and I'm able to think straight, and nothing hurts. Not my shoulder, chest, head or pain shooting down one of my arms, or am I getting the symptoms mixed up with those of a heart attack? I try to get on my stomach again. I can't. I then try to crawl to the dresser on my back, but can't. If I don't get up soon or get help soon, I'll piss in my pants. That should be the worst of my worries. "Least"? "Worst"? "Worries"? "Concerns"? Because I can't lie here all day, can I? So I'll stay here on the floor, unable to call EMS or a friend—someone—unless I'm able to do something to get myself up. Maybe I haven't tried hard enough. "Tighten your abdominals when turning over in bed or standing up from a sitting position when getting off the bed," the physical therapist said over and over again, when I went to her for two months for an aching lower back, and it seemed to work. No, it worked. After doing the stretching exercises she gave me and following her advice, the back only sporadically hurt, when before it was almost all day. I tighten my stomach muscles—"Think of pulling them up to your belly button," she said—and with a great deal of effort I'm able to turn over on my side. I grab hold of the nearest bed frame leg, pull myself closer to the bed, grab hold of the mattress and frame and hoist myself to one knee. I know now I'll make it to my feet. But should I first sit on the bed awhile before I try to go into the bathroom? No. Get to it now, before you piss in your pants. I push my hands into the top of the mattress and stand. I go into the bathroom a few feet away, pull down my pants and boxer shorts, sit on the toilet seat and pee. Good. I didn't make a mess. My boxer shorts are still dry. I don't know what happened, but I feel fine now. I'll call my doctor when I get off here. Or email him—that seems to get a response from him faster—and tell him what happened. I'm sure he'll want me to come in. I'll tell him that all I know is I was feeling pretty good this morning, went out for a jog—a slow short jog—came back, still felt pretty good, was undressing to take a shower after my jog, and collapsed to the floor, feet just coming out from under me; legs, I mean, and I couldn't get up for a while or turn over on my stomach—I was on my back—or move even an inch to the telephone to call for help. Or I won't call or email him. I don't like going to doctors, not even for a regular checkup. He'll probably put me through some tests and find something, or think that something could be there and refer me to a specialist. I don't like going to specialists. I have my reasons. They mainly have to do with my wife. And maybe this'll be the last time this happens to me. What I'm saying is maybe this falling to the floor and not being able to move from where I fell for about fifteen minutes was a fluke and won't happen again. That could be so. I'm all right now, aren't I? Why it happened could in time become less important than that it did happen. That could be said clearer. More clearly? Clearer. What I just said could. Otherwise, it's been a very nice day. I had a long satisfying dream to start it off, and what could be more satisfying than that? Lots of things. Such as my wife was alive, and healthy, of course, or just not as sick as she got, nowhere near it, and I was telling her about the dream I had of her this morning, that long lifelike kiss. So. I stand up. First I grab the grab bar on the wall to the right of the toilet—it was put in for my wife early in her illness and I've come to use it every time I sit on the toilet, and I sit on it here even when I only have to pee—and stand up. I raise the boxer shorts and pants to my waist, zip up, belt up, I suppose I can say, or maybe not, and go into the bedroom and think it'd be a good idea to lie on the bed and rest awhile. I shut my eyes and clasp my hands on my chest. First clasp and then shut and think of the kiss I dreamed earlier today. I picture the kiss. It's realer—I mean it seems as real as any kiss I ever had with my wife. She had such soft lips, just as she had in the dream. And always a sweet breath, again as she had in the dream. I remember that. In fact, I remember thinking in the dream how soft her lips were and sweet her breath was in the dream. She said the same about me once. "You never have bad breath. You take good care of your teeth. Am I permitted to say that?" And also that my lips were never chapped. My eyes stay shut, head is resting comfortably on a pillow, and I feel myself drifting off to sleep. That's always such a nice feeling. And it's okay if I take a little nap now. I'm not going anywhere today but the gym.

And I didn't get much sleep last night, for reasons I don't know. Maybe that's why I fell down. But it doesn't explain why I couldn't get up from the floor for fifteen minutes or half an hour or whatever time it was. And if I fall asleep now, I won't lose the kissing dream when I wake up. It was too vivid a dream not to remember it. And after I wake up I'll write in the notebook I keep on the night table by my bed the dream I had this morning and also my falling down while I was undressing for the shower and not being able to pick myself up or even move for a while. So, am I finished with this? I'm finished. Do I think I'll be able to turn it into anything? I don't think so, or not anything worth saving.

14

Someone Else

"YOU HAVE ONE FOR ME? I have one for you. Choose someone your own age."

"What do you mean?"

"I have to be clearer? After what we've just been talking about? A woman. If you're looking for female companionship, which it seems you are, I suggest you pick someone closer in years to you. Much closer."

"Why? How old are you?"

"At least thirty years younger than you. More like thirty-five years younger. No, why am I circling it? I know how old you are. Your books all say you were born in thirty-six."

"That's right. I never tried to hide it. In the beginning—with my first book or two—I remember a writer friend asking me why I let my birth year be printed on the copyright page. That it's going to hurt me in the long run. Let the reader think I'm still young. But I thought, what do I care if people know my age? And I still think it."

"So, thirty-seven years between us. Which means you were thirty-seven, which'd be when my father was twenty-eight. I wasn't even born yet or was only recently born. Think of it. You're thirty-seven and I'm zero."

"I thought you were older than you say you are. Not a lot, but some. And up till now I had no idea your father is nine years younger than I. 'Was nine years'? Oh, God, I'm such a jerk when it comes to tenses and verbs. But your father had his kids much earlier than I had mine. And you've told me you're not even the first child. I couldn't afford to have even one so early. I wasn't even married till I was forty-five. Wanted to be—long before that—and to have a child. Had lived with a couple of women before Eleanor. But they knew better than I, or were more sensible about it, or something. You know, till I got the teaching job and was able to marry and take care of a family, I was barely earning enough at all sorts of idiotic jobs to keep myself going and also write. But it worked out. A terrific marriage and wonderful daughter and time to write and summers in Maine and everything else."

"Anyway, you must have known how old I was. It was on my application to the graduate program and you said you were the first reader of all the applications."

"You know how long ago that was? And how many applications I had to read? Average year?—two hundred. Sure, a lot of them took me just five minutes each, they were so bad—personal statement and supporting material, mostly. But the whole reading process took up my entire winter break—practically ruined it—and then a few agonizing weeks after the spring term started, where I had to juggle both teaching and reading. Am I glad that's over with. Incidentally, and it has nothing to do with what we're talking about, but you were an instant shoo-in. Maybe, young as you were, and I won't deny that I knew you were very young—right out of college, I think—among the top three applicants I read till the time I retired. So that's three out of five thousand."

"I was two years out of college, but I got my B.A. in three years. But thank you. I won't let it go to my head. It's what I've produced since graduate school that's important, right?"

"In a way, sure."

"Another thing, though. If we ever meet again—"

"You mean there's a chance we won't? How sad."

"Don't act silly. I'm being serious. If we do meet again by accident, I'm saying not by arrangement—"

"And I wasn't being silly. I'd truly regret not seeing you again."

"Okay. But I was saying, please don't ever again kiss me hello the way you did today. I didn't want to. I don't like it. And there's no reason to. Of course what I'm also saying—and you must have picked it up—is that this'll be the last time we arrange to meet for coffee, lunch, or anything."

"Again, that's too bad, from my perspective. I really enjoyed talking to you. Highlight of my week. But what can I do?"

"Nothing. It was once nice for me. Now it's not. And my advice again? One parting shot? Remember? You gave me. I give to you? Or 'suggestion,' we'll say? Go for someone much closer in age to you. To be honest, you look a little ludicrous romancing a much younger woman. Holding hands? Things like that? The difference in looks—in everything—is too great. But I have to go. Thanks for lunch. You sure I can't split it with you? I'll give you cash."

"No. It's all my treat. Always my treat. Or the last time with you. My treat."

"Thank you." She gets up, he gets up, and they head for the door. In front of the restaurant, she says, "My car's over there. The lot on the left."

"Mine's on the right. I'll walk you."

"No need to."

"I'd like to."

"And I'd like you not to." She sticks out her hand to shake.

"One last hug? No kiss."

"Please. Don't."

"Just a little one. The hug. So we end as friends."

"We can't end as friends. Truth is, I don't want to be your friend.

And I know you, with your little hugs. They turn into bear-like embraces and big kisses, nothing of which I want. No thank you."

"I promise it won't."

"I don't believe you and I don't want to chance it."

"You're probably right not to believe me. I probably would turn it into a kiss. At least one on your head, but more likely something on your lips."

"What I thought. Well…"

"All right. No hug or kiss." He sticks out his hand to shake.

"Now I don't know about this."

"Fear not." His hand's still extended. She looks at it and then sticks out her hand and they shake. "You see? No sneakiness or devious plot. But I should go back to the restaurant and use their restroom. I always do before I set off, especially after coffee. You're right. I'm an old guy and I have accidents. Who needs that?"

She smiles and turns around and walks to where her car is. Hell with the restroom, he thinks. He can hold out. And don't think about it and it won't come, and he walks to his car and sits in it without starting it up.

What a fool he is. She'll tell people they know all about this. His turning a hug into a kiss, or wanting to. What she told him about age. That he's so desperate for a woman. Company. What else? Someone to travel with. Or just, simply to go to the movies with. Sleep with, of course, though he never once brought that up or even alluded to it. Or did he? And could he even sleep with a woman—meaning, have sex with one; get it up; keep it up long enough—after not sleeping with one for six years? He thinks he'd be okay. Not all the time, but who is all the time okay? So an understanding woman. And that he seems ready to jump on the first woman he gets even semi-close to. That she'll never want to see him again. That nothing happened but he obviously wanted something to. What was he thinking? Their age difference. Yak-yak-yak. Why doesn't he try meeting someone a lot closer in age to him? He just doesn't. All the women he's taken out to lunch and the one to dinner and thought or was hoping something would happen between them but nothing did, have been thirty years younger than him if not more. One wasn't. Twenty-five years younger. What can he say? He likes younger women. Their looks, spirit, bodies. Other reasons. The old standby: talking to them, he feels much younger himself. But why did he think they'd like him? Did he? Yes, to be honest, a couple of times he did. Well, he doesn't act his age, as some people would say. And he doesn't look bad for a guy a year and a half away from eighty, though he doesn't look like sixty anymore and probably not seventy either. And his body. He's become a little frail the last few years. And he has a pot belly. Not a big one, but he's never had one before. Since he was fifteen, it's always been a fetish of his to stay in shape. He's balder than he was five years ago. His hands have old-man's blotches on them. Liver spots. Forehead too. His ugly neck, which is a dead giveaway as to how old he is. Can't hide it, nor any of the telltale lines on his face. She was so nice. He's dreamed of being in bed with her. Daydreamed it too, imagining what she looked like with no clothes on. But dreamed of sleeping with her or just being with her two nights out of five, he'd say. Usually early morning, room still dark, an hour or two before he got out of bed. In one a few morning ago they're on a daybed and he's on top, sticking it in her. That's how far he got before the dream ended. Just a little ways in. So frustrating when he woke up. He wanted more. In another dream—yesterday? the day before?—she said, "What do you have these on for?" and pulled down his pants, boxer shorts and jeans both and, on a regular bed with a headboard, which his doesn't have, she sat on top facing him—she only had on a T-shirt, no bra—and put it in for him and had no trouble too. He slid in easily and stayed hard. Then she closed her eyes and went up and down on him. It was as close to the real thing as he could imagine. He gets a little excited just thinking about it now. She's so pretty. He wishes both dreams had gone on longer. Maybe he'll have one that will. Such a cute body, but compact. Strong too. She said she runs a mile every morning and works out in a health club every other day. He's written about her. Of course changed her name, and gave her three kids instead of two. Girls, not boys, as she has, and so on. Changed her hair from natural blond to natural red. Made her to be of average height instead of what she is, tall. He used to be about four inches taller than she when she was his student. But he's shrunk the last ten years—arthritic lower back; can't fully straighten up; it's only going to get worse, his doctor says, if he continues to refuse to be operated on or even to take shots—and they're now almost the same height. Made her a poet in his two short stories about her, while she's only written fiction and book reviews. They go to Maine in one of the stories. He fantasized that in real life. Thought if they started sleeping together, and at one point he thought they might. Something about the playful way she acted toward him at the beginning and the things she said they could do together; a movie, concert, dinner at her house where he'd meet her kids whom he hasn't seen for years and who are interested in him because she told him he's a writer with lots of books, and maybe one night a crab house and play. He should have brought that up. "Didn't you once say…?" But what would have been the use? He must have misjudged what she was giving off, probably from wanting it so much. He'd rent a cottage on or near the shore in the same area he and his wife always went to and they'd be there all of July and August, one of his main selling points: out of the Baltimore heat. Both of them writing. Seeing friends he's made over many summers. Eating outdoors if it wasn't too buggy. Lunch in town. Maybe renting a canoe or very light rowboat for a week. Jogging together for a mile or half a mile if he could get his legs to move again that way. They'd bring their cats. Get leashes for them so they can take them outside. His daughter would stay with them for her two-week vacation from work. Her kids for the time they wouldn't be with their father, who always took them to Austria for the summer to be with their cousins and grandparents. He really did think all this could happen. He's such a fool. But he loves much younger women for all the reasons he gave. Does that make him that much of a fool? Yes and no. But she seemed, as he said, to have fun with him. That is, till she got wind he was interested in her romantically. He's sure that's it. All right: he couldn't hold it back. Said a few things he shouldn't have. Once tried stealing a kiss from her, or actually did. The way she wiped his kiss off her lips. It seems the older he gets, the more of a fool he is. But she has to be the last. From now on…that business about someone much closer in age to him. Got it? Now go home. Feed the cat. Let him in if he's out and out if he's in. Go for a walk. Or try for a short run. Weather's still nice. Not a hot humid day like yesterday's was and tomorrow's supposed to be. He'll probably drink too much tonight and not bother about dinner except maybe for a cookie and carrot and handful of peanuts. Should he call her to apologize? Not right after he gets home, but tonight? Say: "I just want to say you were absolutely right. From now on, if I'm ever going to be with a woman again, even if just as a good friend, it has to be one much closer to me in age. I can be a fool, I know—you don't have to tell me—and I hope in time you'll forgive me." No, no forgiveness. Too sappy. Just "I hope I haven't been too much of a nuisance or annoyance to you or whatever I've been." Or be more explicit, but what? Or don't call. Again, what would be the use? She'll see through it as some kind of maneuver to get him in her good graces again, or at least a step or two toward it. But he could be wrong. How so? He doesn't know. The thought came up and then quickly disappeared. Look, she's not interested, in him or anything he has to say, and she definitely won't want to hear from him so soon. Right now, in fact, she could very well be thinking of him as a first-class pain-in-the-ass schmuck. Okay. He doesn't like it but he can live with it. It's not as if he's in love with her. He feels something for her. Excitement, mostly—just standing next to her. And before today, or last time today, that kiss-on-the-cheek hello where he wanted to move his mouth over and kiss her on the lips. So maybe he was in love with her. Is. Was. He hasn't felt anything like that with any other woman since his wife. But he should put the whole debacle out of his head. De-bacle? What's the preferred way to pronounce it? Maybe when he gets home, if he doesn't forget. "But enough. Schmuck. Start up the car and get out of here."

He drives home. His daughter calls a short time after he gets there. He was about to take a run. Cat's in and he's fed him and put fresh water into his bowl, which he's lapping at now.

"Hi, Daddy. How was your day?"

"Just fine. Got a good sleep. Went to the Y around nine. It wasn't crowded. I got to use any machine I wanted to and there was no wait for a stationary bike. Wrote the first draft of a short story I think I can turn into one I like. So at least I'll have something to write the next two weeks. You know how I can get when I don't have something to work on. And I met Iris for lunch."

"Who's Iris?"

"I haven't told you about her? Thought I had. Former grad student of mine—one of my favorites—and now a friend. Terrific writer. Very smart and lots of good conversation and laughs. We've met at Atwater's a few times. It's convenient to where she lives and she likes their soups as much as I do. She's in the thick of getting a divorce, after being married for almost twenty years, and has two boys, I think in their late teens. I met them years ago when I was still teaching and she brought them in strollers to my office, but I haven't seen them since. I really enjoy her company, more than almost anybody's in Baltimore."

"That's good. How old is she? Even with kids that age, it seems she might be too young for you."

"Why? What's too young?"

"Twenty years?"

"Oh, she's younger than that. She had her two boys soon after she graduated the program, and I think she got into the program when she was twenty-two or -three."

"So she's more than thirty years younger than you."

"I guess so. Let me do the math."

"Maybe thirty-five years."

"But not forty. That I'm sure of. If it were forty, she'd have to have had her kids when she was around twenty, and I know she didn't."

"But you do agree she's too young for you."

"I wish she wasn't, but she is. In fact, that's one of the things we talked about today."

"You didn't tell her you were interested in her that way, did you?"

"Of course not. That'd scare her and probably stop her from having lunch with me again, and anyway, that's not the case. No, we talked about a couple she knows who recently hooked up and he's thirty or so years older than the woman. She thought the age gap was huge but that, who knows, a match could still work out between two people with that age disparity between them. Something like that was expressed. I disagreed with her. I thought it too vast, the age difference."

"She may not have believed you. It's possible she thought you were saying that just to protect your own feelings about her. That you didn't want to admit there was a possibility of a relationship like that between you and her."

"What do you mean? You're not being clear. Or I'm just in a deep obtuse state of mind and unable to understand what you said."

"I'm saying, does she harbor romantic feelings to you that you can detect? Some women like much older men, or don't see the age difference as a problem. That if they can have five or ten good years with the man, it'd be worth it."

"Maybe she does. Who knows? But I don't think so. No, I can usually detect when someone does, not that it's happened that often to me in my life, and she doesn't. Also, I'd never pursue it if I thought she did have those feelings. We're strictly for lunch. We always have a good time. And maybe one day we'll go out for dinner together. But where we'd drive to the restaurant in separate cars."

"Why so?"

"So there wouldn't even be a possibility of anything odd happening when we were saying goodbye in the car."

"I don't understand."

"You don't see what I'm saying?"

"Maybe it's my turn now to be obtuse. But why would you make a lunge for her...to kiss her?"

"Something like that."

"You'd never do that."

"I know. But I was just saying. So where was I? Two cars. And of course she'd never make a lunge for me."

"Good thing too. Someone much closer to your age to do the lunging. That's what you want."

"I know. That's what I told Iris."

"How'd that come up? You didn't tell her you were looking for a companion, did you?"

"In a way. Why not? I said I was looking for someone to date, if it got that far. First for coffee. Or at a dinner party at someone's house somewhere. And then maybe for coffee or lunch and then dinner, but someone around my age. I made that clear. Five years younger is okay. Ten at the most. And if she knew anyone, please let me know. That I'm sure she knows the kind of person I'd be interested in. A smart woman, one involved or interested in the arts, and not pushy.

"And kind and gentle and so on, like your mother. For sure, intelligence and gentleness and kindness, foremost."

"Maybe she will know someone. That'd be nice. I'd love for you to get close to someone again. A companion. Even a love interest."

"You would?"

"Absolutely. Someone who'd make you happy."

"Then keep your eyes open for someone for me too."

"Dad. I live in New York. You're in Baltimore."

"Of course. I'm betting on Iris to help find someone for me. She gets around. Teaches. Is very sociable. Knows lots of people."

"She sounds like a wonderful person."

"And I told you. She's a terrific writer. Gets her stories published in better places than I get in to, and early next year a book of them. Maybe the best grad student, or one of three of them, I had in my twenty-five years."

"She sounds perfect, in fact. For a man thirty years younger than you, but with similar interests."

"She's not seeing anyone now, and her divorce is taking a toll on her. I wish I knew a guy close to her age, or much closer than I am, that I could introduce her to. But she's so smart and pretty and talented, it won't be long. I know that's what she wants, even though she doesn't express it openly. Or let's say, it hasn't come up."

"So you had a good day."

"A very good day. As I said: wrote. Lunch. The Y. Beautiful weather too. Sunny and dry and mild. And after I take my run, or as far as I can take it, and shower, I'll open a bottle of good red wine and read on the patio a while. Maybe do a bit of gardening before. And then make myself dinner. A frittata tonight, I think. Easy to make. And I love them. And who knows what other good things I'll do."

"Sounds delightful. It's good you're so active and taking such good care of yourself. And the cat?"

"Huey? Just fine, and so funny. He follows me outside. Follows me inside. Sleeps on my bed every night. A real great companion."

"He does sound funny. He doesn't go on the runs with you though, I hope."

"No. He's too smart for that."

"That's a relief. And listen. I also wanted to tell you I'm planning on coming down in two weeks for a couple of days. It'll be at night. Not too late. You'll have to pick me up at the bus station in White Marsh, though. Will that be okay?"

"Are you kidding? Anytime. Anyplace. It's always a major treat to see you. One of those afternoons we'll go to Atwater's in Belvedere Square, where I had lunch today. And one of those nights, to your favorite place for dinner: Gertrude's."

"I'd like that. Both. Though if you've already arranged to meet Iris for lunch or dinner on one of those days, then I don't have to come along. You don't have to spend all your time with me. I'll have things to do. Although I would like to meet her. She sounds so nice."

"She's said the same about you. I've obviously spoken about you a lot to her. But for the time being, since I don't get to see you as often as I want to—two days isn't enough and goes so quickly—I just want to be with you. And I haven't made any arrangements with her yet for our next meeting."

"Fine with me. But you know, I don't want to be interfering in your regular activities too much while I'm down there. Really feel free to go off by yourself—write in your room; anything you want—as if I wasn't there."

"Believe me, you wouldn't be interfering. So. Speak to you tomorrow, maybe?"

"I've a busy work day tomorrow, so I'll call you after six."

"And oh my gosh. This phone call's been all about me. We didn't speak about what you've been up to."

"We'll do that tomorrow on the phone. Now I've got to go. My train's coming. I love you, Daddy."

"And I love you, my sweetie. Love you a lot."

"Me too to you."

15

Turning

CAN'T SLEEP. TRIED for a couple of hours. Turned over on my back. Turned onto my side. Then the other side I'd turned over to my back from. Then again, every fifteen minutes or so: back, side, side. Turn the bedlamp on. Reached for it in the dark. 3:35. Looked at my watch on the night table. Got to bed around eleven. Took me half an hour or more to fall asleep. Four hours' sleep. Not even that. Got up around one to pee. Reached for the bedlamp in the dark and turned it on. Turned on the nightlight in the bathroom and, after I peed, turned it off. Didn't need to turn it on. More than enough light from the bedlamp to see while I peed. Got back in bed and turned off the light and turned on the radio on the night table to listen to music. Reached for it in the dark. Radio set for the classical music station, which I was listening to when I first got into bed and then felt it was keeping me awake and turned it off. Piece by Stravinsky, one of the early ballets. Too turbulent, no matter how low I had it at, to doze off to. *Music Through The Night*, the program's called. Weekdays, eleven p.m. to five a.m. Weekends, eleven to seven. Got that right. But it's Friday, right? Yesterday the cleaning woman was here, and that's every other Thursday, eight till noon. Then she makes a sandwich with deli and a roll I bought for her the previous day or two, and a Diet Coke I buy for her by the six-pack and put in the refrigerator the night before she comes. Then she drives to someone else's house in the neighborhood for five hours—it's a much larger house than mine and with several occupants and a dog that tears up and chews anything it can find that's made of paper—and then drives home to make dinner for her family. Familiar symphony playing. Mozart or Haydn. I didn't hear the announcer announce who, or radio host, or whatever you call them, but if I had to choose, I'd say Mozart. Slow part of it is quite beautiful and peaceful. Good music to doze off to, but it's not going to last. The symphonies by both of them—by just about all composers—always seem to end loud and fast. Listen to it in the dark. Turn over on my back and extend my legs as far as they'll go. Cat comes into the room whining and jumps onto the bed and stretches out and rests on my legs below the knees, facing away from me. When he lies like that it's always facing away from me, I don't know why. Now I think it's Haydn. Sounds more like him, a little dowdier than Mozart, but what do I know? Been wrong a lot more than right in guessing what composer composed the piece I was listening to. Bach is easy. Almost as easy: Stravinsky and Sibelius and Copland. The hardest? Can't think of any right now.

Turn the pillow over to the cool side and rest my head back on it. For some reason, our wedding ceremony comes into my head. Eleanor's and mine. Maybe just the thought of Bach. Our apartment, while the pianist-friend of Eleanor's only played Bach. First the prelude and fugue of *The Well-Tempered Clavier*. I'd requested it days before. Then part of one of the piano partitas. I asked her what it was after the ceremony. The rabbi asked me if we could start a few minutes ahead of schedule. "I know all your guests haven't arrived yet, but I have a funeral to perform in an hour across town." Windows frosted over from the zero to slightly-below-zero temperatures outside. Also the steam from the radiators in the living room and probably the breath of the forty or so guests. Rabbi: "You may now kiss the bride." Me: "In front of all these people?" Almost everyone laughed. Rabbi smiled and looked at his watch. Or almost everyone who heard me, including Eleanor. The ringbearer—just a kid; four years old; the pianist-friend's son—asked his mother, "What was funny?" Rabbi: "Eleanor. If Charles doesn't make his move, you may kiss the groom." Most everyone laughed. Kid asked his mother, "Why is everybody always laughing?" I looked at Eleanor. We'd only been married a minute. Said, loud enough for everyone to hear, "My dearest. My sweetheart. My loved one. I'll try to say what I want to say without bursting into tears. I love you with all my heart and will always love you and take care of you till death, God forbid, do us part." Rabbi: "Didn't we go through all that in the vows? Oh, well. Kiss, already. And then burst the glass." Me: "I'm sorry. I should've shut up. And you have to get out of here. And our guests are thirsty and hungry. But I wanted everyone here to know, especially Eleanor's parents, that I was absolutely sincere in my saying the vows and not just repeating what you asked me to." Eleanor: "That was sweet, my darling. But are you going to leave the kissing of your bride at the altar?" Several people laughed. She had a very soft voice, often could barely be heard when she was talking, and some guests asked others in front of them what she had said. Ringbearer: "They're doing it again. Laughing. And look at Charlie. Why's he crying?" Probably wiped my eyes, and put my arms around her and we kissed. People applauded. There was no glass to step on. We didn't want that to be part of the ceremony—something about the hymen   but had forgot to tell the rabbi. Someone shouted, "Mazel tov, you beautiful people." Someone else shouted, "Good fortune. Good health. Health before fortune. And good children who don't argue with their parents and all become professionals." People laughed. Ringbearer: "What did that man mean?" Me: "May I kiss the bride again?" Rabbi: "Isn't for me to say. You're free of me now. So, if you don't mind—I see some of the food's already out—I'm going to quickly get a bite to eat and leave." Eleanor: "The check." I get the envelope out of my inside jacket pocket and give it to him. "Now you can kiss me again, if you still want to." We kissed. No applause, but several people sighed. Happiest day of my life? Probably till then. Even though it started badly. Car spun out of control—I was alone in it—on black ice when I was coming back from Zabar's with most of the food for the reception and came within inches—maybe an inch—from slamming into a parked car. And ended badly: about ten of the guests couldn't find cabs. It was five to ten degrees below zero by now, worse on Riverside Drive because of the wind off the Hudson—too cold and maybe slippery for them to walk up the hill to Broadway and all the car services they called were busy for the next few hours and cabs never seemed to cruise on the Drive and who could stand out there waiting for them to?—so I made two trips to drive them home, one to the East Side and the other to the West Seventies and Eighties and then the Village.

Still can't get to sleep. Turn over and over and then turn on the light. Didn't want to. Light might hurt my eyes, or do something to them, and that'll keep me from sleep longer. But wanted to find out the time. Past four. Do stretching exercises on the bed, then stand and pick up the weights on the night table and exercise with them. Curls. Others, for about ten minutes, thinking it'll tire me out for sleep. Then: suppose someone sees me from the street? Didn't pull the curtains on the picture window closed. I never do. Used to when Eleanor was alive. She insisted. "People can look in. Even with the trees." But nobody's going to be walking or jogging past the house at this hour. Even if they were and saw me, what of it? I've got my boxer shorts on. Then the stand-like-a-tree Chinese exercise someone who noticed me slumping at the Y taught me to do to relax my lower back and stand straight. Count "one-one-second" in my head and then get back in bed and turn off the light.

Haydn or Mozart still playing. So soft I forgot it was on. Mozart? Haydn? Now more like Haydn. Then: Why does this thought come? And it's come lots of times before, so it isn't the boxer shorts. Always makes me feel bad. Something to do with the music? Can't see how. Eleanor's in her wheelchair. We're in her study. Five to six years before she died. I've made her lunch. Did that just about every day. She: "Let me try feeding myself for a change." I'm about to spoon soup into her mouth. Tasted it first and it's cooled down enough. "I'm getting so out of practice. And it'll make me feel I'm getting better, or at least by stabilizing, but not worse. When you can't do anything by yourself, or something as simple as feeding yourself, you might as well be finished." Me: "You do plenty for yourself. Working in this room. Teaching yourself Latin. Seeing what needs to be done in the garden and things. I'm fine helping you eat. And we don't want to make a mess. Getting food in the keyboard. Things like that." Just then her hand jerks and knocks the spoon out of my hand and the bowl of soup I'm holding into my lap. "Goddam you," and I slap her hand. She starts crying. "Oh, God, what'd I do? I'm so sorry. Really, sweetheart, I didn't mean to hit you. It was like your hand just now. A reflex I had no control over. Oh, that was so awful of me. Let me clean this up and change my clothes and then I'll take care of you. Or do you want me to take care of you first? Some of it got on you too." She's crying and shaking her head. "Please don't. Please stop. I've so much to deal with now." I get the bowl and spoon off the floor and put them in the kitchen sink. I wipe off the soup that's on her shirt with a paper napkin. "Do you want a new shirt?" She's crying, shakes her head. I take off my pants and shirt, take the belt out of the pants, empty the pockets and memo book in them and stick the pants and shirt into the washer. Boxer shorts are soaked through, too, and I take them off, wipe the soup off the table and floor with them and a few dish towels and rinse them all under the sink faucet and drop them into the washer. She's still crying. "It'll be all right. I promise. I know what I did was very bad." I wipe myself off with paper towels, go into the bedroom and get on new boxer shorts and pants and a shirt, thread the belt through the belt loops, or do that before I put the pants on, and go back into her study and sit next to her. She's stopped crying, is staring at the floor. "I'm so sorry. I've never been sorrier for anything I've ever done in my life, or that I can think of. Please forgive me." I take her hand. She pulls it away, looks up at me. She: "You hate me." "What a thing to say. No, I love you. I absolutely love you." "You resent that I'm sick and you have to take care of me and that you'll have to for the rest of my life." "Honestly; no." "Then why did you slap me?" "It happened. I told you. Some reflex I had no control over. I'll pay more attention to it from now on. It won't happen again. Did I hurt your hand?" "My hand's okay. It's my feelings that are hurt, as if I have to say it. Very hurt. I'll never forget you did this. Nobody has ever hit me before." "I know. Or I don't know, but I assumed. And I'm happy to take care of you. I feel blessed that it's me who can help you. I love you very much and will take care of you till death do us part, God forbid." So that's got to be where it came from. I remember saying it. And the "blessed" part. "May I kiss you now? Or at least hold your hand? But I'd want us to kiss. It would make some of it up. One of them, then? No? Sometime?" "Sometime, probably. But not now and not tonight. Probably not tomorrow either. It's something I don't want to do with you. And lunch is over. I'm not hungry anymore." "You've got to eat." "I'll eat when I'm hungry. And the soup must have been hot in your lap." "No, it had cooled off. I never would have given it to you hot. Warm, yes." "I'm sorry about the accident. Now leave me alone. I want to get back to work. The keyboard seems all right. Nothing got in it." "That's good." I get up and go into the kitchen. "Could you shut the door?" I shut it. That's about how it went.

I listen to the music. Same symphony. Turn on the light. Quarter past four. Feeling sleepy, but this seems like the end of the symphony and I want to hear who it's by. Got to be one of those two, but I've been surprised before. Symphony ends. Again, that long drawn out ending. Slow movement was so beautiful. Announcer says it was the Haffner Symphony. Number 35. "By Wolfgang Amadeus Mozart." Why do they always have to say his full name, or almost always? I suppose not to get him mixed up with his father Leopold or his composer son Franz. No, that can't be. How many people have heard of the son to make them think the Mozart who wrote that symphony could possibly be him? Six kids. Did they all survive childhood? If they did, how did they live after Mozart died, because Leopold was already dead? And if the announcer only said it was by Wolfgang Mozart, it wouldn't sound right. That could be why. Announcer: "Next piece will be a waltz by Franz Lehar." Coincidence. Turn the radio off and shut off the light. Try resting flat on my back, legs straight out, but can't get comfortable. Turn over to my left side, side closer to the radio if I want to turn it on. Cat moves to the other side of the bed. Lie there like that for about twenty minutes. Lehar has to be over by now but what music is on could keep me up.

Dream I'm holding my daughter in my left arm. She's sort of cradled there. Holding her like a football and I was a running back. She looks to be around six months. I'm walking down a flight of stairs that's like the one in the apartment building on Riverside Drive Eleanor and I lived in and got married in and conceived our daughter in, except the stairs in the dream go right up to our apartment door, not to the landing we shared with another apartment in the real building. I've just said goodbye to Eleanor and she closed the front door. "Don't forget to get," were her last words to me. Then I see our cat on the stair landing below me. Not the black shorthair I have now but the furry white one we got in Maine as a kitten and who died on my bed while I was sleeping a few weeks after Eleanor died. "Streak! What are you doing out here? You should be inside: You'll get lost in this big building. Or some other tenant will want to adopt you, you're so sweet, and I'll never see you again and you'll never see me." I try to pick him up with my right hand. Can't while I'm holding Margot in my other arm and there's no place to put her down. And if I put her down, how will I be able to pick her up again once I've grabbed the cat? I walk upstairs to our apartment—"7J," it says on the door, when I don't think it did before, which was the real number of our apartment—and ring the bell. Eleanor opens the door. "What do you want? I thought we said goodbye. I'm not going to kiss you again, if that's it." "It's the cat. He got out of the apartment. I tried to pick him up and bring him back here, but couldn't while I held Margot. Hold her, please, while I get him?" She holds out her arms. I give her Margot. Go down the stairs and pick up Streak. Go back upstairs and set him down in the apartment's foyer. "One more kiss goodbye? It's been so long since the last one, that one no longer counts." "I told you. Not today. Not tomorrow. Probably not the day after that, and who knows till when?" She kicks the door shut. "Wait. The baby." I ring the bell, knock on the door repeatedly.

It's light out when I wake. Probably a little past five. Few days before summer starts, so one of the longest days of the year. Turn over in bed, find a comfortable spot. Close my eyes. Try to sleep but can't. Yawn a few times, but that's as close as I get to it. Get out of bed after half an hour of trying to fall asleep, and dress and go into the kitchen and open the front door. Cat follows me slowly, as if tailing me. I stop, he stops. Get the newspaper by the mailbox, walk back. Cat stays outside. "Want to come in and have breakfast? No? Rather be outside? I've got good stuff for you. Going to open a new can. Okay." I'm tired, can use more sleep. Think maybe it's the bed and I should buy a new one. One I have is about fifteen years old. Margot told me even the most expensive ones are good for only ten years. Lumps. Springs go. Other things. Think about it. If I get one, it'll be the next size down from a queen. I don't need as big a bed as that now. I'll try to nap later. Start to make coffee. Cone, filter, coffee grounds in it on top of a large mug. Put two slices of pumpernickel bread into the toaster but won't start toasting them till the coffee's made. I like the toast warm with my coffee. And keep your eyes on the toaster. Timing switch is off. Kettle I don't have to worry about, since it whistles. Don't let the toast burn. Again, don't let the toast burn. Do half the mornings, or close. Take the butter dish out of the refrigerator and put it next to the toaster and a small plate for the toast next to the dish. Marmalade? Have both butter and marmalade on your toast today. You know you like it better than just butter. Don't be lazy. Takes another thirty seconds. Don't deny yourself what's so easy to get. "All right. Okay. I'll do what you say. But stop nagging me," and I laugh. Someone see me now, talking to myself and laughing at what I say, they'd think I was crazy.

The dream. What's it mean? Could be a number of things. It's a dream. Did I really say that at our wedding ceremony? Made a lot of people laugh. Later, when we were cleaning up the apartment—Eleanor had already done half the work while I was driving the last of our guests home: "Did you mind my saying what I did about kissing you in front of all those people? I don't know what came over me. I knew, just before I said it, it might be something I shouldn't say and it could embarrass you, but I went ahead with it anyway. Wrong?" "Not at all. Different, maybe. And I was off into my own thoughts that I was being married a second time and to you." "That's good?" "Very. And you took the edge off what you said by what you said after, not that I'm saying anything you said was bad." "What did I say after? I forget." "About taking care of me and loving me. What a lovely thing to say. It almost made me cry. My mother cried. Probably your mother too. But my tears, as you know, don't come as easily as yours. You're the softie in our new family. What I should have said then, loud enough for everyone to hear, is that I, too, will always love you and take care of you as best as I can, if it ever came to that. Are you happy?" "I'm happy. I'm very tired too. Who knew one's wedding could be so exhausting? Was it like that with your first?" "No. First of all, it was May, so no cold and snow and ice. And my parents had it completely catered in a rented hall. Quite elaborate. With two servers walking around with finger food on trays and another tending the bar, and after that a sit-down dinner. It wasn't what Howard and I wanted. We would have just gone to City Hall and then a small lunch at a good French restaurant, and saved my parents the expense they really couldn't afford. Well, I was their only child." "I should have just kissed you like the rabbi said. May I kiss you now?" "Of course. As far as I can see, you never need to ask my permission. You should just do it." "Really?" "Really. Although maybe not as much in front of people unless it's a quick one and not juicy, and also not when I'm angry at you."

But the dream. I forget what it was. I can't even remember one small part, which could lead me to the rest of it. I should have written it down. And I'm feeling sleepy now, so chances are good it'll never come back, and it seemed to say something I should think about and the wedding. Anyway, I'm sure we kissed and then we finished cleaning up the apartment and washed and dried all the glassware and cutlery and plates and bowls and platters and put them in the boxes they came in from the party-rental company. Then made sure the cat was in and door was locked and all the lights were off and went to bed and slept until ten the next morning, the latest we ever slept together. It had been such a long day. She was as tired as I was. In bed: "Is it all right if we don't make love tonight?" She: "I was thinking the same thing. But I didn't want to say it and was willing to just let you go ahead, even if it meant I'd probably be asleep by the end of it."

16

My Dearest

THE DOCTORS TOLD ME she could die overnight. At the most, in the next day or two. If that's the case, I said, I want to stay beside her all night. They said, "You look exhausted. And you're very pale. We don't want you getting sick. Go home. Get some rest. Be here early tomorrow, though. You can come here anytime you want. There are no visiting-hour restrictions in ICU for close relatives."

So I get there a little before six. She's sitting up in bed and reading a newspaper when I come into her room and she says, "Good morning." She points to her lips and I kiss her. "How do you feel?"

"Me? Fine."

"Have a good sleep?"

"Not much of one, but I'm all right. How about you? You look good and you're so cheerful."

"I feel good too. I'm going home, you know. I won't be spending another day here. Did you hear the news? I'm not going to die."

"The doctors said that?"

"No, they said the opposite. 'You're doomed, lady,' although with more gentility and finesse. But I'm saying it. I'm the deliverer of good news. Notice no ventilator and hookups and tubes running out of my urethra and arms."

"That's right. How could I have not noticed? You're completely free of them."

"I told them. Either remove them all or I'll pull them out myself. Sure, they could have strapped my arms down, but then I would have screamed bloody murder. You see, I'm going to get better. I already am much better. And every day at home I'll be even better. In a few weeks I'll be all better. Isn't it wonderful? I'll be working in the garden again. Walking a few steps on my own. Cooking us delicious meals and able to sit at a table again. Finishing my book. Everything. Help me pack my things. Or do it for me. And don't forget the radio. I can't do that on my own yet, or it would have been done by the time you got here. I already told the staff here I want to be discharged. They said they'd talk to you. No matter what you think, or how able they are to convince you to take their side, it's my decision to make. What do you have to say about it?"

"Whatever you want. I'd love to have you home."

"I hope you mean that, because it's important you do. You'll be the one attending to me day and night till I'm able to do it all on my own. And you'd love to have me not die, wouldn't you?"

"Don't even joke about that. Of course. There's nothing I want more. I like your attitude. Your spirit. Your everything. If you say you're going to get better and home's the place for you to be, then home it is and you'll get better. I know you. And I'll do everything I can to see you get what you need to get better. Oh, this is great. I'm so happy."

"My dearest. You're a dream."

The doctors try to convince me to transfer her to palliative care. I say it's not what she wants. "She wants to go home."

"She's delirious," the head doctor says. "She's got an infection in both lungs that no medication can help. We've tried all the antibiotics we can. But if she insists on going home, we can't stop her. We'll arrange hospice care for her at home."

"She says she won't need it."

"Believe me, she'll need it. She should do what we say. And you should be doing more to change her mind. She's not going to survive her pneumonia this time. You're aware of that, aren't you? No matter what we do for her here, or what's done for her at home, she only has a few days. At most a week."

"I'm aware you say it, but I think she'll survive. You don't know my wife. Nothing's going to kill her now. She'll be taking care of me in my old age."

"Then you're as delirious as she is. Except you don't have the excuse of an untreatable case of double pneumonia that's affected more than three-quarters of both lungs. I'm sorry. Excuse me for saying that."

"That's all right. I don't mind. I don't mind anything. My wife's coming home."

They want to send her home in an ambulance, but she wants to go in our wheelchair-accessible van. I get her dressed and one of the floor aides wheels her to the main entrance of the hospital while I carry two shopping bags of her things and stuff the hospital gave us. I get the van while they wait out front.

"Goodbye and good luck to you," the aide says.

"And goodbye and good luck to you," she says. "We all need it."

I wheel her up the van's ramp and into the space where the front passenger seat would be.

"Turn on some music," she says. "I want to hear music, and I hope it's lively. By the way, you didn't forget the radio in my room, did you?"

"I got everything. Radio. Clothes you came in with. Hairbrush. All your books you never got to read too."

The car's already started up and I turn on the car radio. "It's Rachmaninoff's Second Piano Concerto," I say, and turn it off. "I used to love it as a kid. Or more accurately, as a very romantically inclined young teenager. But then it became too schmaltzy for me. And the ending goes on forever."

"Then I want to listen to it," she says, and I turn it back on.

17

The Mouse
in the Rafters

"HOW DID I START to write?"

"Yes," the interviewer says. "What first motivated you?"

"That's important to know? I thought we were just going to talk about technique."

"We'll get to that later. But people are interested. You've been writing nonstop, it seems, for how many years? Forty? More?"

"Fifty and more. I've been having my books published for almost forty."

"Fifty years writing. And every day, I've read. That's a lot. So what made you start?"

"And do you want where I first started?"

"You can throw that in."

"You sure the tape recorder's on? I don't hear it turning, and I don't want to do this a second time."

"That little light there? If it's on, we're recording."

"Okay. Columbus, Ohio. I probably didn't have to give the state. It's the only Columbus city, or big one in the country, that I know of."

"Georgia. Not as large as the Ohio Columbus, or as important, not being the state capital the Ohio one is, but it's certainly not small."

"Columbus, Georgia. Of course. I've even been to it. I don't know how I could have forgotten. When I was a reporter in '59 and '60 for a news service in Washington. Flew down in the press plane paid for by a defense contractor—it was what we called a junket—to cover Eisenhower giving a speech at Fort Benning there. Some extravaganza he was attending, sponsored by the Army and the defense industry, called Project Man. I never quite understood the name. Anyway, it was really to show off the defense industry's newest weapons, but using real soldiers demonstrating them. There was even a simulated battle after dark with harmless explosions and rifle and machine gun fire and hundreds, maybe thousands, of soldiers pretending to shoot real bullets and throw grenades and such and fall and die, which we all watched from the stands. Then Ike spoke. Or maybe before the show."

"We can touch on that later, though I don't know where it could fit in. Have you written a short story about it or included it in one of your novels?"

"No."

"So let's get back to Columbus, Ohio. You started to write."

"It had to do with a mouse. A real one. 1955. I was going to Ohio State University for one quarter, having transferred there from City College in New York. I thought it'd be longer than a quarter—at least a year, and maybe till graduation—I was pre-dentistry then—but it turned out I couldn't afford it. My parents, though they wanted me to be a doctor or dentist, didn't see the sense in giving up a free school, so weren't going to help me out with the tuition and living costs. I'd always wanted to go to an out-of-state college, or just one with a campus. To have an authentic college experience, which you couldn't get at City, which was what they called a subway school. I even bought two Shetland wool crewneck sweaters—one beige and the other navy blue—shortly before I took an overnight train from New York to Columbus, so I'd look like a real Joe College. Spalding's was the store. On Fifth Avenue, in the forties, I think—west side of the street. A mostly sports equipment store with a sportswear department. Sort of a huge Davega with clothes."

"Davega? Spalding's I heard of, but not Davega."

"Another sports equipment store, but part of a chain. There was one on 86th Street and Broadway that I used to go to when I was a kid. Actually, between 86th and 87th, again on the west side of the street. You see, I'd been going to City College for two years. As I said, it was free, except for a small registration fee each semester, or maybe it was called a matriculation fee. You went to the registrar's booth in the administration building to pay for it. But that was the total cost for a single semester, plus the books—eight to ten dollars. I remember there was even a student protest and threat of a strike for a day or two—megaphones, handmade protest signs, a march around the school—when the fee was raised from eight dollars to ten, or ten to twelve. Anyway, minimal—what would be a forty-to fifty-dollar fee today. But you have to realize that at the time City College had the most radical student body in the country and had been like that for twenty years."

"What about Columbus? Where you first started to write."

"Right. I got sidetracked. The mouse, who changed my life around, you could say. Goodbye, medicine or dentistry. Though I was a lousy student in the sciences—C's, a D or two, and one F in biology (I got caught cheating with crib sheets on the final practicum and was put on academic probation)—I never would have gotten into one of those schools. I lived in a cheap rooming house for poor students and a couple of derelicts with enough dough they got from street-begging to pay the rent. Ten bucks a week it was, I think. Anyway, that's the number that sticks. And a mouse, just about every morning—five a.m., six—used to run around the rafters in the room I shared with another student. Am I using the word 'rafters' right? The crossbeams that look like they're holding up the roof. But every morning, maybe the same mouse. My roommate slept through it all. Said he was raised on a farm and there were mice all over the place. So, for no explainable reason, since I never wrote fiction before, I got the idea to write a story about it. I wouldn't touch the subject now. No mice, rats, any rodents in my fiction except a chipmunk or squirrel or two, and hasn't been for about forty years. I don't like reading about rats and mice, so I certainly don't want to write about them. Same with vermin. I won't even mention their names to you, except to say 'the city kind.' If I wrote about them, then I'll think about them and maybe dream about them too. But then—this is what must have happened—I probably thought if I wrote about this mouse in the rafters, maybe I'll get tired enough after writing it to fall back to sleep. So I wrote by hand—I didn't have my own typewriter then. That came when I graduated City and my parents—my mother, really—gave me a new Olivetti Lettera as a graduation gift. But a story about a mouse and a poor college student in a rooming house. From the mouse's point of view. Observing the student tossing and turning in bed because he can't sleep knowing the mouse is there. Or that's what the mouse thinks. It was no doubt a very stupid story. And poorly written. But give me some credit. It was my first and it got me started. That I'd unearthed something from myself that I had no idea was there. No, that's too fancy a way of putting it. I'd just never done anything like that before, and there it was. The story, though short, just kept coming till I finished it. In one spurt. It was, as they say, as if it wrote itself and I was just writing down what my mind was telling me to. No, that's not quite it either. But you know what I mean. Though I never could come up with a satisfying ending to the story—it sort of just stops. The imagination did. What it was telling me to write down—it did, writing it, make me tired enough, I remember, to fall back to sleep."

"Do you still have the story?"

"No, of course not. That was fifty-five years ago. Sixty. It was written in a notebook. That story and I think another first draft of one to follow that also just sprung from my head while I was in bed. I probably threw the notebook away after the school term was over and I took the bus—not the train this time. I didn't have the money for one and my parents didn't volunteer to give me any—a bus back to New York."

"Too bad. It'd be quite a literary artifact, your first story, if you had a place to deposit your papers. They'd scoop that notebook right up."

"Yeah, well. And I have a place—the library at the university I taught at for so many years; their rare manuscripts and special collections department—though I seriously doubt they've kept even half the papers and manuscripts I've given them. I do remember telling this girl I was seeing in Columbus that I'd written a short story. She got all excited and wanted to read it. She couldn't read my handwriting, so I think the next time we met I read it to her. I remember we sat on a bench on campus and that she liked the story but told me there was one problem with it. It doesn't end. I said I know, and right there on the bench she supplied me with several endings to it. One where the mouse takes pity on the college student, feels guilty he's keeping him from sleep and, because of that, keeping him from doing well in his studies, and he goes to another rooming house to run around the rafters there. But I was tired of the story by then, probably didn't think much of the first draft of the story that followed, which could be the reason I got rid of the notebook. As for the girl? I forget her name. I think it was Jane. Blond. Pretty. Very smart. Knew several languages. Was getting her master's—so she was older than me—in Italian literature. Never saw her again after I left Columbus, though we exchanged letters for a while and maybe even a phone call. Anyway, have I answered your question?"

"Not quite, but what you said was very interesting and some of it usable. From now on, though, please, I don't want to tell you how to answer my questions, but please try to keep your answers short or much shorter than you did with this one."

"I don't think I can. I've a tendency for going on too long, not just in my speech. It's also what I do in my writing. I didn't used to be that way. My stories and novel chapters were once always very short, though the novels might have been long. So I don't think this interview will go well. We should probably stop it right here. It'll just end up being a waste of your time. I've never been good at interviews. Which is interesting because it's what I used to do when I was a very young radio reporter in Washington. You know—call a senator off the floor, let's say, and interview him with my tape recorder. 'Do you think the House bill will pass in the Senate?' or 'our small soldiers-advisors unit in Vietnam is going to escalate into a full-fledged fighting force?' I also used to do a lot of interviews for my books. Publishers love them.

But they never came out well and, in fact, most of them stunk and I doubt any of them helped sell a single copy of my books."

"I'm sure you're exaggerating."

"I'm not. I don't know why I thought it would this time. Come out well. The interview. Not stink. Or even half well, smell and otherwise. I guess I wanted to help my book in any way I could and also please the publisher so they'll publish my next book. I fool myself from time to time like that. But nothing's going to help my books. Not this one, not the past ones. So if I were you I'd turn the tape recorder off, put it back in its little case and try to find for your magazine a writer a whole lot more successful, interesting and succinct than I."

"Sure we couldn't give it another try? Not that I think it's been bad so far."

"Sure, try. You're here. The tape recorder's still running. If it continues to be a flop, we'll quit."

"Good. Now I know what life experience got you started writing fiction. The mouse in the rafters. I might even title the piece that. What do you think?"

"I don't like it. I told you. Anything with mice and rats and vermin in it."

"Anyhow, being that you thought at the time that your first attempt at writing fiction was a failure—"

"Did I say that? I probably did. Even if I didn't, it probably came out, in what I said, as if I did. No, scratch that. I got a little confused there what I was saying."

"Will do. So I'm asking, what made you write a second first draft of a short story while you were still at Ohio State? And then a third some other place—back in Manhattan, perhaps—and a fourth and a fifth and so on? Till you wrote more than six hundred completed stories, your bio says, more than almost any other writer."

"I suppose, for the second story, I had nothing else to do, once I finished my schoolwork and attended classes and read on my own and saw this girl every other week or so—Beverly. That's right; that was her name. And writing took me away from this nothing-to-doness. You see, I didn't have much money to entertain myself. Movies, going out for beers, etcetera. I told you about my folks not helping me out.

And I didn't hold it against them, by the way. It was my decision to change schools. Actually, about not having much else to do and having little money, I'll correct that. I was working, from almost the first day I got to Columbus, four hours a day, six days a week—lunchtime and dinnertime—as a counterman in a restaurant. A place that catered mainly to students because of its proximity to campus and the food was inexpensive. More like a diner than a restaurant. I remember they served a Salisbury steak. I never heard of it before. I'm still not quite sure what it is, but I remember it wasn't very good. It was on the menu every day, lunch and dinner, their most popular dish because it was so cheap and you got so much of it. It came with a scoop, maybe two scoops, of mashed potatoes, with a pool of gravy in the top of the potatoes. Also, peas or carrots or peas and two slices of white or whole wheat packaged bread, toasted if the customer wanted, and a pad of margarine or butter. The other student favorite was an enormous double cheeseburger with French fries and two tomato wheels on a leaf of iceberg lettuce. If memory serves. But I'm almost positive I got all that right. Truth is, I think being a writer is all about having a good memory. The job paid poorly but it did provide me with lunch and dinner every workday. Maybe a couple of dollars   I don't remember more—for each two-hour shift. Anyway, a dollar an hour. That helped cover, or maybe it covered all of it, my rent. Students weren't much for tipping, and who could blame them? Would I have tipped if I was a customer there, considering how little money I had? So I rarely got anything extra, and when I did, it was more like a dime or nickel, which I was supposed to share with the other countermen on my shift. What the restaurant let me and the other countermen and the clean-up guys eat for free—if we wanted anything better we had to shell out for it—was usually meatloaf or a creamed chicken concoction and peas or succotash, another dish I up till then was unfamiliar with. I had to leave school after the first quarter. Couldn't afford it anymore and my grades were suffering from all the things I was doing. Schoolwork. Restaurant. Now I think it was six hours a day there, not four. At least five. And ROTC. I just remembered that. All lowerclassmen had to be in it because Ohio State was a land-grant college, whatever that meant. I was in the Air Force ROTC and my main instructor there, and I'm not making this up, was Lieutenant Hawke. If this was fiction I'd never name the guy that. Two days a week I had ROTC classes and marching and stuff, so I had to wear on campus a heavy wool uniform and one absolutely neat and clean and the cap and tie just so and shoes polished to a sheeny shine, or an upperclassman ROTC student would stop me and make me salute him a hundred times or do something equally humiliating. Pushups. They were big on pushups. So I also knew I wouldn't last another quarter doing that without telling them to shove it up. I did get the few academic credits I earned transferred to City—CCNY, that is—and I also got my out-of-town college experience out of my system. Joe College comes home. But I wandered off from answering whatever was your original question. As I warned you, I'm an impossible interviewee. It just isn't my forte."

"Forte?"

"Then without the little French mark over the e and only one syllable. My thing. What I excel at. I don't. I'm perfectly lousy at it."

"Nah, you're being too hard on yourself again. I suppose if I let you ramble on I could edit it down and get something out of it. But maybe you're right. We should stop. Unfortunately, there's not enough here what I got to turn it into anything, so I think you'll have to tell the publicity person at your publisher's that for one reason or another the interview didn't pan out."

"I'll think of something. She'll be disappointed. At me, not you, because she hasn't had much luck getting any publication like yours interested in my work. But I already told her the interview probably wouldn't go well. This'll be good, though. What I'm saying is that this interview hasn't been a total loss for me, as she now won't ask me to be interviewed again."

"I guess that's good if you look at it that way."

"That's what I always do. In my writing, I mean. Try to make something out of nothing, which might be the one usable thing I said since we started the interview. But since there's nothing else to go with it, we'll forget it."

"Too bad." He stops the tape recorder and presses what I assume is the rewind button, because it makes that kind of noise. "And thanks for the coffee and cookies you made. Oatmeal. My favorite kind and just what I needed to get me through the rest of the afternoon."

"Want to take a few for the road? I made a batch of them. And if you have a coffee mug in your car, I can fill it up with more coffee from my Thermos."

"I'm fine." He waits till the rewinding stops, puts the tape recorder into its case, collects his notes and pen from the dining table they had the interview at and gets up to leave. "Now as for getting out of here. Which way should I go to get back on 695, left or right, once I get to the street at the end of your driveway?"

"I don't know which way you came, but you can get to 695 either way. Right is the most direct and least complicated and, when the traffic's light, the fastest of the two. But it has its problems. You go half a mile on Rogers—that's my street—to the stop sign on North Hereford, the main drag around here. If you made a right on North Hereford and stayed on it, it'll take you straight into the heart of the city. But take a left and it goes directly to the East and West on-ramps of 695. That could be a little dangerous, though, because you have to cut across the south lanes of North Hereford to get to the north lanes that take you to 695 about two miles away. You also might have to wait a while at that stop sign for all the traffic to pass in both directions. What I always recommend and do myself to get to 695, unless it's five in the morning and I know there's little to no traffic on North Hereford, is go left at the end of my driveway, stop at the first stop sign, and actually the only one in that direction, which is Milona, and go right on it. Stay on Milona all the way, past the first traffic signal till you get to the second, which'll be North Hereford. Make a left at that signal—and you should be in the left turn lane—and the on-ramps to 695 are just a few hundred feet away. You're heading back to Washington. So you'll want to get on the West on-ramp, which is right after the East one, and both are on the right. But I'm as bad at giving driving directions as I am at interviews, maybe worse, and I probably confused you to get here, right? I know we talked and you were also going on-line for them. So just follow them, but the reverse, because if you listen to me you'll just get lost."

"I'll make it. Thank you," and he goes.

18

The Writer

HE'S AT THE Y, on a stationary bike. Woman peddling on the bike next to his, but at a much slower clip, says, "Excuse me. Can I ask? What are you reading?"

"A novel."

"Any good?"

"It's holding my interest."

"I'm always looking for a good book to read. Is it one you'd recommend?"

"I'd have to wait till I got further into it."

"You must like to read. I see you, whenever you're on the bike and I'm on one, too, reading."

"Yeah, I like to read. Also, it helps to pass the time when I'm on the bike."

"What are you, a teacher?"

"Used to be. Retired now."

"What do you do, now that you're retired?"

"Read. Work out at the Y. Do a little gardening around the house."

"That's it? That fills up your day?"

"I also write."

"What kind of writing?"

"Fiction."

"Novels like the one you're reading?"

"Sort of. But different."

"Of course, they can't all be the same. I know that much. Have you been published?"

"Yes."

"Would I know anything you might have written?"

"I don't know what you read. But there's probably little chance of it. My books don't get around much."

"Books? You've been published more than once and not just in a magazine? Did you have to pay to get them published, like what's called a vanity press?"

"No."

"So one that pays you? That's impressive. How many books of yours would you say?"

"A lot."

"All novels?"

"No. But only fiction."

"No memoirs or children's fantasies or spiritual journeys or anything like that?"

"Right."

"I've never met a professional writer before, one with books and who gets royalties, though always wanted to. To find out how they do it. You see, for a long time I've had aspirations to be a writer too. I've had a very interesting and, I'd say, exciting life at times. And I thought all of it, or selected parts that could be connected, would make for good reading a real publisher would want to publish. Unfortunately, I could never get any of it down, not even a beginning, not that I tried that hard. I found out pretty quickly that I wasn't a writer. But what would you say—"

"The answer is no."

"No, no, just listen to me. If we worked out some kind of arrange-ment where I'd give you some of my ideas I have and experiences I underwent and you turned them into a completed work, we could go fifty-fifty on it. Or even more for you if it entailed a great deal of time and work on your part."

"I'm sorry, but I only work for myself. It isn't the money."

"It doesn't have to be a book. It could be a short story or article, with my name changed. Or even it not changed, for a popular mag-azine that pays well. But you'd know more about that part of it than me. Where to send it and so forth. Or your agent would."

"I don't have one."

"You work without an agent and still sell your books? I read where that's unusual."

"My work doesn't warrant having an agent. There's really very little in it for them."

"But you don't write anything shorter than a novel."

"I write short stuff. But collaborating with someone in the writing is just not what I do."

"I can understand that. You want to take the credit all to yourself. I'm not exaggerating, though, about my life. You might not want to pass it up so fast. It could be a book—people have told me that—and all you'd have to do is copy it down, what I say, and then clean it up a little. Polish it but keeping the saltiness in. You know."

"You say you've tried to write it yourself. And it's getting a little difficult, talking while peddling at the speed I want to go. Reading is easier. So try again. Maybe once you start it this time, it'll turn into something. Something here, another day something there. Later the parts can be reassembled in some order. But you want to get something down. Once you start, I'm saying, the rest might follow. Or maybe there's another writer who'd be interested. I don't know. But good luck with it. Sorry I can't be of more help."

"Do you know of another writer who might be interested?"

"I don't. And I wouldn't know how to find one. Nice talking to you."

"Same here. And thanks for the advice you gave."

"It was nothing." He opens the book he's been holding, finds the page and then the part on that page where he left off, and starts peddling faster and resumes reading.

AT THE Y. Sitting, facing out, resting between repetitions, he thinks they're called. Man stops in front of him, hand on chin as if he's studying him and says, "Boy, you're giving that machine some kind of workout."

"I try."

"It's terrific what you do, guy your age. You make the rest of us geriatrics look feeble. I've seen you. You're here almost every day and go from machine to machine. Least, you always seem to be here when I am."

"Every day, it's true, for what little good it'll do me. But no set schedule. Could be ten o'clock. Could be two."

"So when you're done with your work at home you come here to break up the day?"

"You got it. And it works. Exercise and then a shower here seem to reenergize me."

"To go back to your work at home?"

"Yeah, if I feel like it or don't feel like I've done enough that day."

"Someone told me you're a writer."

"I don't know who that could be. I certainly don't broadcast it."

"I think one of the trainers. The real pretty one, short, with the dark bangs. The one who always seems to be folding fitness towels. You must have told her, or she got wind of it some way, and she and I got to talking about what some of the regulars here do. Talking's what I do. One's a congressman. Of this district. But a U.S., not the state assembly or House of Delegates."

"I heard about him in the locker room and I think I even know who he is. Keeps to himself. Wears regular shoes instead of sneakers when he exercises here. And I recognize you from here too."

"Have you written books?"

"Plenty."

"I don't want to keep you from your workout, but how many?"

"Probably too many. Thirty-one, at last count."

"Any more forthcoming?"

"Three. In the next year. That's a first-ever for me, to have that many coming out. It just worked out that way."

"Amazing. She said you were a writer. But I don't think she knows how much you've published or even what kind of books you write. Nonfiction? Fiction? Academic tomes? Because she also said you were once a professor."

"I was. But very few academics have written that number of books. It takes a lot more work per page than I put in for my stuff and they also have to prepare for structured classes and teach. Me? I only write fiction, and no research needed, and after a while I only taught creative writing. So not much work involved, as with real teachers. Read a few short manuscripts for a two-hour class and get the students to talk about them, and every now and then I toss in my two cents. Easy. I was overpaid."

"I bet."

"No, it's true. Not that I complained."

"I'll take that with a grain of salt. But what kind of fiction you write? Detective? Suspense? Fantasies for adults? Or maybe you write for children, with lots of illustrations, and that's why there are so many books."

"Just contemporary life. No genre."

"Any get famous? Best-sellers?"

"Not unless one of publishers is holding back on me. But I would have eventually found out."

"That happens?"

"Just kidding. They've all been on the up-and-up as to the royalties and such, little there's been of them. No best-sellers. Not even close. I've made this crack before, so I'm repeating myself here possibly for I don't know how many times, but I'll say it anyway: just worst-sellers. Plenty. But I shouldn't have preambled the remark. Whatever I did. Prefaced it. Shouldn't have said anything before I said it. It went flat."

"Why? It was good. Worst-sellers. Clever. Never heard it before. Any books turned into movies?"

"One, in France. For TV there. Years ago."

"Then why don't you write a bestseller?"

"It's not so easy. Not that I've ever tried. And it takes a certain skill. Even if I had it you really can't predict, unless you're a well-known writer with a history of best-sellers from a mainstream publisher who's made a small fortune from your books—"

"I get it. You stick with what you know you can do and I guess what keeps you busy and gives you pleasure."

"That's right."

"I can see that. By the way, what name do you write under? In case I want to look up one of your books."

"Ah, don't bother."

"What do you mean? Don't you want to sell your books or create some demand for them at the county libraries?"

"Really, by this time it doesn't matter. And my books are pretty long. But thanks."

"Okay, I won't. I'm not much of a reader anyway. A terrible thing to tell a writer, but I just never find the time. And I don't mean to change the subject, but are you done on that machine? If you're not, don't hurry your exercise or get off it for me."

"I was going to go again. One more round, but there are plenty here to work on. And I can always come back to this one. You take it." He gets off, wipes it down, says, "See you later."

RUBY, ANOTHER TRAINER, one he's spoken to a few times. First time was when she was walking past him while he was working out on one of the machines and gave him tips to get the maximum benefit from it for the least amount of effort.

"Hi, Mr. Epsteen. Write any new books lately?"

"As I think I've told you: I'm always working on something."

"Any coming out?"

"One."

"This one also about life today?"

"Close enough."

"One of these days—I can't predict when, but when I get more free time away from my job and kids—I'll have to read a book of yours. Any particular one you like?"

"No, I have no favorites. Just whatever you'd find."

"Okay. That's what I'll do. I'll keep my eyes out for them. And good luck with the new one."

IN THE LOCKER ROOM at the Y. Sitting on a bench, trying to get a sock on his left foot. For some reason it's always more difficult to do than the right.

"Those are always a bitch," says the man sitting on the other end of the bench and tying his shoes.

"I'm going to invent a sock that slips on easily every time, even if your foot's still a little damp from the shower or pool, and continue to do so long after it's gone through the washer and dryer dozens of times."

"You do and I'll and every other man our age will buy it and you'll end up a rich man. But you're not serious, of course. Or it could be you are an inventor like that."

"In a way, yeah. No, I'm not. There! Success. Sock over the toes. Now the second hardest part. Getting it over the rest of the foot and the heel part where the heel of the foot's supposed to go."

"You'll get there. What is it you do, then, or did?"

"I taught. College. Retired now. Nothing to do with socks."

"I was a teacher too. Grade school. What did you teach?"

"Something they even might be teaching now in grade school. Fiction writing."

"Maybe they are. I taught history and civics. Then you must know a lot about writing fiction."

"Enough to teach. Or maybe I don't. But I didn't get too many complaints about it. Long gone now."

"And literature? You teach that too?"

"Just the first few years. Twentieth Century fiction. Western Hemisphere the fall semester, Eastern the spring. Till they got wise I was no good at it and banished me to just teaching fiction writing to undergraduates and grads."

"Do you write fiction yourself?"

"Yes."

"Books?"

"Some."

"Could you avail me of a piece of information I always wanted to know? How does a writer, with no reputation of being one, break into publishing? I ask because maybe you could help me find a literary agent or publisher."

"Why, do you write?"

"I've some material put away. And lots of ideas for more. I admit, the material isn't right yet. But I figured, get a good literary agent and he or she would help me with what I already have written down and propose for more, and turn it into a very nice book. I'm not looking for money; just to get published. What I have is about the world's first truly professional meteorologist—I don't want to give away more of the story. But a terrific yarn. What he went through to become the seminal figure in his field. People are interested in weather. Everybody is. Not just because it's a science easily explained and understood. It affects everything we do. Wars. Peace. Famines. Feasts. You name it. And our moods every day. And of course his personal life, which was kind of racy and exotic for a scientist. I looked into it. There's never been a fictional book written about him. I change his name and the locations and play with the facts. But it was so long ago. Nobody would care if they found out it was about a real person."

"Maybe you have something there. I couldn't say. But I really have no suggestions as to how to get people in the publishing business interested in it. I'm not represented myself, if that's what you're thinking, or have a regular publisher, so I couldn't help you there. If I were you I'd go online and look into the Association of American Literary Agents, or whatever the organization is called, and see what the agents listed are interested in and if they look at unsolicited work. I'm sure a few would."

"Suppose they say they're interested and then look at what I have and reject it but then steal my ideas?"

"Won't happen. They've enough to deal with. But I guess you have to take that chance."

"Incidentally, what's your name?"

"Charles."

"Charles what? If your books are in the public library, not that I go to them much except to take my grandkids, or even to a bookstore, I could take a look at them."

Just as I type that, the phone rings and I get up to answer it. It's on the dresser. It's a writer friend in Des Moines. We talk on the phone about once a month. He asks how I am, tells me how he is. He has the same disease I have but a worse case of it and for a couple more years. He falls a lot. I wobble sometimes but never fall. We compare the medication we take for the disease. His dose is twice as much as mine. "I'm sure I'll catch up," I say. I ask him how his writing's going. He says he gets in about twenty minutes of writing a day, and often not in the same stint. "I have trouble sitting."

"And I feel best when I'm sitting. I'm lucky. Since I can sit at my typewriter two to three hours straight."

"My standing is good, though," he says, "when I'm not falling. I should probably try writing standing up. Like Hemingway and Thomas Wolfe did, or their biographers say they did. Put the typewriter on top of the refrigerator and type."

"You'd have to be pretty tall for that. Or at least with my refrigerator."

"And dexterous. When I type, my fingers are all over the place. That's why I get one of my graduate students, for a price, to type into the computer what I've sloppily written on the typewriter, and then help me send my work out online."

"Refrigerators must have been shorter when Hemingway and Wolfe were typing on them, wouldn't you think?"

"Probably," he says. "If I close my eyes, that's how I see them, shorter and boxier than today's. I can walk, though. Strange. Not far, not fast, and with a cane—that I can still do. How's your walking?"

"I have trouble with it. But I'm not ready yet to take up a cane."

"So we have different…different…oh, geez, you know what I'm attempting here to say. My mind's going. I couldn't even get that simple sentence straight."

"You got the rest out okay. I wouldn't worry about it. You were saying we show different symptoms for the same disease."

"That's not quite it. Anyway, to my question: how's your writing going? I hope well."

"Sometimes I think too well. I finished a new story after working on it for three weeks. And ever compulsive to have something to work on when I get up in the morning, I was just now writing the first draft of a new story when you called."

"Oh, I'm sorry. Go back to it. I'll hang up."

"Don't worry. I'll get back to it okay. Or I won't. It's not that important to me anymore. One more story? What's it mean? Nobody really gives a damn."

"Come on; I do. I publish you in my magazine about every third issue, don't I? Correct me if I'm wrong."

"You do. I didn't mean you. And you pay generously, for a literary magazine. Yeah, I'll get back to it. Because I might lose it if I don't, not that it matters that much. And I mean it. It really doesn't. I've written way more than enough for one writer."

"You don't know what you're saying. For what would you do if you didn't write?"

"You're right. I'm wrong. But your twenty minutes a day that you're down to, and I hope that's not all it is. Does it add up to completed stories?"

"It's enough. I still turn them out. Just less of it. Much less."

"That's not the way it is for me. I've got more stuff here than I'll ever get published. And listen. With your new book, whenever you finish it and find a publisher, don't send me a copy as you've done with the last ones. This time, let me buy it at my local bookstore. In fact, two. One for my daughter and one for me."

"No way. I have a publisher for the new collection, but he's not giving me anything but contributor copies—fifty of them. I've got to get rid of them some way. When the time comes, if you know of a few people who might like to have a copy, let me know and I'll send you several to give them. Speak to you soon."

Back to the typewriter. Where was I? In the locker room at the Y.

"Charles Epsteen. But don't bother. I mean, the libraries around here have some of my work, or did, for who knows if they haven't got rid of them. They're not checked out enough, or at all, to make room on the shelves, they're sold in the libraries' used book sales for a dollar or fifty cents. I'm not sure if mine are, but I assume."

"Well, I just thought. It might be interesting dipping into something you wrote, if I could remember the next time I was there."

SITTING IN THE SAUNA at the Y after doing a few laps in the pool. Just him and another man, who's been reading a newspaper and starts talking. "This is the life, right? Relaxing. The right sauna temperature. Not boiling hot. No job to go to ever again or cares in the world. Least it feels like it in here. I love it. And great for the body too. Gets out all the poisons."

"But it's so boring. You were smart, bringing in something to read. I couldn't because my glasses would steam up."

"I don't need them anymore. Laser surgery. I've seen you here a lot. Usually around noon, which is the time I get here. Exercising, but riding the bike, mostly. Never in the pool or sauna before. Maybe you were wearing swim goggles and I didn't recognize you."

"No, this is my first time for both."

"World's best exercise, swimming."

"So I've been told. Thought I'd try it out."

"Your lower back. I've seen you walk."

"Yeah. You're very observant. My physical therapist, when I was going to her for it, said swimming and the sauna could be good for it, if I don't overdo the swimming at first, which might make my back even worse. But it took me six months before I decided to jump in. I like lakes."

"You're probably retired. And since you always seem to have a book with you when you're in the fitness center, my guess is you were a teacher. College level. The books always look serious."

"I was. A teacher. The books have nothing to do with the teaching, though. Just for pleasure."

"I've seen you scribbling down things when you were on the bike and a couple of times in the locker room. You a writer too?"

"That's right. The scribblings were of ideas that came to me while I was riding the bike or maybe even between machines."

"What sort of writing? Related to what you taught?"

"Yes. Fiction."

"Now that's really the life. Tell me, do you know the writer in the South who writes these long, complicated novels about lawyers and district attorneys and trial cases and such but always about the law?"

"I think I know who you mean. Good-looking guy. Always a bestseller. And his book jacket photos and full-page ads in the *New York Times* book review always have him with a three-day growth of beard and in a natty sports jacket. One that probably set him back more than I earn from my writing all year."

"But you don't know him?"

"How would I know him? He's out of my league. Or I'm out of his. He's probably a good guy. I've never read him."

"Neither have I. But I read about him in a magazine. He makes a pot of money from his books. One every other year they come out, on average, and almost every one of them turned into a movie. What a life he leads. Writes from eight till noon. Just orange juice and a slice of toast and coffee for breakfast. Then, after writing, he has lunch and spends the rest of the day looking after his ranch-estate. Riding horses. Mending fences. Clearing brush. Tossing Frisbees to his dogs. Things like that. Maybe a round of golf in the late afternoon with his wife or friends. It's a terrific field, writing, if it can go like that."

"Yeah, for some. I can only imagine it. Now I'm going to take a shower. Swim; sauna. I could use one."

"You have a good workout today, besides the swimming?"

"Maybe overdid it a little. First the gym; then the pool. I feel good, though. Back doesn't hurt. So maybe the swim and sauna are good. And the shower will make me feel even better."

"That a way to go. And then you'll do what? Horse around like our Southern gentleman-writer? Or just go home and write?"

"Probably write. I've been known to. Depends how I feel when I get there. I put in my three hours this morning, and that might be enough."

"I won't ask what you're writing. This very successful writer—I forget his name—I read about in a magazine article says he never talks about his work, not even to his wife, till it's been sent to his publisher.

That it sort of spooks the momentum of the book he's writing if he talks about it before it's completely finished and he can start another."

"He's probably right. I don't mind talking about what I'm currently working on, and I've sometimes got some good ideas from it, but I'm also not too eager to talk about it too."

"Maybe I'll see you in the locker room. I know I'll be seeing you at the Y again. Name's Michael. I know yours. Talk to you again soon."

19

Depression

I'M TOO DEPRESSED to write. I take the page I was writing out of the typewriter and crunch it up in my hand and drop it in the wastebasket under my work table. I cover the typewriter with its dust cover. I turn off the light on the table and go into the kitchen. I get a carrot out of the vegetable bin in the refrigerator, snap it in two, put one part back into the bin and wash the other part under the sink faucet and eat it. I take the bunch of celery out of the bin, tear off a stalk, put the bunch back into its bag and the bag into the bin, wash the stalk under the faucet for a few seconds and bite off a piece of it. I don't feel like eating. The carrot was enough. More than enough. I didn't want it and wasn't hungry. I only took it out of the refrigerator and ate it to do something. To take my mind off my depression. I swallow some of the celery I chewed and spit the rest of it out into the kitchen trash can. I think of putting the part of the stalk that's left into the refrigerator, but why bother? I won't eat half of the celery in the bag by the time it starts going bad, and I dump the piece into the trash can. I don't feel like eating anything. I don't know when I'll again feel like eating anything. It's too early to have a drink. I don't even know if I'll want a drink tonight. I go back to my bedroom just to do something. I look at my typewriter and think I'm still too depressed to write. I put on my socks and sneakers just to do something. I don't know if I'll go out. I don't know what I'll do the next few hours. I shaved yesterday, and I usually only shave every other day, but I shave now just to do something. I brushed my hair while I was sitting on the toilet this morning, and I have so little hair I only brush it once a day, but I brush it again just to do something. I could go to the nearby market but I have nothing to shop for. I could go to the Y, which I do every day, but I don't want to get in my car and drive there and work out and shower and drive back. I don't have to shower there—I could shower at home—but I still don't want to go. I go outside just to go somewhere, and think what am I going to do out here? I don't feel like gardening or mowing or checking to see if any tomatoes are ready to be picked. It makes no sense to go to the mailbox because the mail never comes till late afternoon. If I got a letter I'd read it. But there's only one person I correspond with with this kind of mail, around twice a month, and it's usually about what we're reading and writing, and I got a letter from him two days ago and haven't written back. I look around for the cat. If he were here I'd go over to him if he didn't come over to me first and pet him and say something to him, like "How are you, old Buddy?" but I don't see him. "Huey, Huey," I call, but if he's around and hiding, he doesn't jump out and show himself as he often does when I call out to him outside. Maybe I should just walk. I walk along the road by my house for about two hundred feet, when I thought I'd walk much further than that, and turn around and walk back to the house. I don't feel like walking. I didn't when I started out. I did it just to do something. I look around for the cat one more time and then go into the house. So what will I do here? I don't feel like reading. Books, newspaper, magazines; nothing. Nothing I want to eat. Nothing I want to drink except maybe water. I fill up a glass with water from the filter tap attached to the kitchen sink and drink less than half of it, and it's a small glass. I sit in a chair in the dining room, one that's against a wall and not around the dining table, and kick off my sneakers and pull off my socks and stuff the socks into one sneaker and push the sneakers under the chair. I don't know why I did that. Again, I guess just to do something. I could go back to my bedroom and exercise with the weights there and then stretch after, but I don't feel like doing that either. I could also go back there to answer my friend's letter. But I've only written a few pages of fiction, and then discarded them, since I last wrote him, and I haven't read more than ten pages of the novel I was reading when I last wrote him, so I really haven't anything to say to him other than that I feel depressed, not as much as I've ever felt in my life but, still, depressed, and I don't want to tell him that. He's a friend, but not that kind. Do I have a friend I could tell it to if I wanted to tell someone that? I don't think so, and it's not something I want to tell my daughter. It'd just worry her and maybe make her depressed. I could check the computer for messages, which is just about all I use it for, and answering them, except for an occasional movie. But I already checked it this morning and there was nothing there and I'm not expecting anything, and I think it'd only depress me more that I turned on the computer and went to the inbox for nothing. So? Next? I've run out of things to do just to do something. Maybe I should try to nap. So what if it's just a little past noon and I only got up two hours ago, staying in bed longer than I almost ever do, and that I got plenty of sleep last night, or sufficient sleep to get through today till around nine at night, and I'm not tired or sleepy and my lower back doesn't hurt and I don't need to rest it. It's just I can't think of anything else to do now but nap, and I'd much prefer doing it on a bed than in a chair. I go into my bedroom, get on the bed, lie on my back, fit one of the pillows comfortably under my head and neck and close my eyes. Out of nowhere, and almost instantly, and not what I got on the bed for, ideas for stories come—two, one after the other. Not so much plots but the way the stories are written. Form, I think I mean, structure. In the first, in a single paragraph or a new paragraph for each sentence, each sentence starts off with the word "I.""I get up. I go out. I take a walk. I come back. I make myself a drink. I sit in my easy chair. I read. I play with myself. I get back on the bed. I can't sleep. I fall asleep. I dream," and so on. Or longer sentences, or longer ones mixed in with the short ones. "I get up. I wash and dress. I go out and look around for the cat and jog for about half a mile. I walk back to the house and while making myself coffee I think of Louise. I haven't thought of her for years. I think it must be fifteen years at least," and so on. In the other story, again a single paragraph or each sentence its own paragraph, so a very short story because none of the sentences will be very long, each sentence starts off with a different letter of the alphabet, but going sequentially from A to Z. "Alan went to a movie theater and fell asleep a few minutes after the picture went on. By the time he woke up, the movie was over and the theater was empty except for him and a theater employee sweeping up the rows behind him and a young woman whom he didn't know and doesn't think he's ever seen, sitting beside him and staring at the blank screen while holding his hand in her lap. 'Caroline,' she said, when he asked her who she was and what was her name. 'Did you like the movie?' she said. 'Enormously,' he said, 'little that I saw of it,' and so on. It'd be tough, though, finding a sentence that started with a word whose first letter was X or Z. For Z, maybe just "Z-Z-Z," indicating he fell asleep again. But X? That might be harder to start off a sentence with than Z. Still, it might be interesting to try out one of these story ideas to see if it leads to anything. That's how a lot of my stories have been written. An idea comes, mostly from my waking life but sometimes from a dream, I jot it down on a piece of paper, transfer it to my notebook if I didn't jot it down in a notebook first, later start writing the story on my typewriter, sentence follows sentence, and the story's done, or first draft of one. If I don't write down the ideas for these stories soon after I have them or wake up, I usually forget them, and later no going back over what I was thinking or dreaming will retrieve them. That's how I am, especially when the ideas come from dreams. But I don't feel right now like sitting up with my legs over the edge of the bed and getting my notebook off the night table and writing the two ideas down. I'm saying I'm satisfied with where I am: lying on the bed, on my back, pillow under my neck and head, eyes closed. But maybe I should write at least one of the ideas down. Again, it'd mean sitting up, getting the notebook off the night table, opening it to a clean page and writing something like "Story!!!"—underlining the word two or three times—"Each sentence in its own paragraph, or all the sentences in a single paragraph, but each one starting off with the pronoun 'I'" Or, what the hell, same thing for the A to Z story: "One paragraph for each letter of the alphabet, or a single paragraph for all the letters, but going sequentially from A to Z." Will I remember what I was referring to for the A to Z story? I think so, or I can make it clearer. But both ideas for possible stories aren't very good. In fact, they're pretty bad or, at least, I now feel, aren't good enough to be worth getting up for to write down in the notebook. And I think I might even have done one of them years ago and published it—the "I" one, though maybe it was "He" that started off all the sentences in the story; I'd have to check, though with all the stories I've published, it might be nearly impossible to find out. Anyway, I probably won't want to write a story using either of those two ideas. In fact I don't know when I'll want to write any kind of story. I really don't want to do anything. So what are you going to do then? Maybe get off the bed and go out again. But why go out? Maybe I'll feel better after I take another walk. This one longer than the last one, and by the time I come back from it, my head cleared, so to speak, I'll want to write a first draft of a story or continue writing the story I was writing before I put it aside. I don't know. I don't feel like I want to do anything. You already said that in almost the same words. Say something different. Then just get up. You know you're not going to nap now. And it isn't the end of the world. You've been there before. I get up. Okay, I'm up. What do I do now? You'll think of something. I go into the bathroom. I pee, not because I have to but because it's a good precaution to take. By that I mean… Just get on with it. I wash my hands, dry them on the hand towel in the bathroom, brush my hair twenty-five strokes, which I do every morning but forgot to today—ten strokes for each side and five for the top. I go into the dining room and put on my socks and sneakers. I look out the window of the kitchen door. The cat's sitting on the doormat, which means he wants to come in. I thought he'd be there. I let him in. He goes over to his food plate on the floor by the refrigerator and sees nothing in it. He then goes over to the shopping bag of paper by the trash can and does when he's hungry and there's no wet food for him to eat or when he's dissatisfied—I'm almost sure I'm reading this right—with what I've put on his plate, and that's to put his front paws into the bag of paper and knock the bag over. "All right. All right. Food's coming. Don't make a mess for me to clean up." I open the refrigerator and take out a can of cat food that's about half full. I spoon some of it onto the plate and put the plate back on the floor. I expected him to walk over to it but he doesn't. "Huey, your food. You wanted something to eat besides the kibble. There it is," and I pick up the plate and set it down so it makes a noise. He looks left, right, behind him, but not at the food, and then goes to the door. I open it and then the screen door and he goes out. I see his water bowl outside has a bug in it of some kind. I empty it into a hedge, fill it with fresh water from the kitchen faucet and bring it outside and set it on the ground. He goes over to it, smells it and walks away. I'm outside, so I should probably go for a longer walk. Maybe I'll feel better after it or during it. I walk past the church playground across the street. Maybe I should run. Sort of exhaust myself for a few minutes. I have my sneakers on. And I'm not carrying anything. Usually when I go for a walk I carry a book with me and stop at the end of the walk in front of the church and sit on the bench in my favorite part of the grounds there, my little tucked-away garden, I've come to call it, and read for about twenty minutes. But now no book to hold me back, I start to run. I run for about half a mile. It felt good. I like that I'm panting. I don't do that enough. I like that I ran and, for some of it, as hard as I could. I like that I'm outside and not feeling so bad anymore. I like that I think when I get home I'll uncover my typewriter—maybe pour a mug of coffee out of the thermos and bring it to the back of the house—and write. Probably, best, the first draft of a new story, since the one I was writing this morning wasn't going well. Maybe a story—I've been thinking of this one awhile—about my brother who died fifty-five years ago when the freighter he was working on went down—sunk, sunk—in the North Atlantic and was never—no part of it—found. How, after so many years, the narrator still sometimes cries when he thinks of him and the drowning and the freezing temperature of the water—it was late December when the ship sunk, and what he must have gone through when he was drowning, and when they were kids, his brother eighteen months older than he and they were best friends, always best friends, never, that he can remember—and he remembers speaking about this to his brother—a single argument or flash of anger between them. That's all the story would be. A chronologically-told series of happy reminiscences from the time they were very young—being bathed by their mother in the same tub together when they were two and three—till the moment he learns by phone the shipping company and various countries' Coast Guards had lost all contact with the freighter. Would that be enough for a story? I think I could make it be. Just one short sentence at the end, almost like a news headline, saying radio contact with the freighter has been lost for three days and the fear is the ship sunk in the most violent storm in that part of the North Atlantic in years. So maybe two headline-like sentences and no phone call. Or his father calls him and says, "What's the name of the freighter Dan's working on?" I'll see. Another I've been thinking of writing is about a lonely and solitary widower who talks to himself during the entire story. No quotation marks, though, and every word in it said aloud but where nobody can hear him or is around. The reader would know soon after the story started that every word is spoken by him and none of it is in his head. For instance—and the story would have the man take a long walk around his neighborhood, so would begin when he leaves his house and end when he gets back there: "I shut the front door. Should I lock it? No need to. Neighborhood's safe and I'm not going to be gone that long. Nice day. Could be a bit less humid. There's my wedding—I mean, my weather report for the day. The cat. Where the hell is he? Dewey, don't scare me. I worry about you when you're outside, more times than I don't. He might go out on the road that runs past my house and not jump back to the shoulder fast enough to get out of the way of a speeding car. Speed limit's posted as 25, but cars and pickup trucks often go fifty and sixty on it. I've given up holding my hand for them to slow down or shaking my fist at them or yelling out, 'Slow down, will ya?'" So there would be quotation marks, but only for things like that. "There's Clay. Very neighborly neighbor. He put up my mailbox—even dug the hole deeper for the stand—when a car or something demolished it. 'Anytime,' he said, 'though for your sake, I hope it doesn't happen again.' It'd be nice to be as handy as he is and to have such a sunny disposition and a wife who, whenever I see them outside together—gardening, weeding, walking, a few times jogging, bringing the recycling and trash cans to the street for the designated pickup days—seems to adore him." Does this sound like someone talking out loud to himself? No. Sounds more like writing. "And today? Clay mowing his lawn. Seems to do it once a week. All right. His business. Excessive? Who am I to say? 'Good exercise,' he called it. I'll pretend I don't see him. If he calls out to me, that I don't hear him. Because why would he think I could, over the lawnmower noise? If he shuts the mower off to call out to me, that presents a problem, but I'll do something to get by him without saying anything. A smile and wave should do it. Because I don't want to talk to anyone now. To my wife I'd speak to gladly. Ecstatically. Rapturously. Can I use those two adverbs there that way? What of it? And who's stopping you? But no such luck with her, and faster you get off the subject, the better. Keep walking. Just keep walking. I pass Clay. He doesn't call out to me or shut his mower off and maybe doesn't even see me. Too intent on doing the perfect mowing," and so on. But a story told like that. He makes the entire loop, home to home. I can even call it that: "The Loop." But would it be enough for a story? Maybe not. Most likely not. But I could try if everything else I want to write doesn't work. My wife's slippers. Moccasin slippers, fleece-lined, ordered from L.L. Bean as a Christmas gift. Men's size, large, because her feet were so swollen the last years of her life, she couldn't fit in any women's slippers. I wear them sometimes. I should really throw them out. Every time I look at them or put them on, as I don't have any slippers of my own, I think of her. All this in a story. "But he can't. Something always stops him. He once, even, took them back out of the kitchen trash can he'd put them in. That she wore them to keep her feet warm when the weather was cold and there was a draft in the house." I'd call it "Slippers." No, that one he couldn't turn into a story. Not enough there. Or one where every paragraph starts with "This was in" or "This was on." As: "This was in November, 1961," and "This was on June 27th, 2002, around five a.m.," followed by an incident in the narrator's life, but all the paragraphs making up an entire life. Not done chronologically. Halfway through, it could describe the narrator being born in a New York City taxi on the way to the maternity ward of a hospital, and the whole piece could begin with his daughter's birth. Maybe. Or a story about a man's cat being run over by a speeding car in front of his house and the man going into deep mourning over it. "What's with you?" friends could say. "You loved him but he was only a cat. You're acting as if it was even worse than the loss of your wife." Again, a possibility. Or one about all the places he passes in his car one day that remind him of his wife. That bring back memories of her and him there together. Bookstore. Coffee shop. Their favorite restaurant for lunch. Farm truck. Medical center, just a couple of miles from his house, she was taken to Emergency to a few times her last two years. Or one he'd call "The Kiss." Been thinking about this one since the incident that inspired it happened a month or so ago. A man's at a bagel shop buying what he always does there almost every other week, three everythings and three plain, and bumps into an old friend of his wife's. "What a surprise," he says. "Of all places. Haven't seen you for what must be years," and is about to kiss her cheek, when she turns her face toward his and kisses him on the lips. He thinks about this kiss the rest of the day. That it was close to being a fervent kiss, but that he hasn't kissed a woman on the lips in any kind of way for years and how he's missed it. Other kisses. The first time, on a couch in her apartment, he kissed the woman he later married. Their kiss at their wedding, when the rabbi had to part them and said, "Come on, we have to finish the ceremony, or maybe we have. Okay, you're married." And his last kiss on her lips, soon after she died in her hospital bed at home. Maybe it could be a story. Girls he kissed on the lips while he was still in high school. A prostitute he wanted to kiss when he got on top of her and before he put it in, saying, "Please, just one, and then I won't ask again and we'll do all the regular stuff." Kissing games at birthday parties when he was still in grade school. With another woman on the street on their first date, which ended up in bed in his apartment. Anyway, lots of possible stories. One has to work. And I'm feeling much better after my run. Much, and I go into the house, fill up a mug from the thermos of coffee, go back to my bedroom and set the mug down by the typewriter, but far enough away from it so the carriage doesn't knock over the coffee, take the dust cover off the typewriter, put paper in and think how should I start one of these stories, or a new one entirely made up here? I write: "A man goes out for a walk." "I unlock the kitchen door from the inside. The cat walks up to it and I warn him: 'Now be very careful. Don't go out on the road. Also watch out for our neighbors zipping up and down the driveway. Good cat. You'll listen to me. Now go on,' and I open the door and he goes outside." "He gets out of bed, puts on his boxer shorts, turns on the radio to the classical music station, does his morning exercises with his barbells, goes into the kitchen, lets the cat out and makes coffee and toast and sits at the dining table with them and reads the front page of the newspaper." No, first he has to get the newspaper at the mailbox and then sits down at the table with it and the coffee and toast. "He can't stand it anymore. He's going to have to move. Because every place he passes in town when he has to go anywhere, brings back memories of his wife." "He tells his wife, 'I love you. Did I ever tell you that?' 'Multiple times,' she says." Or: "'You tell me that a lot. I'm beginning to believe it.' 'Believe it,' he says. 'I'm so happy with you. Are you happy with me?' 'What a question,' she says. 'Because what do you think?' 'That you're happy with me.' 'I'm very happy. Extremely. Couldn't be happier.' 'Just as I'm extremely very happy with you. Listen,' he says. 'What do you say today we don't do what we seem to always do in the morning after we get out of bed and wash up and dress? You know, let's not go our separate ways at breakfast. Eat alone. Browse through the newspaper alone at the table. And then go to our respective work rooms to work for the next few hours. Today, let's go out somewhere for breakfast. To a place we've never been to for any kind of meal but heard good things about. Or we just go to it even if nobody's told us anything about it and we haven't been there before.' 'Sounds good to me. I could use a little change. Got any ideas where we could go?' 'Johnny's in Roland Park might be a good place,' he says. 'I've heard it advertised on the radio on the classical music station.' 'Then it must be good,' she says, 'or odds are it'll be, considering the audience they're marketing it to. Okay. Let's get washed up and go. I don't know about you, but I'm starving.' She puts out her arms. He lifts her off the bed into her wheelchair, wheels her into the bathroom, lifts her onto the toilet and then back into the wheelchair after she's done. He helps her wash up, dress, brushes her hair and ties it into a ponytail, and pushes the chair outside. Their van's gone. 'Damn,' he says. 'Everything was going so well.' 'You didn't park it somewhere else yesterday?' she says. 'Where else would I park it other than our carport? No, it's been stolen. Now what? Ah, let's not let it ruin our day. Let's take a stroll, and then I'll call the police. There's no hurry. Like the last time, they won't find it and we'll end up with a brand-new van.'" I can't think how I can make the story go further. Maybe if I wrote the last few lines again, it'd just take off on its own, though I doubt it. Try another. "He feels good today. Air's fresh. Humidity's low. Sky is clear and temperature's perfect. Everything smells nice too." No. But something will come.

20

The Kiss

HE'S LEAVING A MARKET and she's about to enter it and he says, "Dolores, what a surprise," and she says, "Charles. I had a sneaky feeling I'd see you here or sometime today. Don't ask me why. A sudden flash in my head when I got out of the car. So I'm psychic after all." "What do you mean 'after all'?" and she says, "I thought we once talked about it. Maybe I only did with Eleanor. Anyway, this is wonderful. Hello," and she moves her head toward his, he's about to kiss her cheek but she kisses his lips.

They step away from the door and talk. Her kids. His daughter. Her husband. What she's been working on. What he is. Does he have a new book coming out? Oh, what's she talking about? He always does. What about her? The one she was writing the last time he saw her, which was a few years ago. She finish it?

She'd been his graduate student about twenty years ago. After she got her master's she'd stayed on for a while teaching expository writing. She used to come to his office a lot to talk. She'd bring containers of coffee for them and sometimes cookies or muffins. Books she'd been reading or recently read. Had he read it? She'd be dying—"frothing at the mouth"—for somebody to talk about it with. Novel she'd been working on. Interconnected story collection she'd been working on. She hadn't had much luck selling her fiction. How did he do it? Did he have any new tips for her?

She and her husband—what's his name? Burleigh.—invited Eleanor and him for dinner several times over the years. Burleigh was in finance, made lots of money. She came from money. They were always great dinners and the other guests were always pleasant and interesting. And Burleigh was into wine, so always the best wines he ever drank. He and Eleanor had them over for dinner a few times too. By then, Eleanor was in a wheelchair and he did all the cooking.

Then Eleanor died. Dolores came over to the house a few days later with food she prepared for him—enough, if he froze most of it, for two weeks—and two good bottles of wine from Burleigh's wine cellar. "We're going to invite you to dinner a lot," she said then, "so be prepared for it. When you're ready, of course."

She called a month later. He said he wasn't ready yet. Burleigh called a couple of months after that. "I'm still not ready. Really, I don't know if I'll ever be." "If it's only that you don't want to drive at night, one of us will pick you up and drive you home." "I just don't want to go to someone's house for dinner or lunch. Things have changed for me. I've become a little strange, I know. You'll have to forgive me. You both have been very patient and kind." "I'll call again in a few weeks. We're going to have you here, though, that's for sure."

She called several months after that and invited him to lunch at his favorite restaurant. An informal place. Sandwich and soup and good coffee. Conversation went well. Books. What she was writing. A story coming out in a literary magazine. "They even pay. A hundred bucks. My first publication. I'm so proud of myself. You told me not to give up and to keep sending and gave me the name of the magazine and editor, so I owe it all to you." He talked about the long novel he was writing.

Sort of an elegy. "Sounds wonderful," she said. "I'm going to buy ten copies when it comes out and give them to relatives and friends."

That lunch was about three years ago. She called a number of times since for lunch and he always refused. Sometimes lied. "My stomach's been acting up. Nothing serious but it does interfere with my eating." "I'm coming off a bad flu. Maybe some other time." Other lies.

Then he bumps into her today. Her older daughter's in college now. Younger one's a year away from college and they've been busy visiting a number of schools. Burleigh's working as hard as ever. He tells her about his daughter. Finishing up a doctorate in literature, like her mother, but not in Russian literature. They promise to meet for lunch soon. She'll call him. "And I won't accept a no. And then dinner at our house. Something simple. I'll also invite Barbara and Glenn, if you don't mind. They love you and speak about you often. Burleigh or I will drive you there and then back to your home. It couldn't be easier for you." "No need to. I can drive. It'll be fun seeing you and Burleigh and Barbara and Glenn. Give them all my regards."

He goes to his car. She goes inside the market. He sits in the car, doesn't start it up, thinks of that kiss on the lips. Her lips were so soft. The first woman he's kissed on the lips since Eleanor. Last time he kissed Eleanor was a few minutes after she died. He's missed so much kissing a woman on the lips. When Dolores and he said goodbye in front of the market, he thought they'd kiss again on the lips and was looking forward to it, but she just said, "Oops, got to run. I only have two items to buy and not much time. This has been great. I'll call you," and waved and went into the market. Did he shut his eyes when they kissed. Did she? She probably didn't and he probably did. He doesn't remember. It was all so quick. Normally, he'd shut his eyes. Maybe he didn't because it came without warning, was such a surprise. The other times he saw her since Eleanor died. For lunch. And when she brought food over. Did she kiss him on the lips? He doesn't think so. He thinks he would have noted it, at least that time at lunch. So why today? He doesn't know. Did she know or sense how starved he was to kiss a woman on the lips? Why would she? Nothing that he gave off. So what made her do it? He doesn't know. Did her turning her face toward his so they could kiss on the lips mean anything to her?

How could he know? Probably not. No, definitely not, or almost definitely. It's just the way she is. Freer with her kisses than most women, or women he knows. She might think a kiss isn't a kiss if it isn't on the lips, or think that when it's between a woman and man. Wouldn't it be nice to be with a woman he kissed on the lips several times a day as he used to do with Eleanor and with other women he lived with before her, though nowhere near as much. Eyes shut, eyes open, eyes half closed. All kinds of ways for them both. Deep kisses. Light kisses, but on the lips. Did he ever kiss Eleanor on the cheek? Must have, for some reason, once or twice, or more. Nearly thirty years together. Had to a number of times, but otherwise, why would he? From the first time they kissed, it was on the lips. Kissed her almost every night after they went to bed. If she turned off her light first, he kissed her. "Wait a sec. Don't fall asleep yet," he knows he said a few times, which she got a laugh out of. If he was about to turn off his light and she was still reading in bed, he kissed her or she kissed him. It went either way. But more him than her. She didn't find it as important. Kissed her on the lips when he left for work. Kissed her when he got back from work. Kissed her just before he wheeled her into her classroom when she was teaching. Almost always. But a quick kiss and even if her students were just filing in. She didn't mind. "Have a great class," he'd say. Their wedding ceremony kiss. That was a long deep one. The kiss after their daughter was born. They were still in the birthing room. The nurse had cleaned off the baby and put it under some lamp for a few seconds and weighed her and handed her to him and he cooed over it and gave the baby to Eleanor or set it down beside her. "Now pucker up for a kiss," he said. "It's all right to, right?" he said to the obstetrician or nurse. So many kisses. "You're really a good kisser," Eleanor once said, and he said, "And you're a great kisser." "Good kisser meet great kisser. Give me a good kiss."

Dolores taps on his car window. He rolls it down. "You waiting for me?" she says. "No. Just sitting here thinking." "Didn't think so. Can I ask what you're thinking?" "The novel I'm writing." "That'll keep you busy. Remember. When I call you for lunch, or email you—I have your email address—you don't refuse. And when Burleigh or I call or email you for dinner at our house, again, you don't refuse.

We want to see you more. You're one of our favorite people, and we miss you." "Same here with me. Thank you. It's very nice to hear." "Before I rush off, what's your novel called?" "'Man and Wife.' It's only a working title. I doubt it'll be the one I use. But I can't continue to write something unless I have a title for it, even a temporary one, once I've done the first draft." "I can understand," she says. "I'm sort of the same way. I must've got it from you. Adieu, my friend. I feel so lucky to have run into you. Wait'll I tell Burleigh." She blows a kiss to him. He does the same to her. She goes to her car. He stays in his, thinking of other times he kissed Eleanor. He remembers so many. And vividly too. For sure, their first kiss. They were sitting on the sofa in her apartment. He'd been sitting in a chair across from her on the sofa. It was their third date. They'd gone to a Greek restaurant in her neighborhood and she'd invited him up. He said, "Would you mind very much if I sit next to you?" "Not at all," she said. "Plenty of room." He sat beside her, took her hand, said, "I suppose you know what's coming next," and she said, "If it's what I think it is, go ahead." Times she greeted him at the door to her apartment and said, before one of them shut the door behind them, "Come on, a kiss." The first time she came to his apartment—it was in the afternoon—and he said, "This is a memorable event. The first time we kiss in my apartment. I won't forget it." "If I do," she said, "you can always remind me." The kiss after their wedding ceremony in her apartment, now theirs. "That was quite a kiss, the ceremonial one," she said later that day after all the guests had left. "A lot more than the bride typically expects to get after the I do's are said. You were really scaling it, as the expression goes, and I was all for it." "As long as we're talking about kissing," he once told her, "I think the best one we ever had was when we were on our honeymoon in that Connecticut inn for two days and the pregnancy test kit we used there indicated you were pregnant." "That was a good one. I don't usually remember things like that, as you do, or not as well, but that one stands out. No doubt the ardor behind that kiss had a lot to do with what we'd just found out. We were so happy." "We're still happy." "Of course," she said. "But to me the best kiss we ever had was after we'd split up for around three months and I called you to ask how you were, though no doubt to see, on the sly, if you'd already hooked up with another lady since we went our separate ways. You came over to my place and rang the bell and I opened the door and you said, 'Hi' and stuck out your hand to shake and I impulsively, you can say, or whatever why I did it, since we hadn't officially reconciled yet. We had only agreed to your coming over so we could talk some more than we did on the phone the previous day. Anyway, I put my face close to yours—you still had your hand out to shake mine—and we kissed on the lips. That was some kiss. I almost stopped breathing. But it was worth it." "Yeah," he said. "I remember it exactly like that too."

21

Mornings and Evenings

SO MANY THINGS to do in the morning. Get out of bed. It's almost always a struggle. Lower back hurts and it's difficult sitting up on the edge of the bed and then standing up without tottering or falling. Sometimes I fall back on the bed into a sitting position and then try standing again and again till I'm up. Then in the bathroom, sitting on the toilet. First thing I do when I get in there. Have to grab hold of the grab bar that was put in for my wife and which I now use every time I sit on the toilet and then stand up from it. Sit on it to shit or pee, makes no difference now. If I pee while I'm standing I usually dribble a little on my leg or boxer shorts, if I wore them to bed. Then I dress, which isn't difficult except for the socks. At night I leave them on the floor by the side of the bed I get up from, either the pair I wore that day or a clean pair I took out of the top dresser drawer.

Next I make the bed. I can't stand an unmade bed once I get off it in the morning. Then I go into the bathroom again, this time to wash my hands and face and brush my teeth and hair. If I need to shave, which I do every other day unless I shaved the previous day but am meeting someone for lunch, let's say, today, I do it after I've had breakfast. By then I'm much steadier on my feet and have better control of my hands, although I still manage to cut my face or neck or both every two to three shaves. I have in the medicine cabinet that stick, I forget what it's called, to stop the bleeding. Stip stick, or stick stip. Something. I'll remember it. If I've cut my lip, it takes more than just that stick. A dry washcloth. Pressure. After washing up, I go into the kitchen. Most times the cat's already there waiting for me. He usually—I'd say nine times out of ten, or maybe four out of five—stays all night on my bed and jumps off it when I start to make it and runs to the kitchen door to the outside, wanting to go out after being in the house the last twelve hours or so. He makes it easy for me. Uses the kitty-litter box in the other bathroom about once every two months, even when there's snow on the ground or it's raining, and mostly just to pee. In the kitchen, after I've unlocked the door and let him out, I empty his water bowl into the sink and refill it with fresh water. Do I need to? I don't know. It's a habit I got into, and I suppose fresh water's better for him than water that's more than a half day old. I do only give him water from the regular faucet rather than from the filtered-water tap attached to the sink, since it takes longer, because I have to hold a lever down and the water comes out much slower than it does from the faucet, to fill up the bowl with filtered water. Next I pour fresh kibble into his kibble bowl and get the opened can of wet cat food out of the refrigerator, or if the cat finished it for dinner the day before, then a new can of cat food from the kitchen cabinet all the cans of food for both of us are in, and open it and put two teaspoonfuls of it on his plate, which I washed the previous night and left in the dish rack next to the sink along with the washed teaspoon, and set it on the floor by the water and kibble bowls. What I also do after I let the cat out is get the bowl of water that's been outside by the kitchen door since yesterday morning, empty it in one of the house plants outside if they're all not already soaked by a recent rain, dump it on the ground if they are soaked, refill it with fresh water from the kitchen sink and leave it outside by the door. If there are no houseplants there—they've all been brought inside for the winter—I also just dump the water on the ground or sometimes heave it into a nearby bush. If the weather's gotten so cold that the water outside freezes in a few hours, I don't leave any water out there for him. He still goes outside when the temperature's that cold—he even goes when it's snowing or has snowed, but less so when it's raining—though not for as long. After I put the water out there in the morning I go to the end of the driveway and pick up the news-paper by the mailbox. If it's trash pickup day, I bring the garbage can with me. On Thursdays I bring a different trash can of recyclables with me—plastic, paper, metal, glass, all mixed together, along with broken-down paper cartons if there are any, which I've broken down a day or two before—and leave it, as I do the garbage can on Mondays, at the end of the driveway. If there happen to be a number of broken-down cartons, which would be unusual, or the one I'm leaving there is very large, I make two trips. Sometime later in the day—the dump truck always seems to do both pickups between 8:30 and nine—I bring back to the carport whichever can I brought out there. Back in the house, I put the newspaper on the dining room table. So many things to do, as I said. And I'm not even talking about the little things, or not most of them. Cleaning the spoon I used for the wet cat food. Also the can opener I had to open the can of cat food with if the lid couldn't be removed by pulling the tab. Of course, that doesn't happen much; about once every ten to fifteen cans. And after breakfast, dumping the coffee grounds into the kitchen trash can and cleaning the automatic coffeemaker and dishes and utensils I used and wiping the kitchen counters and maybe every three mornings or so sweeping the kitchen floor and the area around where I sat at the dining room table. I can't seem to eat there without dropping a few pieces of food. If it's something like yogurt or banana that falls off the spoon to the table or floor, I clean it up with a paper towel. But preparing the breakfast. That's the major morning effort. First the coffeemaker if I hadn't done it the night before, which I do pretty often so there'll be one less thing to do in the morning. Then, while the coffee's being made: two slices of toasted bread or half a toasted bagel, sliced sideways, with butter and jam or marmalade; a bowl of sliced banana, yogurt or kefir and granola; and a side dish of two or three fruits: strawberries, blueberries, peach and so on. Mostly, whatever's in season. In the fall I make a cranberry compote about once every three weeks—not in the morning but later in the day—and spoon a little of it on the granola mix. Did I say I almost always put a fork and tablespoon on a place setting on the dining room table the night before? Doesn't save me much time, but again, I do it so I'll have one less thing to do the next morning. After I prepare breakfast, or "make it" I should probably say, I bring it to the dining room table. By that time the cat usually wants to come in and I open the kitchen door and he goes straight to his food. After he gobbles down the wet cat food and eats a little of the kibble, he goes to the door and will wait at it till I let him out. Since he throws up what he eats in the morning about once every two weeks, I like to get him back outside fast as I can. My pills. I forgot about them. First one is for my Parkinson's disease. I take it right after I get to the kitchen in the morning and open the door for the cat. Then, about ten minutes later, a pill for my enlarged prostate. Then, a few minutes after that, a third pill for an esophagus problem. All with water, of course, maybe half a small glass. After I have breakfast, I let dissolve on my tongue and then swallow a pill for high blood pressure. What have I left out? To go back a bit, while I'm sitting at the edge of the bed waiting till I feel something enough to stand up—strong, relaxed, steady, confident—maybe a couple of those—I open the top drawer of my night table and take out my eyeglasses and cellphone, where I left them the previous night before I turned off the light. I don't keep them on top of the night table overnight because the cat likes to get up on it in the dark and swipe them to the floor, along with any pens I might have left there. My watch, which I only put on my wrist or take with me in my pants pocket if I'm going to be out of the house for more than a few hours, I keep under the book I was reading in bed before I turned off the light. If my cellphone needs recharging or looks like it might sometime today—one or two of the three bars has gone blank—I recharge it when I get to the kitchen but after I've let the cat out and taken my first pill. So that's about it for the morning: a lot of things to do and probably a number of other little things I don't remember right now and have left out. Then, cat back outside, unless it's pouring and he doesn't want to go out, and dishes and such washed and placed in the dish rack to dry and eventually put away, I go back to my bedroom and sit at my work table and work on the story or novel I've been writing. If I finished a story or chapter, I guess I can call it, the previous day, I try to write the first draft of a short story or the next chapter or section of a novel. If it's stories I've been writing and nothing comes or nothing worth continuing, after I sit down at my typewriter to write the first draft of one, I get a little anxious that I won't have anything to work on the next day. If it's a novel I've been writing, I usually, since by now I probably have a good idea where the book's going, don't have much trouble starting a new chapter or section the day after I finished the last one. And I didn't make clear that the kitchen door in my house is really two doors: the regular one and the storm one. So when I say, for example, I'm opening the kitchen door for the cat to come in or go out, I mean both doors. Evenings are much easier for me. Nowhere near as many things to do. Before retiring for the night, to use an old way of saying it, I make sure the oven and stove burners are off, the living room and kitchen doors to the outside are locked, the central air conditioning or heat is turned off if either has been on till now during the day (so turning one of them on is another thing I might have done in the morning), and all the lights outside and in the house except for my bedroom, of course, are out. I also dump whatever food might still be in the cat's bowl and on his plate. If I don't, and he's done this several times before I took this precaution and a couple of times when I forgot to, he's liable to eat it sometime after I go to bed and throw it up soon after that. Then I brush my teeth, floss, maybe water-pick, swish around in my mouth a capful of Listerine mouthwash or the generic equivalent of it and spit it out into the sink; undress, if I haven't already undressed; get under the bed covers with the book I've been reading and, when I'm not reading it, keep on the night table till I'm through with it; turn the radio on to the classical music station in case it's playing a piece I want to hear—usually it's not; and read till I feel my eyes getting tired and I can't concentrate on the page anymore. Then, if the radio's on, and tuning it on may have been one of the first things I did when I came into the room, I turn it off. Put the bookmark in the book where I stopped reading. Put the book on the night table. Put my watch and maybe a pen or two under the book. Put my eyeglasses and cellphone in the top night table drawer. Feel for a handkerchief under the pillows to see if one's there. If it isn't, nor on the night table, I get up and look for it in the side pockets of my pants on the chair by the bed or get one from my dresser and put it under a pillow. Turn off the light. Or maybe get up to pee once more before I fall asleep so I can stay in bed three and sometimes four hours straight. Find a comfortable position on the bed. Stretch out my legs far as they can go, mainly to make sure the cat's not in the way of my feet. If he is—I think I already said he stays on the bed almost every night and is often on it when I come back to the bedroom for the last time today—I nudge him with my foot or say, "Huey, move!" or both, and he usually gets up and moves to the other side of the bed.

Designer: Jacob Covey
Editor: Conrad Groth
Supervising Editor: Gary Groth
Associate Publisher: Eric Reynolds
Publisher: Gary Groth

Fantagraphics Books, Inc.
7563 Lake City Way NE
Seattle, WA 98115

www.fantagraphics.com
facebook.com/Fantagraphics
@fantagraphics.com

ISBN: 978-1-68396-172-7
Library of Congress Control Number: 2018949570
First Fantagraphics Books edition: February 2019
Printed in China